DOOR TO DOOR

A Door to Door Paranormal Mystery

T.L. Brown

Copyright © 2020 Tracy Brown-Simmons

All rights reserved.

The characters and events portrayed in this book are fictitious. Any similarity to real persons, living or dead, business establishments, events, or locales is coincidental and not intended by the author.

No part of this book may be reproduced, or stored in a retrieval system, or transmitted in any form or by any means, electronic, mechanical, photocopying, recording, or otherwise, without express written permission of the publisher.

ISBN: 978-1-7359290-1-9

First Edition: October 2020

Book Cover Design by ebooklaunch.com
Created / printed in the United States of America

PRAISE FOR AUTHOR

With a novel premise, engaging characters, and a wholly original world, T.L. Brown's first-in-series will draw you through her magical doors - and refuse to let you go...

- Book review site Jill-Elizabeth.com

for my husband, Gordon
and
for my mother, Linda

CONTENTS

Title Page
Copyright
Praise For Author
Dedication

CHAPTER 1	1
CHAPTER 2	13
CHAPTER 3	27
CHAPTER 4	41
CHAPTER 5	54
CHAPTER 6	73
CHAPTER 7	90
CHAPTER 8	104
CHAPTER 9	119
CHAPTER 10	137
CHAPTER 11	152
CHAPTER 12	169
CHAPTER 13	191

CHAPTER 14	210
CHAPTER 15	232
CHAPTER 16	254
CHAPTER 17	272
CHAPTER 18	293
CHAPTER 19	312
CHAPTER 20	334
CHAPTER 21	353
CHAPTER 22	372
Acknowledgements	385
Books In This Series	387
About The Author	389
Find T.L. Brown Online	391

CHAPTER 1

Thud.

I sat up. A quick glance around the room told me the Furious Furballs – my three cats – were not the source of the sound. Jack slept at my side. I knew the noise wasn't part of a dream.

Climbing out from under the covers and into a sweatshirt, I crept down the stairs, William and Mystery padding along at my heels. At six in the morning, the house was dark except for a lamp in the living room. I paused on the last step and listened again. Nothing.

The floor creaked as I walked to the front of the old colonial. Peering out a window, I checked the stoop. The streetlight cast a yellow glow on the front of the house. In the snow, on the first step, I could just make out a package.

"What is that?" I rubbed my breath from the glass to get a better look. Was it something for my birthday? If it was from Jack, why didn't he have it delivered to his office? Maybe it was from someone else. Would Mom have something delivered? I supposed it was possible.

Staring out the window wasn't going to answer any questions. I opened the front door. In a blast of cold air and a sprinkling of sparkling snow, I stepped out and picked up the box before shivering myself back inside. It was barely damp from the weather.

The package was about the size of a shoe box, only wider and wrapped in brown paper. It was tied with shipping string and addressed to Emily Swift, 7 Apple Tree Lane, Kincaid, New York. Both the zip code and postage were missing.

I chewed my lip. Who would deliver a package at such an early hour? Were there even any tire tracks left by a delivery truck? I walked back to the door and cracked it open a few inches, resting my nose against the door jam. I peeked out with one eye. No tracks. The only footprints in the snow were mine. It hadn't snowed in hours.

It was time to wake up Jack.

❊ ❊ ❊

"Jack, you need to get up. Someone left a package at the front door."

"Mufnh." He rolled onto his stomach, covering his head with the pillow. Jack is generally a good sport. Being a professor at the local community college provides him with all kinds of opportunities to practice patience. Still, he's not the most understanding of men when poked awake before the alarm.

"Jack! Someone dropped off a present for me." I pulled at the pillow, but he gripped it tighter.

We wrestled for a moment.

"What time is it?" His head reappeared from under the pillow and he rolled his eyes toward the clock. "Sweetie, just come back to bed. You can open it after the alarm." He patted the mattress with his hand.

Leaning over, I flipped on the light. "No. It's my birthday – my thirtieth birthday – and I need your help with this weird package. I need to open it. *Now*."

Jack opened one eye. I lifted my chin.

"Okay, okay," he said. "Just let me throw on some sweats. It's cold in here."

❉ ❉ ❉

After what seemed to be an awfully slow roll out of bed, Jack shuffled into the living room. His short salt-and-pepper hair stood up in little horns all over his head. He rubbed his eyes before putting on glasses to inspect the package. He blinked.

"Well," he nodded, "it's for you."

"Thank you, Sherlock," I said. "But where's the postage? Look. No stamps." I turned the package over, showing him every angle. "No delivery logos either. Nothing on any of the sides."

"Could it be from someone you know? Hand-delivered?"

"Then why put my address on it?"

"I have no idea." Jack yawned. I raised an eyebrow and he shrugged. He pulled out a pair of scissors from the writing desk. "So open it."

I eyed the package. "What if it's a bomb?"

"It's not a bomb. If you were so worried, you wouldn't be bobbling it between your hands like that." He waved the scissors at me. When I didn't reach for them immediately, Jack took my hand and placed them in my palm.

"Fine. If I blow, you're going with me." I held my breath and cut away the shipping string before unwrapping the brown paper. The box itself was plain. I lifted the lid, wincing in anticipation of a ticking clock and a nest of wires. Instead, the box held old packing paper and an even older-looking book. The bluish cover was worn with a faded, gold-embossed 'S' pressed into the center. A letter was tucked in beside the book. My name, written in my mother's handwriting, appeared on the envelope. I sat on the couch and sighed, partially out of relief, and partially out of annoyance. All this worry and mystery for nothing.

"See?" Jack echoed my thoughts. "Nothing to worry about." He patted me on the knee before disappearing into the kitchen to make coffee and feed the Furballs.

Shaking my head, I picked up the envelope. Inside was a short note from Mom.

To my beautiful daughter Emily,

> *On your thirtieth birthday, it's important for you to have your father's journal.*

Dad's journal? I put the letter down and dug back into the box. The book was heavy and thick. The embossed 'S' was probably for Swift, my father's last name. Then I noticed the lock. It reminded me of those old drugstore diaries with a tiny lock and key designed to keep out snooping siblings and nosy mothers. I pulled out the rest of the packing paper looking for a key. Nothing. I went back to the letter.

> *Your father used this book to keep a record of his travels, associates, and transactions. He carried it with him whenever he traveled. The details of his work might be valuable to you in the future. His notes are private, of course, and you should keep them to yourself.*
>
> *I know he would have wanted to share this with you on your birthday today. I'm sorry that he isn't with us to do so himself.*
>
> *Give my love to Jack and the kittens,*
>
> *Mom*

I sunk back into the couch cushions, holding the letter between my fingertips. My father, Daniel Swift, died 17 years ago when I was 13. He was a traveling salesman, although I never knew exactly what he sold. I remembered my father as a quick-moving and smiling man. He wasn't home a lot, but I always looked forward to the times when he would surprise us by stepping through the front door, arriving out of nowhere.

Sometimes he'd bring me a present. The best gift was an amazing flute. I didn't know how to play any musical instrument, but whenever I would put it to my lips, I could play whatever tune I wanted.

For some reason Mom wasn't very happy about it, despite my sudden musical talent. In the end, my father won out. I was allowed to keep it as long as I promised to never play it in June. When I asked why, Dad winked and told me that sometimes we just needed to humor Mom. As I folded and unfolded the letter in my hands, I wondered what happened to the flute. It seemed like one day it was just gone. Kind of like my Dad.

I didn't think about my father a lot. He died in an accident when traveling. Although I missed out on the more meaningful father-daughter moments during my teen years, I had a nagging suspicion with his constant traveling, any time we spent together would've been sporadic at best. Still, I would've liked to understand why he chose a life as a traveling salesman when he had a wife and child at home.

Then there was my mother. I frowned at the letter. She had a way of catching me off-guard, but usually with some wild new project. She surprised me with the book. Why now? Sure, it was my thirtieth birthday, and yes, it's sort of a big deal. But stuff related to my father? That should be too important to hold back. At the very least, she could've given me the book when I was old enough to understand whatever he'd written inside. I reread the letter.

Your father used this book to keep a record of his travels, associates, and transactions. He carried it with him whenever he traveled. The details of his work might be valuable to you in the future. His notes are private, of course, and you should keep them to yourself.

"That won't be hard to do." I examined the book. "There's no key to open it."

I fingered the lock. It was tarnished, yet it held the book covers tightly together. The book wasn't going to give up its secrets easily. Picking the lock was an option, but I didn't want to break it. I'd have to be careful.

"Well?" Jack brought in two steaming mugs of coffee.

"I'm going to go find something we can use to pick the lock," I said heading for the stairs. Back in my bedroom I ran my fingers through the top contents in my armoire. I needed something thin enough to fit into the keyhole. A sewing needle wouldn't work and a bobby pin was too big. I found a couple of old keys I'd collected over the years, and for a moment I wondered if one would work. But none looked as if they'd fit. As I dug through the various pieces of costume jewelry, lockets, and bracelets, something small and thin in the back of the middle drawer caught my eye.

My father's hat pin.

The pin was not quite two inches in length, with a small replica of an old-world globe affixed to one end. The stem was gold and ended in a tiny S-shaped point.

Before my fingers even touched the little piece of jewelry, I knew it would fit the lock perfectly. When I picked it up, a warm tingle ran through my fingers.

Jack sat examining the lock when I came downstairs. He'd lit the fireplace and the room was warmer. "I might have something in my toolbox we can use," he told me as I stepped off the bottom stair. "But it is pretty small."

"I don't think we'll need to do that." I held up the pin.

"What's that?"

"My father's hat pin."

"Really? Where'd you get it?" He held out his hand.

I passed the pin to Jack as I sat down beside him. "A few months after my father died, someone came by the house and dropped off the things he had with him during that trip. This was one of them."

"It was tough on you." He squeezed my knee.

"No one survived the train wreck. They told us there was hardly anything left. God, it was horrible." I closed my eyes and rubbed the skin between my eyebrows with a fingertip. "Before the hat pin was delivered, I was convinced he wasn't dead. That he escaped. You know how kids are. Dad, the traveling salesman, survives the wreck, but has amnesia so he doesn't come right home. He's out there trying to find out who he is. I had a wild imagination."

Jack tweaked my nose. "You still do."

"Yeah, well, at least now I know the difference between make-believe and the real world." I swatted his fingers away. "Anyhow, there were some other things too. I remember a long coat and a pair of boots being delivered with the pin." I considered the little antique in Jack's hand. "But no hat and no book."

"Who delivered your father's stuff?"

"You know, I don't remember. Probably someone from work, but I'm not sure."

"You could ask your mother," Jack said. "I'm sure you'll be talking to her today."

"You can say that again." I reached for the hat pin. When I touched it, I felt another little tingle tease my fingertips.

"It's an interesting pin. I'm taking a wild guess that the globe represents traveling around the world?"

"I'm guessing," I said. "I never thought about

it. I finally admitted to myself that he wasn't coming back when my mother gave it to me. It was as if the pin was a sign he was really gone."

"I'm sorry." Jack put his arm around me and gave me a hug. He kissed the top of my head.

"Oh, it's okay." I shook off the dark feeling as I sat up straighter. Parents die and some die when you're still growing up. "It was a long time ago and no one can change the past. I'm sorry he's gone, but that's just the way it is. Sometimes accidents happen." I didn't meet Jack's eyes. It was time to get down to business and I reached for the book. "Now, let's see if my hunch is right."

Taking care not to damage anything, I inserted the S-shaped end of my father's hat pin into the old book's lock. It slid right in. I wiggled it, turning the globe slightly to the right between my thumb and finger.

The lock made a little *Click!* as it opened. I looked up at Jack.

He grinned. "It worked."

"Indeed it did." I opened the book, revealing softly yellowed pages with my father's handwriting flowing across them. I ran my fingertips over his notes, hearing the sound of the kitchen door opening and his voice calling out to my mother. *Lydia! Where is my beautiful wife?*

"By the way," Jack said. "What kind of hat did your father wear?"

I cocked my head to the side, remembering.

"Believe it or not, a top hat."

※ ※ ※

The book was a treasure trove of sketches, hand-drawn maps, and a lot of departure and arrival dates. Some pages consisted of nothing but strings of numbers. Jack said they could be geographic coordinates, but I had no idea. I skimmed the handwritten notes about the places my father traveled to, the people he met – or planned to meet – and even some of the items he picked up on these trips. The word 'Delivered' was written by shipments ranging from tea to jewelry. Other pages contained lists with cryptic notes jotted in the margins such as: 'Not available after The Split' or 'Available to Senior Salesmen only.'

"This is incredible." Jack turned through the pages. I detected a bit of the professor coming out. "We should show this to Martin and get his feedback. He might be able to give us an idea of what these dates refer to if they correspond with big enough events."

Dr. Martin Shaw was a history professor on campus where Jack taught English. He was a good friend to Jack, but I didn't want to show the book to anyone else just yet.

"Remember what my mother's letter said? I should keep this to myself. I don't plan on passing it around for everyone to go through, Jack. Even if Mom hadn't said anything, it was my Dad's. I'd like to see what he's got in here first." I pulled the book from his hands.

"Sure, sweetie, I understand." Jack nodded, his brows dipping into a little frown. "If you change your mind, I'm sure Martin would be happy to help you figure out what some of these things might mean."

"I know." I closed the book and looked at the mantle clock ticking off the morning's minutes. My breath caught when I realized how late it had become. Two hours had flown by.

"Jack?"

"What, sweetie?"

"Look at the time. It's eight o'clock!"

Jack lifted his eyes to the mantle before turning back to me. He shook his head. Where had the time gone?

CHAPTER 2

My mother, Lydia McKay Swift, is a lovely, whimsical sort of woman. For as mysterious as my father's work had been, my mother's was just as puzzling. Growing up it was easier to tell my friends she was an artist, which was sort of true. She composed music, painted, sculpted, danced, and wrote poetry. Every now and then she could be found wearing big, bulky work clothes over her slender frame as she sawed, hammered, and constructed various pieces of furniture or other odd items in her workshop.

Mom never worked outside the home, but she was not your typical housewife. The house was usually in a mild state of chaos as she moved from project to project. Still, I think she was successful. Paintings and sculptures disappeared soon after they were completed. Sometimes I wondered if my father took them when he went on his travels. Perhaps he sold them for her.

When I was around 15, I asked my mother if she had any of her artwork since nothing was ever out on display. She just waved her hand at me and said, "Oh those? They weren't mine, dear."

And that was that.

After Jack left for campus, I sat down at my desk with the book and phoned Mom. I looked out the window at the snow-covered trees while I waited for her to pick up. After several rings, she answered, singing prettily.

"Good morning, my beautiful Emily! Happy birthday to you!"

"Hi Mom, are you busy? Did I call at a good time?" I picked up a pen and started to draw circles on my notepad.

"Of course you did! I would have called you first, but I wasn't sure if you would sleep in on your birthday."

"Funny you should mention that," I said. "I did get up earlier than planned. I don't know who you used to send your package, but it arrived at around six a.m."

"Sounds like perfect timing!" she said, her voice still singing in my ear. I shook my head. Sometimes my mother and I had two different conversations – at the same time.

"Anyhow, Mom, it was creepy because I didn't know who it was from. There wasn't any postage on it either. By the way, how did you send it?" I wasn't going to let it slide that easily. When I wanted answers, little could distract me. Of course, Mom had years of practice in that department.

"By courier, dear. Aren't you more interested in what was inside?"

"Oh, I am, Mom. Really. But like I said, it was strange to get a package that early. And there weren't any footprints in the snow either. That seems weird, don't you think?"

"Well, you are a curious person," Mom said. I could picture her head bobbing up and down. "But sometimes, dear, there's no great mystery. And sometimes, there's no explanation for a great mystery! I've always said that when life delivers you little pieces of delight, don't question it. You just say thank you and carry on. Who knows what kind of inspiration might show up at your door when you least expect it?" She was cheerful. She was ramping up. Soon the conversation would take off in a different direction. I had to keep her focused.

"Mother..." I started, closing my eyes. *Breathe.*

"Oh Emily, it's nothing! I simply contacted an old service specializing in discreet deliveries. They deliver at all hours! I wanted the package to arrive before your birthday, and I was running a little behind. As for the missing footprints, we'll just have to accept that odd little tidbit for what it is."

I could hear the smile in her voice. Fine. I wasn't going to pursue it. She was right; I should be more excited about the present itself. I now had my father's private journal. Opening my eyes, I picked it up from the desk, my fingers tracing the faded gold 'S' on the cover.

"Alright Mom, I give. I'll let it go for now. But someday you'll have to tell me how you know about a 'discreet' delivery service, okay?" I cleared my throat. "Anyhow, the book. This is Dad's journal from work?"

"It is. Now that you're thirty, you should have it. I'm so sorry he isn't here to tell you about it himself, Emily." Sadness crept into my mother's voice. She never talked about my father's death. She never remarried or had a relationship with anyone even years after my father was gone. "But he's not with us now. You should have the book."

"But what is it? If it's from his work, is it some sort of sales record?" I turned through the pages. My eyes roamed over lists of numbers, dates, and locations. There were a lot of drawings, some with odd little notes. A sketch of a rabbit missing a powder-puff tail caught my eye. Beside it my father had written: *If a Rabbit has no tale, can he still tell a story?* At the bottom of the page, he included a string of numbers: *4.23.67.7.78.* None of it made any sense to me.

"I believe so. But I've never read it."

"You never read it? Why?" Why wouldn't she look inside my father's – her husband's – book?

"My dear, you had the hat pin."

I resisted the urge to bang my head on the desk. "Yes, speaking of the hat pin, why didn't you tell me that was the key?"

"But I didn't have to," Mom said. "You used it to open the lock, didn't you?"

"Yes, yes I did." I let out a slow breath. "So Mom, you never looked inside to see what was there? To read what he wrote?"

"No, I decided it was better for you to look at it first. You're more like your father than like me."

"Your note said the contents are private, that I shouldn't show anyone. What is it about this book? What am I missing?"

My mother was quiet for a moment before I heard her sigh through the phone. She wasn't telling me something, which wasn't that unusual, but I sensed something big lurking in the corners of our conversation.

"Mom?"

"Maybe it's time for me to come for a little visit."

❊ ❊ ❊

After phoning Jack to tell him my mother would be spending the night on Friday, I put aside the copywriting project work I had planned for the day. That's the beauty of working from home and being my own boss. Except when deadlines moved up and I found myself scrambling to complete a project at two in the morning. Except when I was hustling for a new client. Except when I was the only one to do all the work. That's the downside of being your own boss.

Still, I always pulled a rabbit out of the hat at the last minute and survived the little entrepreneurial challenges that came up. It was that way when I was in college. Back then report deadlines were always met, but only after a night of frantic research and coffee-fueled creativity.

Jack used to tease me by saying when I got out into the real world, there would be no hats to pull a rabbit from.

Hats. Whatever happened to my father's top hat? I slapped my forehead. I didn't even think to ask Mom about the hat during the phone call. Damn. I bit the bullet and I dialed her number again. I wasn't sure if it was good or bad fortune when I reached her voice mail.

"Hello! This is Lydia. If you are looking for a little inspiration, just leave me a message at the beep and I'll send some your way!" A tone followed.

"Hi Mom," I said. "I completely forgot to ask this morning, but do you have Dad's hat? The one he used to wear when he traveled? I don't remember seeing it when... When they delivered the hat pin, I don't remember the hat being with it." I took a chance Mom had it in her possession. "Can you bring it with you when you come down? Thanks. I'll talk to you later. Love you."

It was only ten in the morning and it looked like my thirtieth birthday was going to be a memorable one.

* * *

I spent the next few hours going page by page through my father's notes. Whenever a date or a location caught my eye, I recorded it on a separate notepad. I didn't want to mark up the pages with my own handwriting or post-it notes, so this seemed like a good alternative. I planned to look up some of the places and dates online to learn if there was anything special that might clue me in on some of the more cryptic references Dad made.

As I jotted down my notes, I began to refer to my father's journal as The Book. Capital 'T' capital 'B.' It just felt right.

At the very beginning of The Book, my father sketched a map featuring three prominent cities: Matar, Anwat, and Vue. He drew what looked like mountains in the northern part of the map, and a body of water in the southern part. Another possible city was called Port of North, which sat on the northern edge of the sea. Now, I'm no expert in global geography, but nothing sounded even remotely familiar.

I started my research with Matar. Nothing came back on a city, but I did learn that Matar was the name of a star. I continued to search on the name, but I couldn't pinpoint where the city was located. I searched on Anwat next.

Apparently there was an Anwat – an Anwat Gar, to be specific. It's located on a fictional planet from the He-Man and the Masters of the Universe series.

Probably not the same Anwat.

Strike two.

Next up: Vue. I couldn't find one city named Vue buried in the search results for Vue the car, Vue the restaurant, and VUE: Visual Understanding Environment.

I punched 'Vue Anwat Matar' into the search engine. Nothing. I typed in Sight Sea, the name of the body of water on the map. Some information on hotels in Greece and Turkey showed up. Well, at least they weren't located on some fictional planet with He-Man and his friends.

I tapped my fingers on the keyboard, staring at the screen. My father included other notes on the map. Between the cities he wrote: *Hidden cluster? Is Rabbit there?* I paused. He mentioned a rabbit on another page. I flipped a few pages forward to the sketch of the tailless bunny. I read the note again: *If a Rabbit has no tale, can he still tell a story?*

What if Rabbit was a person? I read the numbers my father wrote at the bottom of the page: *4.23.67.7.78*. Could it be an IP number? I didn't know if my father ever used a computer, but it couldn't hurt to check.

I typed the string of numbers into my browser. A second later the page returned reported 'The address 4.23.67.7.78 cannot be found.'

"No kidding," I said to the screen. Nothing was being found.

❋ ❋ ❋

Jack planned to take me out to dinner for my birthday. As much as I looked forward to our evening together, I spent the entire day fixated on the notes in The Book. Daylight disappeared. It seemed as if there were an endless number of pages. I would get lost staring at a map or trying to figure out the hidden riddles in my father's notes. Daniel Swift was becoming even more of a mystery. I realized how much I didn't know the traveling man with a quick smile and a top hat.

"Where did the time go?" I whined to Mischief as I dressed. The slender white cat sat watching me from the corner of the dresser as I dug through a drawer. William wandered into the bedroom and made as if to jump up on the dresser too. Mischief's pointed hiss convinced him to watch from a safer spot on the bed.

"It's The Book. I lose all track of time when I'm going through it." I pulled out a red sweater with a deep V-neck. I'm not a vixen, but it was my birthday, after all. Why not celebrate? "This is going to have to do."

Mischief blinked at me and yawned.

"Thanks for the vote of approval." I scratched her under the chin before she made a couple of strategic jumps and curled up in her kitty bed. Red sweaters, humans, and William forgotten, her eyes slid shut and that was that.

"So what do you think, William?" I asked. He stretched, his body taking on a yoga pose. He threw out a few cat murmurs, but he didn't have much of an opinion either. "You two are no help."

I paired the sweater with a black pencil skirt that came to just below my knees. Black tights slipped into a pair of black heeled boots that lifted me by three inches. Pulling my hair up into a twist, I brushed my bangs to the side. I looked into the mirror. Not bad. I was ready for my date – who was running late. Reservations were for seven-thirty and it was already seven.

Last month I told Jack I didn't want a birthday party. I love my little circle of friends, but I wanted to celebrate this milestone with a nice dinner followed by a quiet evening curled up in front of the fire. After Jack asked about a hundred times if I was really sure I didn't want a party, he finally promised we would stick to dinner for two.

I stopped by my office on the way downstairs, grabbing The Book and my notepad. I knew it was my imagination, but I felt a tiny little thrill whenever I picked it up. It was a connection to my father.

I had a list of questions for my mother when she came on Friday. She knew about The Book all of this time, but never told me she had it. Why keep it a secret? She said she never looked inside, but told me to not share it with anyone. How could she not read it? She made sure I got The Book on my thirtieth birthday, and not my eighteenth, or twenty-first, or even as a graduation present. So why now? Why not before? And where was the damn hat?

I was becoming more and more fixated on my father's missing top hat. Perhaps my curiosity was stirred because the hat pin was The Book's key. I sat in the living room so I could keep one eye on the window while I waited. I held The Book between my hands.

"I just don't know what to do with this," I said to the empty room. I ran my fingers across the worn cover. Come on, this was my father's journal. It shouldn't be this hard. I closed my eyes and turned to a random page. The old paper was smooth under my touch. I stroked the page. Tell me where to go next. I opened one eye. Great. Yet another one of Dad's cryptic notes:

Templeton.

Not in Matar during EoS?
Friend?

My father underlined Templeton twice. Templeton was probably a person, and maybe someone important. I knew from the map that Matar was a city or town. I had no idea what EoS meant, but two out of three wasn't bad. One thing was clear, my father wasn't sure if this Templeton was a friend when he wrote the note.

Templeton. I didn't remember my father ever mentioning the name when I was little. My mother never talked about a Templeton either.

"Tem-ple-ton," I annunciated each syllable. "Who are you?" Picking up my notepad, I wrote the name down and underlined it twice, just like my father had done so many years before. "And are you a friend or not?"

Staring at the page, I continued to talk to myself. Mystery, my silky, black kitty, sat his portly self at my feet. He was listening to me.

"E-o-S." I tapped the letters with my pencil. "E-o-S. Have I seen this before?" I flipped back and forth between the pages of The Book. Something was whispering from a corner in my mind. I skipped sketches of doors, more map drawings, and other wordless doodles. "Here," I stabbed the page with my finger. "This is it."

When in Matar, look for
Anne Lace. Her special-ty

helps people see.
May have knowledge
regarding Eve of Silence.
Will need Rabbit's help.
Contact prior to
Solstice.
Avoid Walled Zone.

EoS had to stand for Eve of Silence, right?

"Oh, yeah, that sounds good," I shuddered. Mystery offered one of his semi-silent mews from the floor. I touched my fingertips to the top of his head. "Okay, so we have Eve of Silence, a woman named Anne Lace with some sort of 'special-ty,' another reference to someone called Rabbit, and we're supposed to stay away from the Walled Zone –" I flicked back a few pages "– which is on the map with Matar."

I jotted down the new information. Which Solstice did my father mean? Winter or summer? The winter one was right around the corner. "And you, Templeton," I turned to the first mention of the name. "Were you in Matar during the Eve of Silence or not?"

What was up with my father? I chewed on a thumbnail. This journal of travels and sales sounded a lot less like a list of business transactions and more like something out of a spy novel. I put The Book down on the coffee table and stared at it. I willed it to give up its secrets.

The sound of Jack's car pulling into the driveway brought me back to the real world. Patting Mystery on the head one more time, I pulled on my heavy wool coat and stepped outside.

It had snowed earlier in the day, dumping another five inches of the white stuff throughout the city. I loved it. It always snowed on my birthday. I picked my way down the slick sidewalk. After climbing into the car, I leaned over for a kiss. Jack obliged.

"Who was here?" he asked.

"What do you mean?" I dug around my coat for the seatbelt.

"I mean, who just left?" Jack pointed toward the front door.

"No one was here." I stopped my search and looked up. I felt a strange pit open up in my stomach. "No one was here, Jack."

"Well, someone was walking down the sidewalk and away from the house when I pulled up. The wind blew snow across the windshield for a second so I couldn't make out who it was."

"Wait here." I climbed from the car and checked our sidewalk. The pit in my stomach pushed a taste of nervous acid into my mouth.

There was only one set of footprints.

Mine.

CHAPTER 3

"I'm just saying I don't think you should be so upset by it," Jack said as the waiter poured us each a glass of red wine. He lifted his glass, toasting me before taking a sip. "I'm sure there's a reasonable explanation. Let's focus on the birthday girl instead."

"You wouldn't be a little freaked? Who was there? What were they doing?"

"Sweetie, it was probably someone who had the wrong house and they realized it before they rang the bell. Then they left. No big deal."

"Jack, there weren't any footprints."

"The wind was blowing. Maybe the snow covered them."

"The snow is too deep."

"Sweetie..."

"Jack, there were no footprints this morning when The Book was delivered, remember? What if it's the same guy? Or person – whatever!" I ripped a piece of bread off the crusty loaf sitting between us before plunging it into a dish of olive oil.

"I think this book has you a little on edge."

"Gee, you think?"

"Sweetie," Jack began again. "I know there's a lot you don't know about, but let's keep everything in perspective. There's an explanation for everything."

"Sometimes there's no explanation for a mystery," I said as I thrust another piece of bread into the dish.

"What do you mean?"

"That's what my mother said. Sometimes there's no explanation for a mystery."

"Well, when Lydia gets here on Friday, you can talk about it then. If there is some mystery behind the book, she probably knew it would come up. I bet she's expecting you to ask questions. The fact she's coming here to talk to you face-to-face about it should tell you something."

"Maybe." I took another sip of wine. My eyes wandered across the dining room as I pictured the sketches and words from The Book. Templeton. The name played cat and mouse in the edges of my thoughts. Who was he? Was he a friend of my father's? I knew I should drop the subject for the rest of the night. Jack was patient, but I didn't want to push it. Forcing a smile, I picked up my menu. "Do you know what you're ordering?"

He raised an eyebrow at me but decided to roll with it.

The restaurant was packed on this first day in December. The dinner crowd laughed and yelled, and the combination of noisy patrons and clattering from the kitchen created quite the din. Still, the food was always excellent and the service was top notch. Jack ordered lamb while I opted for the seared tuna.

Over dinner Jack described his workday – the semester was winding down and more than one student anxiously requested an appointment. I tried to focus on the conversation. I nodded and rolled my eyes at the appropriate spots, but I was beginning to feel a little chill crawling down my back. I didn't dare say anything to Jack, but I felt like someone was watching us. Watching me.

During dinner, I stole little peeks around the dining room to see if I recognized anyone. I couldn't turn around to check behind me. Jack would probably lose all good humor at that point.

I didn't want to be this paranoid. Yet that prickly feeling walked up and down my spine. I wasn't imagining it.

"I'm going to run to the ladies' room. I'll be right back," I said as I stood. I left my napkin on the chair and weaved in and out around the other tables, avoiding the wait staff and their towering trays.

I scanned the crowd for someone I might recognize. I didn't see anyone who looked familiar and was just about to turn into the lobby when something – or rather someone – caught my eye in the mirrored wall. I stopped short.

A tall man sat at the bar behind me. He had turned to watch as I walked on by. He swirled the wine in his glass studying me – no, appraising me from head to toe. Our eyes met in the mirror. I felt the same creepy shiver as before, but I was tired of being on edge. I felt angry. I needed to take action on something. Anything. I spun around and marched over to the bar.

A split-second flash of surprise ran across his face as I stepped in closer. Good, he didn't expect me to walk up to him. I took a quick inventory. He was somewhat attractive, with black hair cropped short and light eyes that looked as if the blue had faded from them, leaving only a dark ring around each iris. His features were cut a bit too sharp for my taste. I guessed him close to Jack's age, but probably older. A smirk slid into place as he looked down his nose. His arrogance hung in the air between us.

I got straight to the point, lifting my chin. "Hi. You were watching me. Do I know you?"

His mouth moved into a sly smile as his eyes traveled to my lips and then lower to my cleavage. I felt the color spread up from my V-neck and into my cheeks.

"You... *could*." A low voice brushed over my ears. He tilted his head and blinked, his gaze rising. The exchange gave me chills, and not the good kind.

"I don't think so, buddy." I spun fast on my heel and made a beeline for the lobby, heeled boots clicking like mad. Once inside the ladies' room, I leaned on the counter and stared into the mirror. Oh yeah, that was smooth. I needed to get a grip. I shook my head at my reflection. Enough was enough. Jack was right. I was making myself crazy over nothing. So my father's book was strange, and my mother was acting weird, but what else was new? I'd just have to deal with it until I was able to pin her down for more answers.

I kept an eye peeled for the pick-up artist when I left the bathroom, but the dark-haired man was gone. Good riddance.

"Where did you go?" Jack asked as I sat down at the table.

"Got lost on the way." I gave him a half-hearted smile. He winked at me. I considered telling him about the guy in the bar, but we were interrupted by singing.

"Happy birthday to you," sang several members of the wait staff. A piece of gourmet pumpkin pie was placed in front of me. A lit candle sat in the center of the dessert. "Happy birthday to you. Happy birthday, dear Emily, happy birthday to you!" The restaurant broke into applause as the wait staff cheered. I blushed and Jack frowned.

One waiter called out above the noise. "Make a

wish!"

I grinned, leaning over to blow out the candle. Jack still wore a puzzled look on his face, but I was caught up in the moment. I didn't stop to ask what was wrong. Closing my eyes, I took a deep breath and tried to think of a good wish.

Unbidden, the name flashed against the wall of my mind. *Templeton.*

Oh, what the hell. Who is Templeton?

❋ ❋ ❋

"What's wrong?" I asked around a mouthful of pie after the wait staff left and the other diners went back to their conversations.

"I didn't tell anyone it's your birthday," Jack said.

"What do you mean?" I waved my fork, pumpkiny-goodness dangling from the end. "God this is good, Jack."

"I mean I didn't order you any pie. I didn't tell the staff it's your birthday. Emily, I don't know where that pie came from." He pointed to my plate.

I froze, my fork poised halfway between my plate and my mouth. Jack didn't order the pie. And it was pumpkin pie. I always had pumpkin pie on my birthday. Who knew that but my family and closest friends? Sometimes there was cake, but it was for other people. I set the fork down and waved over the young waiter who told me to make a wish.

"Something wrong?" He wiped his hands on his apron, blinking at me from under a set of truly unruly eyebrows.

"No, not at all. Well, no." I hesitated. "It's just we didn't order this pie, so we're wondering where it came from."

"Oh, right." The waiter patted his pants before fishing a piece of paper out of a pocket. "I forgot to give you this. You must've been wondering what was up." He laughed. "Here. Your friend told me to give this to you."

"My friend?" I glanced at Jack before taking the folded paper from the young man. I opened the note. Unfamiliar, slanted handwriting appeared in black. The note simply said:

Happy thirtieth birthday, Emily.
Enjoy your dessert.
T.

I handed the paper to Jack. He read it, his brows pulling together.

"Who is 'T'?" he asked.

I shook my head, surprised at what I was thinking. "You won't believe me."

"Try me."

"Let's get out of here. I'll tell you on the way home." I pushed the pie away and stood to leave.

As we left the restaurant, I could've sworn out

of the corner of my eye I saw a top hat balanced on a shelf high above the coat rack. When I looked again, it was gone.

※ ※ ※

"And so you think this Templeton from your father's book is the person who sent you the pie?"

I had to admit, the fact that Jack wasn't suggesting we make a little visit to the psych ward 'just for an evaluation' was pretty amazing. The idea sounded crazy to me too.

"Well, no. Not really. I mean, I don't know what to think! Jack, you have to admit this has been a weird day, from the moment we opened that book, to dinner tonight. And who sent the pie? We can't write it off as just some bizarre coincidence."

Jack stretched back into the cushions and ran a hand through his hair. We had tucked in on the couch as planned, no work glowing up from a laptop, no pile of papers to be graded, and the only book gracing the coffee table was The Book. Jack stared at it. This was not how we envisioned the evening ending.

"Em," Jack began, "was you father involved in anything illegal?"

"What? No. Of course not!"

"I'm only asking because you are right. Things

were a little weird today, and I don't want you to get hurt."

I pulled my knees up to my chin and fingered the hem of my pajama bottoms. "I don't know. At least I don't believe he'd willingly be involved in anything illegal. I guess I don't know for sure."

"Not the way you wanted to spend your birthday, is it sweetie?"

I dropped my shoulders and sighed. "No. But here we are. Look." I reached for The Book. "I've been going through it all day. There are so many pages, Jack. It's never-ending." I flipped through several. "Anyhow, I've been trying to put things together and there does seem to be some sort of story here. I've been taking notes and trying to make connections between the references."

"Story?"

"Yeah, story. See." I pointed to a page. "He keeps referring to these three cities: Matar, Anwat, and Vue. But I don't think they're real cities. Well, I think they're real, but I don't think the names are right. I think it's some sort of code. I think the entire book is written in code. Code names, fake names for cities, lists of numbers that might mean something else altogether."

"I guess that's possible," Jack said. "Of course the next question would be, why? Why keep your travel record, or sales record, in code? Unless?"

"I know, unless you were involved in something bad or illegal. But what if that's not it at all? What if you were one of the good guys, but had to keep your work secret?"

"What do you mean?"

"What if you were pretending to be a traveling salesman, but maybe you were really a spy or something? And this –" I held up The Book "– was your top-secret record."

Jack wasn't convinced. "Well, maybe. Em, do you really believe that?"

"I don't know what to believe. But my father was a good person and I don't believe he would be involved in anything bad."

"Your mother might be able to tell you more about his actual work. Ask her for help. Tell her what's in The Book. Show it to her. And tell her about the pie being delivered to the table." Jack paused. "Actually, would your mother know something about that? Do you think she would have a piece sent since she wasn't there tonight?"

"That's possible," I said. "But the note was signed with a 'T'."

"True." He rubbed his forehead. "You know, maybe for the next couple of days you can come to campus with me. Do a little work in the library. You can use my login for the WiFi."

"Why? You don't want me to stay home

alone?"

"I think maybe if we learn just a little bit more about what's going on with your father's book, then we won't wonder what's going to happen next. And we'll be close to each other if something comes up."

"I suppose I could ride with you. Do a little research while I'm there. Maybe I can browse some scholarly articles or something."

"Exactly."

I slid my fingertips across the cover of The Book. It held many secrets, and maybe some of them were not so good. I thought about the references to the Eve of Silence, the Split, the Walled Zone, and Templeton. Some notes did sound a little menacing. And the more I thought about it, I didn't know if this Templeton was a good person or not. My father had wondered if Templeton was a friend, and maybe the answer was no. There were others too. The woman named Anne Lace and someone called Rabbit – who didn't have a tale.

But there were answers in The Book; I knew it in my heart. The memories I had of my father, though few, were good ones. He was a friendly man with a big smile. And for as flighty as Mom could be, she was less scattered when he was home. Everyone liked him.

In fact, my mother's family adored my father. Relatives used to give him lists of things to pick up during his travels. I never paid much attention to that part of the grown-up talk, but several times he brought back large quantities of tea leaves for Mom's great-aunt Sadie – a small but spry seventy-something year old. Once, Sadie tried to pay my Dad and he refused to take the money. She pressed it back into his hand and pulled a tiny little purse from her pocket, waving it. She told him...

I sat up straighter. What did Aunt Sadie say?

"Em?" Jack asked.

"Just a second." I flicked through the pages of The Book. "There. That's it." I pointed to a list my father made. It said:

Emily:

1. ~~Flute~~

2. ~~Sand Castle~~

3. Purse from Anwat

4. Smoked mirror (Vue)

5. Shoes for travel

6. ~~Door Dust~~

Flute, Sand Castle, and Door Dust were crossed out as if they'd been acquired.

"What is this?" Jack read the list. "Were these presents from your father?"

"I think they were, or at least supposed to be. I remember getting the flute, but I don't know what happened to it. I do remember a jar of sand, but no sand castle." Some of my childhood memories were coming back to me. "Actually, I remember Dad telling me it was a sand castle in the jar, but it was up to me to put it together. When I asked him for water so we could make one, he told me it wasn't that kind of sand castle. I have no idea what happened to it. And I have no idea what he meant either."

"Door dust?"

"No clue, but it's this I'm interested in." I tapped the third item on the list: Purse from Anwat.

"Okay, but why?"

"When my father traveled, sometimes he would pick up stuff for my mother's family. He brought back huge packages of tea leaves for my mother's great-aunt. All of us called her Aunt Sadie."

"And?"

"And I remember he didn't want her to pay him. He kept telling her it was a gift, but she insisted on giving him the money. Aunt Sadie pulled out this tiny, green purse and said it was okay, because she had a purse from Anwat." I poked the list with my finger. "Purse from Anwat, Jack. She knew about a place in this book. If my Aunt Sadie knew, others probably did too. If my father was involved in anything illegal, it's highly unlikely my great-great aunt was also involved."

I sat back, half-excited, half-relieved.

"Is Aunt Sadie still alive?"

"You know, I don't know. I think my mother would've told me if she passed away. She'd be at least ninety now, but longevity runs in that family. She was very active." I pictured her pulling in the driveway during those summer visits. "I think she used to drive in from another state. She always traveled alone. I wouldn't be surprised if she was still alive."

"You should ask your mother. If your Aunt Sadie is alive and well, call her. Ask her what she knows about Anwat. Ask her about the other places too."

"I will. Wow." I put The Book back onto the table. As fast as the day had passed, it still felt like years since The Book landed on my doorstep. It felt like years since I turned thirty. I rubbed the back of my neck and gave a deep, shuddering sigh.

"Em." Jack reached for me, putting his hand on my shoulder. "Come here. It's been a long day."

I let him pull me against his chest and the two of us settled deeper into the cushions. I closed my eyes as he kissed my forehead.

"You'll figure this out," he said.

"I know. And now I think I have a place to start."

CHAPTER 4

It was another cold and snowy December day in upstate New York. My house sits on a quiet neighborhood street called Apple Tree Lane, which consists of homes built around 1920. Years ago, when Kincaid was a small town, an apple orchard stretched along the northernmost point. The town eventually grew into a city, but a nod to its agricultural roots remained in a surplus of green spaces and parks. However, out where the orchard once thrived it's now a sub-division of cookie-cutter homes and cul-de-sacs. Only a few apple trees remained.

After feeding the Furious Furballs, I checked on Jack. He was still asleep. I poked him and watched as he pulled the covers over his head. A barely intelligible sentence indicated he wanted to sleep for another 30 minutes. Typical.

Grabbing The Book from the dresser, I headed back into the kitchen to pour myself a cup of coffee.

I'd have to resist delving too far into The Book if I wanted to get any work done. Tapping my fingers on the kitchen table, I decided it wasn't practical for me to go to campus with Jack and spend the day at the library. I needed to make some headway on work projects. I also hoped I'd be able to find out if Aunt Sadie was still alive and if she could shed any light on my father's book. At the very least, maybe she could explain the Purse from Anwat.

I sipped my coffee, trailing my fingers over The Book's cover, tracing the 'S.' Today I would dive deeper to see if I could turn up anything that might help me make some sense of Dad's notes. I picked up my pencil and wrote 'Priorities' at the top of my notepad. First, client project: complete sales letter draft and verify with Sommers agency that new web copy is a go. Second, call Mom and ask about Aunt Sadie. Third, call Aunt Sadie and ask about The Book and the Purse from Anwat. I chewed on my lower lip, rolling the pencil back and forth between my fingertips before writing: Fourth, learn more about Templeton. I underlined Templeton twice. Number four was going to be a tall order, but someone had to know who he was. I would check with my mother on that one too.

My mother. I glanced around the kitchen. Mom would be arriving tomorrow. Better set some time aside for cleaning. Number five, mop kitchen, dust living room, pick up spare room.

Good enough.

* * *

"You're sure you won't come with me?" Jack stood in the kitchen with his travel mug in one hand, leather briefcase in the other. It was eight o'clock and he was leaving for campus. His first class wasn't until ten, but there was always plenty of paperwork and academic drama to attend to.

"I'll be fine. I think last night we just ended up over-reacting and –"

"We?"

"Yes, we." I pressed my lips together, pausing. "Okay, I'll admit I've been a little over-sensitive since The Book showed up, but you're the one who suggested I come to campus with you."

Jack took a deep breath. I could tell he was torn. He hadn't been that concerned until someone sent the piece of pie last night. Still, he believed there was a rational explanation, and he wasn't going to speculate on anything until I talked to my mother and my Aunt Sadie. He was confident the answers would come.

"Call me if there's anything strange, you got that?" Jack pointed his travel mug at me. "And check in with me after you talk to your mother."

"I will." Stepping forward, I gave him a quick kiss.

"And give Tara a call too. Run this by her. Maybe plan a lunch and tell her what's going on."

"I just might do that." Tara Parker-Jones was my best friend and managed a small specialty bookstore downtown. The hyphen in her last name wasn't the result of marriage. Tara's parents had a bit of a bohemian flair. At her birth, they each contributed a last name: Parker from mom, Jones from dad. Sometimes when I was about to crawl the walls from working alone at home, I'd meet her at our favorite environmentally-friendly coffee shop, *The Green Bean*. They served the world's best homemade quiche and even better lattes.

"Good. Tell her I said hello." He kissed me again.

"I don't suppose you could stay home instead?" I batted my eyes. He gave me a pointed look and I shrugged. "Hey, merely testing your self-control. So go. Be careful though. It's still snowing."

"Really?" he said over his shoulder as he stepped out into the windy morning. Unlike me, Jack wasn't the biggest fan of winter weather. I grinned and locked the door behind him.

I checked my Priorities list. I decided I needed to focus, clear out the cobwebs before tackling client work or doing research with The Book. I also decided I needed to be in a peaceful state before calling my mother. This meant grabbing the yoga mat and busting a few moves. This is also about the extent of my exercise regimen.

Several poses later I settled into a crossed-legged seated position and practiced some deep breathing. There. I felt yoga-fied.

After showering, I sat down at my office desk and clicked on the laptop. Ignoring email, I opened a file holding the latest copywriting project I was working on. I hesitated. It probably made more sense to call Mom first to learn if Aunt Sadie was still among the living. I'd also ask if she'd ever heard of a man named Templeton. It dawned on me that this Templeton could very well be a woman. I knew that little. I called Mom.

Aunt Sadie was indeed alive and kicking. She lived in Pennsylvania – or as Mom called it, down P.A. – near her family, and since it was winter, she'd most likely be home. In nicer weather the old woman still traveled by herself. My mother never heard of anyone named Templeton, and unfortunately my father's top hat was not among the items returned to her after he died. She assumed it was lost in the train wreck along with most everything else. Still, someone had managed to get the hat pin back to us. It was all so strange.

I decided to call my Aunt Sadie right away. I didn't know if she would remember me. Well, nothing ventured, nothing gained. I tapped the numbers into my phone.

I was just about to hang up after the seventh ring when an elderly, yet clear, voice answered.

"Hello, this is Sadie," she said into my ear.

"Hi Aunt Sadie? Um," I cleared my throat. "I'm sorry to bother you. This is Emily. Emily, um, Emily Swift." I realized Aunt Sadie hadn't seen me since I was a child. I wasn't sure the old woman would remember me at all.

"Emily! You're Lydia's daughter, aren't you? How are you, dear? Now wait here, is everything alright? Is Lydia okay?"

"Oh, she's fine, Aunt Sadie, just fine. I'm sorry, I didn't mean to worry you. Everyone here is fine." Great, give the poor lady a heart attack.

"Thank goodness! You gave me a scare. I hadn't heard from any of you folks up there in a while. Eventually, when you get to be my age, when the phone rings, there's a good chance you'll pull out your funeral clothes after you hang up."

I winced at the words, but figured it was true. "I'm actually calling because I have a couple of questions about my father, and I think you might be able to help me out. Do you remember him? Daniel Swift?"

The voice on the other end was quiet for a long moment. I heard a deep breath being drawn before Aunt Sadie spoke again. "I remember your father. He was a good man, Emily. I liked him. We all did."

In light of the past twenty-four hour craziness,

I appreciated her words. "Aunt Sadie," I began again, "do you know what my father did for a living?"

"He was a salesman. You didn't know that?"

"Well, yes and no. I knew he traveled a lot, but I'm not sure what he sold or even who he worked for. I remember him bringing you tea, though, and that's main reason why I called." I fidgeted with my pencil. "You tried to pay him once and he didn't want to take any money. You said it was okay because you had a 'Purse from Anwat.' Do you remember that?"

Aunt Sadie chuckled. "There's not a lot I've forgotten, Emily. I move a little slower, but my mind still works as fast as ever."

"I'm sorry! I didn't mean to imply–"

"Don't worry about apologizing. Now, are you a high-strung sort?"

"These days, Aunt Sadie, I am."

"Well, then. Let's start at the beginning. You want to know about your father's work and about the purse I had?"

"If that's alright with you. Yesterday was my birthday and my mother sent my Dad's old journal to me. He wrote about his work travels in it. There's a lot that doesn't make any sense to me, and I'm trying to figure it all out."

"Is that right?" Aunt Sadie said.

"So can you tell me about the purse?" I'd finished playing with my pencil and started to flip through The Book. I wanted to have the map in front of me.

"A Purse from Anwat is special. The legend says whoever has one won't ever want for money."

I frowned, but I wasn't sure if it was because I didn't understand the legend, or if it was because my great-great aunt believed it. "You mean it would make someone rich?"

"Hardly. No, a Purse from Anwat makes sure you'll always have enough for what you need. I suppose if you needed thousands of dollars, it'd make sure you had it. If you only needed a hundred, you'd get that instead."

"So, it's kind of like a lucky charm?"

"You might say that."

"But where is Anwat? I don't think it's a real city," I said.

"Oh, it's a real place, alright. A little off the beaten path, but it's real."

"Have you been there before?"

"Me? No. But I think your father used to travel in that neck of the woods pretty often."

"But where is 'that neck of the woods'? I looked it up online and the only thing I found is a reference to a city in an old cartoon."

"I don't think that's the same place," she chuckled.

I smiled. Aunt Sadie was quite the trip. I flipped a few pages further into The Book. "I don't think it's the same place either. Have you ever heard of Matar? Or a city called Vue?"

"Matar, sure. Vue, I don't think so. I think Matar is in the same region as Anwat. I'm not the best person to talk to about these places, Emily. Don't you have someone else who can help you?"

"My mother is coming tomorrow, but I'm not sure how much she knows."

"Hmm. Well, I'd check with her. She might shed some light on where these places are," Aunt Sadie said. "But isn't there a fellow salesman who can help you find out more?"

"I have no idea who my father worked with. I never met any of his co-workers."

"That's going to make it tough then."

"Well, there is a name that came up in The Book. Several, actually, but one in particular caught my eye. Templeton. Do you know anyone by that name? Did my father ever mention a Templeton to you?"

"Tem-ple-ton," Aunt Sadie repeated. "No, can't say I recognize the name."

Damn. "Okay, well, it was worth a try," I said. "Do you know what my father sold?"

"I believe he had quite the extensive inventory. I think most salesmen carry a variety of items. I'm sorry, dear. I wish I could be more help," Aunt Sadie said.

"Oh no, no! You've helped. Really," I assured

her. "Trust me. I've gotten more information from you than anyone else so far."

"God help you then," Aunt Sadie laughed. "Look, Emily, I think what you need is to get in touch with another salesman, someone your father knew and trusted. Ask your mother if she can find someone for you. If not, well…"

"I'll just have to figure it out, won't I?"

"You will. I know it. I seem to remember you were a lot like your father when you were little. A real go-getter."

The sentiment was nice, but since I realized I didn't know what my father was really like, it was a hollow compliment. "Thanks Aunt Sadie."

"You said you just had a birthday?"

"Yup. I turned thirty yesterday."

"Well, that makes sense then."

"What makes sense?" I turned to the page where my father had written Templeton's name.

"As I understand it, most salesmen don't take up the trade until their thirtieth birthday. Of course, there might be a few young ones who start traveling before then, but my guess is there aren't that many. On the other hand, some come into it a little late."

I sat at my desk trying to make sense of what she had just rattled off. "Aunt Sadie," I said, "I don't have any idea of what you're talking about."

"Get ready, because I think you will soon enough," Aunt Sadie said. "That's all I have for you today, but you can call me back when you know more about your father's work. Maybe I can help then. In the meantime, remember if you keep digging, you're bound to find answers you're looking for. Talk to your mother. See what she has to say. And keep your eyes peeled. You never know what'll find you when you're too busy looking for it."

It was an interesting way of looking at the situation. "Okay, Aunt Sadie. Thank you. You've been a great help. I really mean it."

"You take care of yourself. And keep a sharp eye on that book of your father's."

"I will. I'll call again and let you know what I find out."

"You do that. Good-bye, dear." Aunt Sadie hung up.

I set the phone down and moved my attention back to The Book, its faded 'S' seeming to sink deep into the cover. I wondered about it. Did the 'S' stand for Swift, or could it stand for something else, like 'salesman'? I traced the letter with my fingertip. "Salesman," I said. "But what kind of salesman?"

A crash downstairs sent me jumping from the chair. Two of the three furballs raced by my office door and tore into the bedroom. William stole behind the bed and Mystery slipped into the open closet.

"What the hell?" My heart drummed in my chest. I forced myself to be still, listening. I breathed through my mouth. Nothing. The wind and snow whipped up outside my window, but the rest of the house stayed silent. Grabbing my phone and hovering my thumb over the '9' on the call screen, I crept down the stairs into the living room. I held my breath, entering silently while my eyes darted to every corner. A large plant stand was knocked over. The spike plant living on top was now on its side on the floor. Dirt was everywhere. Great.

This had William's paws all over it. He was like a bull in a China shop with cabin fever in winter. "You wait until I get a hold of you," I threatened over my shoulder. "You better not have freaked out my plant!"

It was only when I turned to get the broom that I noticed little Mischief, her white tail puffed out and her head low. Her back to me, she stared from the kitchen toward a partly open pantry door. She hissed.

Dialing '9-1' with my thumb, I grabbed the broom kept in the corner by the fireplace. Before I lost my nerve, I rushed into the kitchen and kicked open the pantry door, slamming it into the shelves behind.

"Hi-yah!" I yelled as I made my move. The

pantry was empty except for canned goods and other boxes. Once again closing the call screen on my phone, I leaned on my broom.

"This is getting ridiculous. And you," I said as I turned to Mischief. "What's gotten into you?"

Mischief continued to stare past me into the empty space of the pantry in the 'I-can-see-things-you-can't-see' way that only cats can do. It was unsettling. I pulled the door shut. I'd had enough creepiness for one day. I called Tara's number. This was definitely a two-latte morning.

CHAPTER 5

"And you have no idea who sent the pie last night?" Tara asked wide-eyed, light eyelashes framing soft, brown eyes. She leaned forward, her thin hands gripping a coffee cup for warmth. Her fair hair slid forward, mussed from the woolen hat she wore to the shop. No matter where she went in winter, Tara layered on the sweaters, scarves, and gloves. Because she's such a tiny wisp of a thing, people have a habit of taking her for granted. What they don't know is that she's a shrewd and savvy businesswoman. Because of her management, the owner of the bookstore where she worked decided to give Tara free reign and semi-retired to Florida. *Pages and Pens* flourished and Tara developed a reputation for procuring hard-to-find and rare books. She did a significant amount of business online. Her customers lived all over the world. We met as freshmen in college. She's a bit of a matchmaker and was the one who introduced me to Jack.

"Not a clue," I answered, savoring another bite of my lunch. *The Green Bean's* quiche of the day was spinach-artichoke-Swiss.

"Wild." Tara shook her head. I filled her in on the latest, from the early morning delivery, to

The Book, to the birthday pie. I wrapped up by telling her about the conversation with Aunt Sadie.

"I know. I wouldn't believe half of it had it not happened to me. Did I tell you there were no footprints in the snow when The Book was delivered?"

"Maybe the snow blew over them," Tara said. She sipped her coffee and her eyes closed for a moment as she savored her drink. "Mmm. I love these lattes."

"Nope. There wasn't any wind and the snow was too deep," I said. "And Jack saw someone leaving the house last night, but again, no footprints."

"And Lydia arrives tomorrow?"

"Yes, would you like her to stay with you?" I raised my eyebrows.

"I love your mother, you know that." It was true. Tara adored her. After a visit from my Mom, my friend often disappeared into her apartment for a week or two, compulsively writing through all hours of the day and night. She said Lydia never failed to inspire her.

"That's because she's not your mother. Anyhow, it's a good thing she's coming. Maybe she can answer some of these questions. I just wish she wouldn't have waited all of this time, you know? Why not tell me when I was eighteen, or twenty?"

"Does your age really matter here?"

"No, I suppose not. I'm annoyed she didn't give me The Book sooner, that's all."

"Well, ask her about that too."

"That's the plan," I said. My list of questions was growing.

"So, besides the weirdness, how was your milestone birthday? Emphasis on milestone." Tara grinned over her latte.

"Cute, real cute. You just wait. You're not far behind me," I reminded her.

"Didn't you miss having a party? I think I want a party," Tara said.

"No, I didn't miss having a party, and yes, you can have a party, Miss I'm-So-Special. I'll throw you one."

"Good! I can give you a list."

"Of what? Presents?"

"No silly, guests. I might have a friend or two you don't know about." Tara waggled her eyebrows up and down.

"Oh, for the love of Pete." I rolled my eyes. Tara, little unassuming Tara, had a hot little black book that would make most women blush. Men couldn't resist her. I had my theories, but I wasn't sure I wanted to go there. Speaking of men. "Hey, I almost forgot. Some guy tried to pick me up last night."

"What?" Tara's little nose wrinkled. "When you were with Jack?"

"Yup. Well, no. Jack was back at the table. I had this feeling I was being watched, so I decided to make a trip to the bathroom. I went through the bar and saw this guy looking at me. I mean really looking at me, Tara. I was already on edge with everything that had gone on, so I just marched on over and told him I saw him watching me. I asked if I knew him or something."

"You did not!" Tara laughed.

I grinned. "I did. And he kind of gave me the ol' up and down and told me that 'I could.' I about died."

"Smooth." Tara rolled her eyes. "Was he at least cute?"

I thought about the man. He looked at me with such an intensity it made me uncomfortable. But was he handsome? There was something about him that was clearly unappealing.

"He was good-looking, I suppose. About Jack's age maybe? A few years older? Dark hair. I didn't pay attention to his body, but he was tall. Probably fit. His eyes were almost a translucent blue." My thoughts turned to Jack. When I looked into his eyes, I felt warm. It was not the same with the man at the bar. "Faded. They were cold."

"And you're certain you never saw him before?" Tara asked.

"Yup."

She cocked her head to the side. "Would you

know him if you saw him again?" Her gaze traveled over my left shoulder.

"Why do you ask?" I had a bad feeling. A bad, bad feeling. I clenched my jaw.

"Because there's a tall guy, with dark hair who parked himself at the counter about five minutes ago and he's been watching us the whole time."

"What color are his eyes?" My heart thumped so hard it made my throat hurt.

"He's too far away. Can't tell. But I think he's good-looking. I wonder if he's single? Oh, wait. I think he knows I'm talking about him." Tara pretended to check her wrist, presumably for the time. "You better look. We're creeping each other out and probably for no reason."

I nodded. Faking nonchalance, I turned toward the café counter. It was him, the man from the bar. "Ho-ly hell," I said.

He didn't try to hide or pretend he wasn't staring at us. For a moment, the noise of the café seemed to drain away, and all I could hear was my heartbeat, which sounded loud and slow even though it hadn't stopped racing. I studied the sharp angles of his face: his prominent cheekbones, the long line of his nose. I had missed the thin sideburns last night.

A good thirty seconds passed before he reached for a long, dark coat sitting on the stool beside him. He stood, pulling on the garment while we watched each other. Mental bells and whistles went off when he pulled out a top hat. Placing it on his head, he gave me that slow, sly smile before flicking his finger against the brim and disappearing into the second wave of the café's lunch crunch.

"Wait!" I bolted from my chair. I didn't want to lose sight of him.

"Emily!" Tara called after me as she jumped up. "What are you doing?"

I didn't care. I was following this jerk and getting some answers. I twisted around the scattered tables, knocking into chairs in my haste. Ignoring sharp comments to 'watch where the hell' I was going, I caught a glimpse of a top hat heading toward the back of the café. When I rounded the corner, he was gone.

"Dammit!"

"I'll say!" said a young girl to my right.

"What?" I turned to her.

"Some guy just went into the ladies' room," she said.

"Some guy? Was he wearing a top hat?"

"Top hat?"

"Yes, a top hat!" My voice slid up an octave. "You know, like a Dickens Christmas Carol hat." I waved my hands above my head as I tried to explain.

She didn't seem to be impressed with my pantomime, but the light bulb went off. "Oh yeah, like an actor! Yeah, he was wearing one."

I hurried down the hall to the door marked 'Ladies.' As my hand landed on the knob, I felt the door wasn't somehow quite right. But I gritted my teeth and pushed hard – before landing smack in the middle of the café's busy kitchen, tripping over my own feet and falling to my knees. In the process, I knocked over a trash can and slid in some tomato sauce.

I scurried to my feet. Crap! This wasn't the ladies' room! One of the chefs stared at me as I righted the garbage can, while two busy waiters pushed by and went back into the hall. I cleared my throat, my cheeks warm.

"Um, sorry, I was looking for someone." I started to back up. "Did a man in a top hat come through here?"

"No." The chef was a man of little words. He pointed a wooden spoon at me. "You need to leave now."

"Sorry! Going!" I scooted back out into the hall. But the door was marked 'Ladies,' right? What the hell?

I looked at the outside of the kitchen door. The sign read 'Kitchen – Employees Only.' But that was impossible – I'd gone through the door marked 'Ladies.' I looked for the young girl, but she was gone too. A woman stepped into the hall through a door several feet away.

"Were you just in the ladies' room?" I asked.

"Yes." She frowned as she looked at the tomato sauce on my knees.

"Was there a man in there? Wearing a top hat?"

"No, I was the only one in there." She scowled before turning and walking away.

I stood in the hall, baffled. Tara rounded the corner, her eyes once again big as full moons.

"Holy-mother-of-freaking-god-please-don't-do-that! What are you, nuts?"

Taking one more look at the sign on the door, I nodded. "I just may be, Tara. Let's go back to the table."

❄ ❄ ❄

"Okay, let me get this straight. Some girl told you he went into the ladies' room, and when you went into the ladies' room, you ended up in the kitchen instead? Maybe you went through the wrong door in all of the commotion." Tara sat across from me, her fine eyebrows raised.

"Well, it wasn't the right door, that's for sure." I took a sip of my Irish latte. Tara decided that the excitement called for more lattes – this time with shots of Bailey's and Jameson.

"He was definitely watching you," she nodded. She mulled over the events while she sipped her own hot drink. "And it was the same guy from last night? You're positive?"

"Absolutely."

"You need to tell Jack."

"Absolutely not."

"What? Em, this is a bit too much. There are a lot of whack-jobs out there. If he's following you... Ohmigod! What if he's the one who was at your house? The one Jack saw coming down your sidewalk last night?"

"I'd say that's possible."

"And you are not telling Jack?"

"Nope." My mind was running a mile a minute. Since The Book landed on my doorstep, I had nothing but confusing puzzle pieces to find and shove together. Every new path I explored only turned up new questions. Until now.

Tara threw her hands up into the air. "I give up."

"Don't, because I need your help." I'd left The Book at home, but I carried a small notebook in my purse. I flipped to a clean piece of paper and began writing. When finished, I ripped off the page and handed it to Tara. "Here. You have clients all over the world. Ask them if they've ever heard of these places or of any of these names. It's a long shot, because I don't think they're actual city names, but maybe they're close."

Tara read the list before looking up at me. "Matar? Anwat? Vue? I've never heard of these places."

"Me neither. But they're from a map in my father's journal. I want to show it to you and get your take on it. I wish I would've brought it along. I was in a hurry." I remembered the open pantry door and shuddered.

"That's good. I'd like to look at it, considering my profession and all." Tara gave me a pointed look before she went back to the list. "Sight Sea? What's the Walled Zone?"

"No clue. Maybe a mountain ridge or something. He drew little pointed sketches on the map. Like this." I wiggled my finger in the air. "They made me think of mountains."

"I wonder. Walled Zone sounds like a military term though, doesn't it?"

"Yeah, that's true. I didn't think of that." I handed Tara my pencil. "Put down that it could be a military zone."

"Okay, this is all well and good, but why aren't we telling Jack about you being followed?" Tara waved the pencil at me.

"Because the 'pick-up artist' from last night was wearing a top hat today," I said.

"It's Christmas-time. Maybe he's part of a holiday play or something."

"Maybe, but I don't think so." In my mind's eye I watched two puzzle pieces fit together.

"Come on, out with it," Tara said.

"My father wore a top hat too. Just like the one this guy was wearing."

"Really? That's, um, strange!" Tara laughed before apologizing. "I mean, I'm sorry, but top hats weren't all the rage when you were growing up."

"Oh, I know, but trust me. Weirdness ran in the family. You've met my mother, after all. She's just the tip of the crazy iceberg in our family."

"True. You are a bit nutty."

"Hey, I'm the most normal one of them all," I said. "I guess I didn't think anything about it back then. It's not as if he wore it constantly. Just when he left for work, or if we took a little trip. Come to think of it, we took a couple of daytrips by car and he brought the top hat with him."

"So let me put this together. You think because this stalker is wearing a top hat and because your father wore a top hat," Tara hesitated. She was a little suspicious of what I was suggesting. Okay, probably a lot suspicious.

"That he knew my father, yes," I finished.

"Alright, if that's true, and I promise, I am only going to ask this one more time, why aren't we telling Jack?"

"Because I think he will be a little bit more than freaked –"

"I'm freaked."

" – and I don't see how making him worry will make it any easier for me. I need to find out what the hell is going on and who our top-hatted friend is."

Tara stared at me, chewing the inside of her

cheek. I could almost see the wheels turning in her fair-haired head. She was weighing risks and possible outcomes. Her business-savvy brain was clicking along. *Clackety-clack.* I waited.

"Fine," she said. "We won't tell Jack – yet. But we need to be smart about it and you need to stay safe. Don't get cocky. Keep your doors locked when you're home alone, and make sure you're with another person if you need to go out. Call me with anything that's out of the ordinary, especially if you're followed again, okay? Oh, and keep your phone charged and with you at all times."

I saluted my friend. "Got it."

"So what's the next step?"

"Outside of you doing a little geography research and me entertaining my Mom? Not a thing."

"Nothing? What about 'Top Hat'?"

I took another sip of my booze-charged latte and looked Tara in the eye.

"I think he knows where to find me."

✤ ✤ ✤

Once home, I supposed I should've been more worried. Top Hat, as we were now calling him, was obviously following me. I even believed he was the mystery visitor who didn't leave any prints in the snow the night before. I wondered if he was the one who delivered The Book in the first place. I had a lot of questions for my mother now.

What would be the point of hanging around though? Why sneak in to deliver The Book, and then turn around and openly stalk me? It didn't make any sense.

"I bet he sent the pie too," I said.

"Muurrrh?" William asked from the floor. He weaved in and around my ankles while waiting for dinner. Mystery sat in the doorway, his big yellow eyes on guard.

"I said, I bet Top Hat sent the pie to the table last night. If he's the 'courier' my mother used from her 'discreet' delivery service, then maybe he knew it was my birthday. Maybe she told him I liked pumpkin pie instead of birthday cake. Maybe he thought it would be a fun prank to send me a piece during dinner." I dumped the wet food into a bowl. "Maybe the 'T.' on the little note stands for Top Hat."

"Mur," William replied before walking out of the kitchen, his tail trailing behind him. He had little patience for my chatter when he was hungry.

"Well, do you have a better suggestion, Bub?" I called after him. Mystery still sat in the doorway. "Well?"

He closed his eyes.

"I thought so." After putting down two bowls

of cat food in the kitchen, and delivering a third one to Mischief upstairs, I returned to the chili cooking on the stove. On the way home I stopped at my favorite bakery for some crusty bread. A blustery day like this one called for stick-to-the-ribs comfort food. A blustery day like this one also called for a bottle of red wine – especially after being stalked and giving pursuit in return. I had stopped at my favorite wine shop on the way home, too.

Things stayed quiet after I left *The Green Bean*. As I replayed the day's events over and over in my mind, I kept coming back to the sign on the door leading into the kitchen. It most definitely said 'Ladies.' And yet, I remembered having a quick feeling at the last moment that the door was not quite right in some way. Something was off. Well, yeah. It was the damn door to the kitchen.

I shook my head. Stupid door. Stirring the chili, I added my secret ingredients: a block of semi-sweet dark chocolate and a spoonful of peanut butter. The kitchen smelled fabulous.

Could Top Hat have switched the signs? That made little sense. He'd beat feet out of there before I could catch up to him. Besides, even if he'd waited around, I left the kitchen just about as fast as I entered it. There had to be another explanation. What about the young girl who said she saw him go into the bathroom? Was she in on it?

Giving the chili one last stir, I turned the burner to simmer. The Book sat on the kitchen table. I pulled up a chair and started to flip through its pages.

"I don't even know what I'm looking for," I complained to the empty kitchen. Turning past the map and several pages of numbers, I landed again on the list my father had written.

Emily:
1. ~~Flute~~
2. ~~Sand Castle~~
3. Purse from Anwat
4. Smoked mirror (Vue)
5. Shoes for travel
6. ~~Door Dust~~

"Door dust," I snorted. "Maybe that's what I need, some door dust. Like I even know what the hell door dust is." I flicked the corner of the page with my fingertip while I studied the list. A few seconds later I noticed another page stuck to the one I was reading. I rubbed the pages between my thumb and finger and gently separated them.

Another cryptic note from my father stared up at me:

Emily, the first door must
be the North.

"The first door?" A tiny tingle danced on the tips of my fingers as I ran them over the words.

"What does he mean the first door?" I pulled my notepad closer and started a list.

The Book appeared on the front doorstep.
The door marked 'Ladies' led into the kitchen.
Reference to 'Door Dust' – whatever that is.
The first door must be the North.

But there was something else. There was something that I couldn't quite remember, but it was right there at the edge my mind. I tapped my pencil on the list, stopping on the ladies' room entry. How did I end up going through the wrong door? What am I missing? What happened when I chased Top Hat? What happened when I touched the doorknob? It didn't feel right. But what does feeling right mean? I stared across the kitchen, seeing nothing. What had happened the moment my fingers connected with the doorknob? It wasn't right, I repeated inside my brain. Where have I heard this before? A memory flickered to life. I sucked in a sharp breath. That dream.

Two weeks ago, I had a terrifying nightmare about being chased. It didn't start out scary, but like many dreams, things eventually took a turn for the worst. I was outside, maybe somewhere downtown Kincaid, carrying an invitation in my hand. The paper was old and yellowed, crumbling around the edges. 'Swift' was scrawled across the top in wet, dark ink. I didn't recognize the handwriting. Thin letters slanted to the right. Below, the time and date had faded, and I could just barely make out the month: December. The invitation asked me to appear in court. A gold seal with an 'S' was pressed into the bottom. Nothing made sense.

I looked for anything familiar as I walked, but the storefronts were dark and I was lost. The setting morphed from an empty city street into a wooded path as the dream continued. I knew in my bones I was late for something important. There was some place I needed to be. Out of nowhere a door slammed shut behind me. It was a loud, but hollow, sound echoing in my head. Things grew darker and I began to walk with one hand held up as I searched for a way out. I gripped the invitation to my chest with the other. I wasn't sure which way to turn and I was worried about who or what slammed that door.

I pressed forward. The ground was uneven and I lost my footing more than once. The wind began to move through the branches above, their leaves whispering around me. They told me they had a secret. I stopped, listening. Wait! Was there another noise? Was something else moving around me? Nothing. It's nothing, I told my dreaming self.

Nothing? A soft voice. It was too close. I held my breath as a cool breeze slid across my cheek. Fingertips touched the back of my neck.

That's when I ran.

I raced through the dark, stumbling over roots and rocks. I managed to keep my balance and plowed forward. Ahead a light flashed and grew brighter as I thrashed through the underbrush.

There! I saw it! My getaway door. I tried to pull myself out of the woods and closer to the door, but the forest floor was not letting go. Behind me I heard twigs snapping and branches being shoved out of the way. Someone was getting closer. I tried to move, willing my feet to break free. I reached out and in the strange way dreams allow you to do the impossible, my fingertips grazed the doorknob. This was the 'right' door. I could feel it in my bones. This was the door I needed to go through – now. I stretched further, but I couldn't quite get my fingers around the knob. What was happening? Why wasn't I able to move?

I kicked my feet and threw myself forward, dropping the invitation as the darkness rushed up behind me. No matter what, I had to get through that door. Just as a hand wrapped around my ankle, I shook myself awake. I was in bed, sweaty and scared, with a sheet twisted around my foot. Jack slept like the dead beside me.

The dream drove me to the couch and sitcom reruns. I didn't dare fall back asleep that night.

Growing up, I was a child plagued by bad dreams. I had an overactive imagination that was a gift and a curse. I still had scary dreams from time-to-time as an adult. However, like most bad dreams, a couple of weeks of time faded this one from memory. It just wasn't relevant then. It was now.

The thought of the fingers on the back of my neck did me in and I fought the involuntary spasm that followed. It was like being home alone and thinking about a horror movie – and then hearing a noise downstairs.

Like this morning's noise. The one that inspired me to kick open the pantry door.

I couldn't wait until Jack got home.

CHAPTER 6

I managed to reign in my little panic attack and after pouring a big glass of wine, I sat back down with The Book and my notepad. I added to my list:

Nightmare about going through the 'right' door.

I know dreams aren't real. They're manifestations of fears, stresses, tidbits from life, and probably even part of the brain's way of entertaining itself. Or something like that.

But there was a difference now. I sipped my wine and thought more about the past year. Out of nowhere during the day, I would remember a snippet from a dream, like most people do. Something happens through the course of the day and you think, oh yeah, I dreamt about that last night. You spend a few minutes seeing scenes from the dream in your mind's eye and then move on.

Lately, these flashes were like phantoms. I couldn't quite hold them in my mind long enough to flesh them out. The storyline stayed the same. I needed to find the right way out to escape something. I needed to find a getaway door. Although I couldn't be sure, I sensed I always did.

Except for today. Then again, chasing Top Hat

at *The Green Bean* wasn't a dream. It was real.

When I told Tara I wasn't going to tell Jack about the mysterious man, I meant it. Jack is pretty easy-going, but if he knew a guy was following me, he wasn't going to brush it off. I'd have one heck of a time getting anything done under his watchful eye. Now it seemed as though I had a bigger issue. There was no way in the world I could tell Jack what I was starting to believe. He'd think I was losing my grip. He might be right.

I rested my hand on The Book. There were answers inside. I just had to figure it all out. My father, The Book, the doors, maybe even Top Hat. They were all connected. So, what now?

Getting to Top Hat was the next logical step. I had to talk to him. But how to find him? Even though he was at the restaurant last night and *The Green Bean* today, he was following me. It didn't mean he hung out in either place. No clue there. Or was there? If I was being followed, then wherever I went, he might show up. Maybe that's how I'd find him, by letting him find me. What did Aunt Sadie say? You never know what will find you when you're too busy looking for it?

That settled it. I'd go out and give Top Hat a chance to show up again. I'd have to be alone. He wasn't going to talk to me if I was with Jack or Tara.

My phone buzzed with a text message: *On way home. See you soon.*

Damn. Jack would be home in thirty minutes so going anywhere now was out of the question. I'd have to wait until tomorrow. Tomorrow! Mom would be arriving. I closed my eyes. Well, maybe I'd have time to go somewhere in the morning. When Jack left for work, I'd head out to... To where? Some place public. No sense taking any more chances than I needed to. And I would call Tara and tell her where I was going. Hopefully, I could avoid admitting I'd be going out alone. Even better, I would text her so she couldn't ask me a bunch of questions at once.

I decided it made sense to try out my little plan at the grocery store. It was the perfect place. Public, and I wouldn't need to make up an excuse. When I saw Top Hat, I wouldn't chase after him. I'd wait for him to come to me. Maybe I'd try to wave him over. I pictured myself gesturing to him from the produce section.

Maybe not.

It didn't matter. I had a plan. Even though the whole situation was downright bizarre, I felt like I had some control over what might happen next. Or so I liked to believe.

❉ ❉ ❉

Over dinner I told Jack about the morning's feline frenzy and the tipped plant, but glazed over the part where I thought someone might have been in the pantry. I omitted the whole episode at the café with Top Hat. I wasn't going to worry Jack until I had a better sense of what was going on. I told him I met Tara over lattes, and that she was going to help me figure out where Matar, Anwat, and Vue were located, if they even existed. That much was true.

Jack filled me in on the latest in departmental drama and student angst. I worked to focus on the conversation, but I was distracted by my plans for tomorrow. It didn't take long for him to catch the 'be back later' look in my eyes.

"Hello? Earth to Emily?" He waved a hand in front of my face.

"I'm sorry," I said. "I'm thinking about tomorrow when Mom gets here. I have so many questions. I'm not sure where to start."

"Start by filling her in on everything that's happened since yesterday morning. She might give you some information without you having to ask for it."

"That's a good point. I'll do that. And I think I'll run out to the grocery store before she gets here," I added.

"I can help you with getting things ready tonight." Jack paid no attention to my grocery store reference.

"Great. Thanks." I felt a little guilty about misleading him, but it was for his own good. Well, our own good.

"Tell you what, I'll finish up here in the kitchen and you make sure the spare room is all set. How long is she staying?"

"Just overnight. She'll get here late in the morning and then leave after lunch on Saturday. She said she's working on a new art project that's taking up a lot of her time."

"Painting again?"

"I think she's still in welding mode." I hung a damp dish towel over the oven door handle. "I'm afraid to ask."

Jack shook his head and smiled. Picking up The Book, I went to make the spare room presentable. After changing the sheets and running a dust rag over the dresser, I checked my email. A message from Tara had arrived during dinner.

Hey. Did a little digging and you're right. Nothing came up for cities with the names Anwat, Matar, or Vue. I couldn't find any good info on the Walled Zone either, although I'm not ruling out the possibility of something military-like. I do have a client in Spain who says that Matar means 'to kill' or 'to butcher' in Spanish. (I'm sure that makes you feel good, considering.) Anyhow, I'll keep looking. Call me tomorrow. I'll be at the shop all day.

Great. Matar means to kill or butcher in Spanish. That's comforting. I clicked out of email and looked at my calendar. Client work wasn't going to be put off anymore. I needed to earn my paycheck. I'd have to bite the bullet and get back into it. The Book and everything to do with it would need to wait.

No time like the present.

※ ※ ※

I worked late into the night and completed several items on the most pressing project with the Sommers agency. They had approved the web copy I provided to them, and the sales letter was one of the best I had ever written. I sent the files to the client along with an invoice. I so rocked.

Earlier Jack stopped by my office on his way to bed. Laptop tucked under one arm, he reminded me that my mother would be arriving soon enough, and that I should probably get a good night's sleep. I promised I wouldn't be too late. Jack raised his eyebrows. He knew better. I blew him a kiss goodnight.

Before closing down my laptop, I noted the time. It was well after midnight. I knew I should take Jack's advice and go to bed, but I hadn't looked at The Book all evening. Opening to a random page, I again read my father's note about the mysterious Templeton.

Templeton.

Not in Matar during EoS?
Friend?

I hadn't forgotten about ol' Templeton, but Top Hat's appearance and the door issue took priority. I realized if Top Hat knew my father, then he possibly knew this Templeton as well. Add that to the list of questions I planned on asking him.

Tomorrow could be the big break. In fact, everything might be answered between pumping Top Hat for information and getting actual facetime with Mom. Maybe that was being a little too optimistic, but I was hopeful.

I closed The Book and left it on my desk. Better to put a little distance between my father's journal and my night's sleep. It was just too distracting.

After slipping on a nightshirt, I crawled into bed beside Jack. He gave a little snort but rolled toward me, automatically pulling me under his arm. I cuddled closer, my ear against his bare chest. I could hear his heart beating its familiar *ta-tum! ta-tum!* and within minutes, I fell asleep.

❋ ❋ ❋

Considering the past couple of days, I wasn't surprised to find myself in yet another door dream. In fact, I made a point to tell my sleeping self that I knew I was dreaming. I was curious to see what would happen next.

A wooden door stood in front of me, the top disappearing into murky shadows above. I couldn't see a doorknob, so I tried to open it by pushing against it with both hands. It didn't budge. Could it be locked? I knocked on the rough surface and waited. No one answered. I pushed again. Nothing. Frustrated, I banged my fists against the wood, risking a splinter. In my bones I knew this was the right door. I knew I was supposed to go through.

"Do you need a little help, Emily Swift?" A voice asked from behind.

"I can't get this door open," I answered. Ugh! Was it stuck? I pressed my full weight against it and pushed before kicking it twice. The sound echoed. My hands roamed to its edges. Was there a handle I couldn't see?

"Is it the right door, Emily?" The voice spoke directly into my left ear. That got my attention and I turned to look. No one was there.

"I don't know. Yes. I think so."

"Why do you want to go through?" This time the voice sounded like it was inside my head.

"I want to know what's on the other side." Putting my palms against the door, I shoved as hard as I could. The door groaned, but held its ground.

The voice laughed. "Curious, are we?"

I stopped. The voice was not only in my head,

but all around me. The air seemed to crackle with energy. I turned around, facing the darkness. I couldn't see anything in the dim corners of my dream.

"Who are you?" I called into the nothingness. My mouth was dry. I felt as afraid as I had in the nightmare where I was chased.

"Someone who can help you open that door."

I wasn't alone anymore. It's just a dream, I reminded myself. Nothing can hurt me.

"I don't want to hurt you, Emily. I want to help you." The voice dropped even lower.

"Why?" I whispered back.

"Because I can."

A wicked shudder ran through me. It's just a dream, it's just a dream, I chanted silently. I turned back toward the door and leaned against the rough wood. It hummed under my hands. As I pushed, it began to swing open, groaning against its hinges. Pressing forward, I managed to make a two-foot opening. It was plenty of room to slide through. I entered a long, narrow room, with walls lined from floor to ceiling with books. It looked like an old library. A lit lamp sat on an empty desk. I turned around to see if the voice had followed me inside.

"Who are you?" I asked again.

"You know my name."

I hesitated, biting my lip. I didn't want to say it out loud. Instead, I let my thoughts conjure it:

Templeton.

The door slammed shut.

* * *

After the dream, I didn't get much sleep. I did, however, wake Jack and made him get me a drink of water. I didn't explain my dream to him – he was thankful – but spent the rest of the night tossing and turning and jumping at every little creak in the house.

At about five in the morning, I fell asleep. At six, the alarm sounded. I smacked my hand against the clock and buried my head in the pillow. Jack didn't even seem to notice it was time to get up. My whole body felt like I'd spent the night lifting weights. Every muscle was exhausted. Rolling over onto my back, I thought about what had happened in my dream.

Dream or not, imagination or not, I knew the voice belonged to The Book's mysterious Templeton. It didn't matter to me that my brain turned him into a disembodied voice. It was real enough, and I was more determined than ever to find out who he was and what connection my stalker Top Hat had to The Book and my father.

Two hours later, after Jack left for work, I sent Tara a quick text saying, *Mom here later. Running out for her fav tea. Text me later.* She replied: *Ok, but keep eye out for you know who. DON'T do anything stupid!*

I would definitely keep an eye out. I frowned at her 'stupid' comment.

I hopped into my car, a seven-year-old grey Subaru with a cranky heater. A couple of whacks usually brought it to life, but today it wasn't going to play with me. I shivered in my wool coat and reached for the radio. Instead, the car's weather-band squawked and infiltrated the FM station. I learned yesterday's precipitation in inches. I shut it off.

My plan was to park close enough for a quick getaway, but I'd take my time wandering the aisles. I'd be on the lookout for Top Hat and when I saw him, I'd move to a semi-private area. The idea was to give him the opportunity to come to me. If too many people were hanging around, he might not take the chance. I wasn't going to chase him this time. And I didn't want to be all alone when I finally got to ask him what was going on.

On the way to the store, I thought about last night's dream. The desire to get beyond the door was overwhelming. The conversation I had with the mysterious voice was already fading, but I knew it belonged to Templeton. It had to be him. And, he helped me open the door. The library on the other side wasn't familiar, but it wasn't unusual for people to dream about places they've never been.

I don't put a lot of stock in what dreams might mean. If I dream about a snake, it probably has little to do with sex or male appendages, and more to do with a snake. Then again, looking back at the past year of door-related dreams, I was rethinking my position. I wondered if a dream about a library could represent knowledge. The fact that I was so intent on getting through the door to this 'knowledge' also made sense. I wanted to figure out what everything meant, especially the cryptic notes my father left behind in The Book. I decided to stop at Barnes & Noble before going home. I could buy a book on dream interpretations. There had to be a bunch in the New Age section.

I found a parking spot up front, so I only had a short distance to trot through the slush and slop. I wore my old boots, but they must've developed a hole along a seam. I felt cold water leaking in around my toes.

I squished my way through the morning crowd, snagging a small shopping cart as I went. I hit the store at prime time. Those on their way to work stopped in for a bagel and a java-to-go at the coffee counter. I jockeyed through, keeping my eyes peeled for a tall man in a top hat. Fortunately, most people wearing hats chose the knitted cap variety, so I figured he'd be easy to spot.

I did need to pick up some items, so I poked along, grabbing bagged lettuce and a bottle of dressing. Most aisles had either other shoppers filling their own carts, or employees stocking shelves.

None wore top hats.

I pushed my cart back to the last aisle in the store: the beer aisle. I doubted many customers would be buying beer before nine in the morning.

Well, I was wrong about that one.

I wandered back and forth, from produce to pasta. There were plenty of other customers roaming the aisles, and plenty of employees moving pallets of goods out from the storeroom. There was even a spark of excitement when a terribly embarrassed man in a terribly big parka knocked over a small display of Christmas wrap – before backing into the 'Warm Up to Winter' soup display. He sent canned goods rolling down several aisles.

In the commotion, I caught something out of the corner of my eye. Whipping my head around, I just caught a glimpse of a top hat turning a corner.

Crap! I tried to turn my cart in the little throng that gathered to help or make fun of Parka Man. A couple of people moved, but I was blocked by an elderly couple toddling along in front of me. I swerved several times before I realized I should just dump the cart and go. So I did, excusing myself past grandma and grandpa before turning down the aisle to catch up with Top Hat. I caught a flash of his coat as he left the aisle by the other end. My boots slid on the wet floor, but I kept my balance. That earned a smirk from a stock boy.

I raced down the aisle and turned right, spotting Top Hat just ahead.

"Hey!" I called, but he didn't stop. A few fellow shoppers turned their heads and looked at me. I caught up to him and clamped my hand down on his arm. My heart sped up to panic mode. This is it! A shot of fear ran through me. He turned.

It wasn't him. Oh god, it wasn't Top Hat. My mouth popped open.

"Can I help you?" The man pulled away from me.

Jerking my hand back, I felt my face burn through several shades of red before landing on scarlet. "I'm sorry! I thought you were someone else, a friend of mine. Sorry."

I backed up as the older man turned away from me. But he's wearing a top hat. Why?

"Excuse me, sir?" I started after him. *Don't touch him!* I shouted inside my brain. "Sir?"

"Yes?" He sighed, facing me again. He did not look happy about the whole experience. I knew how he felt.

"Can I ask why you're wearing a top hat?" He couldn't complain to the store manager and get me banned, could he?

"Not that it's any of your business, but I'm on my way to a Dickens Brunch. Charles Dickens." Punctuating that last bit with a look reserved for idiots and obnoxious children, he spun around and walked away. His coat fanned out behind him like an entourage.

"I know Charles Dickens," I said to his back. Brilliant. I rolled my eyes at myself. Time to make my great escape. I picked an aisle at random and headed for my cart. When I returned to where I'd left it, it was gone.

"Oh, are you freaking kidding me?" I threw my hands up. The smirking stock boy walked past. "Hey, did you see what happened to my cart? I left it right here. It was a small one with, like, ten items in it."

He shrugged and kept walking. Great.

I stood in the middle of the grocery store trying to decide on what to do next. I checked the time on my phone. If I wanted to stop and find a good book on dream interpretations, I'd have to leave now.

Defeated, I left the store, hesitating and ducking when I saw the Dickens Brunch Guy ahead of me. No need to repeat the embarrassment.

✳ ✳ ✳

A huge Barnes & Noble sat just down the road from the grocery store. While I love a quaint little specialty bookstore like Tara's, I also love the hustle and bustle of B&N. During the Christmas season the place is packed with merry shoppers.

I took the escalator to the second floor where the New Age section was tucked into a corner. Not too many people were hanging out in this particular area, but a few young and trendy types nestled into deliberately placed couches and overstuffed chairs. Books, laptops, and to-go cups balanced on their thighs.

I browsed through a short row of books that promised to tell me all about my dreams. As suspected, most of the authors believed libraries represented knowledge or furthering one's education. Another popular theme was wisdom. I looked up doors and wasn't too surprised to read that they often represented a change or transition. I could see that. A note said to see the entry for 'portal.'

I flipped to the index and found the page. Portal – representing travel, magic.

Travel? Okay, that made sense. Magic? Interesting.

"Accosting strangers at the grocery store is an unusual hobby." A voice floated from behind me.

The hair on the back of my neck stood on end

and I closed my eyes before turning around. I took a deep breath and opened them.

Top Hat.

CHAPTER 7

He leaned against the wood shelving that lined the aisle, his arms crossed and his top hat dangling from his fingertips. It was black and even I could tell it was well-made. This was not part of a costume. Real money and craftsmanship went into it. I watched as the corners of his mouth turned up into a fake smile. We weren't four feet apart.

Time stopped. Even the din of the store faded away into the background. The floor under my feet seemed to tilt then, tipping me forward. I wanted to put my hands out to break my fall, but my arms felt heavy. Instead, I dove toward those cold eyes, my stomach lurching as I fell. In that moment, everything went dark and I heard the sound of a train and an explosion. I wanted to scream for help, but I no longer had a voice.

Breathe, Top Hat said inside my brain.

My head snapped up. I was still standing, my fingers gripping the book on dreams. He watched me, cocking his head to the side. I hadn't fallen. The cheery noise of shoppers and cash registers wafted up from downstairs. What just happened?

He raised an eyebrow.

"Who the hell are you?" My voice betrayed me,

shaking as I spoke.

"Oh, come on Emily. You must know who I am by now." He shook his head and sighed.

I licked my lips with a dry tongue. It dawned on me. How had I not seen the obvious? After all this time.

"You're Templeton."

"Ah, she's finally figured it out!" he said, extending his right arm forward with a little hand wave as he bowed at the waist. He looked up from his bent position, peering through dark lashes. "So nice to meet you, Emily Swift."

I looked around. Was I alone? Was I in danger? Think Emily. You have a lot of questions for this man, don't blow it!

"Do you know what dreaming about a library means?" The words tumbled out of my mouth. Yet another example of my genius under pressure.

Templeton straightened and crossed his arms again. He shook his head. "Meanings are only relevant to the dreamer. What do libraries mean to you?"

"Well, reading, studying, wisdom," I babbled. "Knowledge."

"Have you considered the dream might be giving you a literal message, such as go to the library?" He picked an imaginary piece of lint off of his coat sleeve.

"No," I said. "But this wasn't any library I've

been in. It's not the library here in town or on campus." Why was I talking about this? This is not what I wanted to discuss with him.

Templeton's gaze began to roam around the room. I knew I'd better start asking my questions fast if I wanted real answers. He had that habit of disappearing.

"Alright, whatever. Doesn't matter. Who are you really? Why are you following me? Why are you playing this little cat and mouse game?" I felt a surge of confidence. My adrenalin kicked in. "I don't have time to play any games with you, Templeton – if that's who you really are. If there's a point to your stalking me –" here his expression switched from annoyed to what probably passed for amused "– then let's have at it. You have something to say? Then say it. You want something? Then out with it. You don't scare me." That last part wasn't true, but I said it anyway.

Templeton listened to my rant without blinking. "I am not stalking you, Emily," he said as if talking to a child. "Let's just say, I'm making sure you stay out of trouble."

"Excuse me?"

"You turned thirty and received your father's book, did you not? I simply want to, oh, make sure you don't unintentionally stumble into any unpleasant situations."

I pointed an accusing finger at him. "So you did

deliver The Book. It was you." I felt shaky again. Templeton was my mother's 'discreet' delivery service?

"Well, I helped deliver The Book." The smirk was back.

My stomach gave a little twist. What was he insinuating? Was he capable of harming someone? I couldn't answer that question.

"Emily, Emily, Emily," Templeton tsked as he examined the brim of his hat. He certainly favored the theatrical. Another imaginary piece of lint was found and removed. "I'm someone who cares. I'm someone who cares about your future." He raised his eyes to mine. "I want you to consider me… as a friend." His voice was soft.

"Listen Templeton," I said, giving myself a little shake. "I don't understand why turning thirty is such a big deal, except for a few gray hairs I'd rather not have. I want to know what you know about my father and his journal. In fact, I want to know what The Book is. You obviously know something I don't know. I want you to tell me what that is. I'm not playing any more games with you or anyone else for that matter."

"You have a lot of requests. What do you offer in return?"

"How about I don't call the police and tell them you're stalking me?"

"I wouldn't waste the precious time of law enforcement if I were you. Besides, I doubt they could help much anyway."

"Fine. Did you know my father?" I got to the point.

"I did." Templeton didn't even flinch. Not even a tiny flutter of surprise walked across his face.

"How did you know him?"

"He was a Salesman."

"Yes, I know he was. But how did you know him? Did you work with him? He wore a top hat too." I gestured to his hand. "Is this part of a uniform? Was there a salesman uniform?" I hadn't intended to ask about the top hat, but words just kept pouring out of my mouth.

A frown puckered Templeton's brow. After a moment he asked, "Emily, what do you know about your father's work?"

Without warning, a thick lump formed in the back of my throat. What could I tell this strange man? That I had no idea what my father did for a living, that no one ever made a point to tell me? That when he died, all of these important little details disappeared too? That I was beginning to realize I knew next to nothing about my own father?

I shook my head. I couldn't speak.

"I see." Curiosity flickered in his eyes. "I think you should go find that library from your dreams, Emily." He spun his top hat in his hand and placed it on his head.

"Wait!" I realized he was about to pull his disappearing act.

"The library isn't far. You just need an invitation to find the right door." He turned away.

"Wait!" I cried out again, this time reaching for his arm. My fingers missed his sleeve. The sound of popping and bells filled the air as holiday music blared. Confetti and balloons rained from the ceiling and a horn blasted behind me. Santa Claus had arrived. My chin jerked toward the chaos. The sound of kids yelling roared up from the first floor. I recovered quickly, but when I turned back to Templeton, he was long gone.

***

"He just disappeared?" Tara's voice rose again. I winced and pointed the phone away from my ear. After deafening me with shouts of how stupid I was for trying to get Templeton to stalk me, she calmed herself to a dull roar.

"Please stop yelling," I said. The car was cold. I smacked the dash twice, but the fan still wasn't playing. I could see my breath.

"Sorry." I heard Tara sigh. I imagined she was trying to calm down, devoting her energy into not ripping off my head for what I had done. She cleared her throat. "So poof, eh? Nowhere to be found?"

"I couldn't find him anywhere. I literally only

looked away for a second. The bathrooms were right behind me. The guy coming out of the men's room said no one was in there. No one in the women's either. And you have to swipe a card to go through the employee door. Nada. Just like yesterday. Gone."

"Really super creepy."

"You have no idea."

"Now what?"

"Now I go home and pump my mother for information on this weird delivery service she uses. I need to find out if she knew what my father did for a living. If Templeton knew my father, I need to be on a level playing field so I can figure out what he wants."

"I don't like this," Tara said.

"Me neither, but it seems like I don't have much of a choice."

"Well, good luck with that. Hey, I do have some more info that might be of interest to you."

I sat up straighter. "What?"

"Well, some of my more 'in the know' customers are asking their people if they've ever heard of any of the places in your father's book. I emailed you about Matar, right? Well, it seems that a friend of a friend has a colleague who says he's heard of an old city called Matar, but it was destroyed by a civil war or something. He was vague on the details. Of course, he didn't have any other information and had no idea where it was located."

"Do you think he was telling the truth?"

"No way to know."

"Damn. Okay, well thanks anyway."

"I wish I had better news."

"Me too." I tapped my fingers on the steering wheel and checked the radio's clock.

"On your way home? Straight home?"

"Yeah, my mother will be here soon." I closed my eyes, mentally preparing for an afternoon with my mother. "We might see you later."

✳ ✳ ✳

Mom arrived a little after eleven o'clock, her car bouncing into the driveway, sliding in on the ice. I winced, but of course she stopped before anything was hit. I was glad to see her.

"My beautiful daughter!" She swished through the door, bringing with her a swirl of snowflakes. "Happy birthday!"

"Mom, it's not my birthday." I hurried after her, trying to catch her white winter coat before it hit the floor. A fair amount of sparkly glitter covered it. I didn't bother to ask. This wasn't unusual. Who knew what she'd been working on?

"But it was your birthday, dear. I brought you a pie!" Mom presented a foil wrapped pumpkin pie. "Tada! And I brought one for my darling Jack, too. Apple for Jack!" She laughed as she glided toward the kitchen.

Mom continued to shed clothing as she went – a glove on the desk, a scarf flung over the back of my rocking chair, a pair of earmuffs ended up hanging from a doorknob.

I followed, picking up as she went along, wishing she would have left the big faux fur boots by the door. So much for our mopping. She set the pies on the kitchen counter.

"Now, I think Jack said he likes his pie at room temperature, so we'll leave that out. You should put the pumpkin in the fridge, though. It will sweat if you don't." William walked into the kitchen, pressing his tail against her leg in a kitty hug. "Well hello there, Big Guy." She scooped up my big grey and white cat. He nuzzled her face. "You get more handsome every time I see you," I heard her whisper into his ear.

"Don't give him a big head," I told her. I made space in the fridge for the pie. I admit to having a weakness for my mother's homemade pie crust. And this was no wimpy pumpkin-cheesecake pie like the one Templeton sent me on my birthday. This was a whole traditional-thick-custard pumpkin pie. Life was good, but better with pie.

"How was the drive?" I put the kettle on for tea.

"Not bad. A little slippery here and there. I just pointed the car in your direction, closed my eyes, and hit the gas."

I looked up to find my mother rummaging through a bulging shoulder bag. "Excuse me?"

"Teasing, darling!" She wrinkled her nose. "Now, what did I do with that letter?"

"What letter?"

"A letter came for you yesterday."

"A letter was sent to your house? Who is it from?"

"I don't know, dear. I'm not one to open people's personal mail. It was addressed to Emily Swift."

"That's strange."

"Not really." Mom kept digging through the leather bag, setting paint brushes, rolls of film, a memo pad, a bunch of candles, knitting needles, a hammer, and several other assorted odds and ends on the table. She began to hum.

In spite of myself, I smiled. Where did this woman come from? She was small and slender, and at fifty-five still very pretty in a girlish sort of way. Her strawberry-blond hair, pulled back from her face and held in a clip, now had more white than color, but her blue eyes were as bright and twinkly as they were when I was little. She was graceful, but often a bit on the disheveled side. In fact, her hair was already slipping out of her clip in wavy wisps, floating around her head. She stopped the archeological dig through her bag and pursed her lips.

"I know!" She snapped her fingers. "It's in my overnight case. I'll be right back." She scampered off to the living room.

I stuffed the flotsam and jetsam back into my mother's shoulder bag. She returned to the kitchen, waving the letter.

"Here it is. Addressed to Emily Swift." She handed it to me.

"Why am I not surprised there isn't any postage or return address on this?" I gave her a pointed look as I sat down at the kitchen table. This had 'discreet' delivery service written all over it. The tea kettle began to whistle. Mom finished filling the metal tea baskets with leaves before pouring the hot water over the filters. Bringing two steaming cups to the table, she sat across from me.

She smiled and nodded toward the letter in my hand. "Are you going to open it?"

"I don't know."

"Why not?"

"Because a lot of very strange things have been happening since you sent me The Book."

"Ah." She bobbed the basket up and down in her cup with her fingertip. Her head bobbed in time with her finger.

"I met someone today who said he knew Dad."

"Really? Today?" She stopped bobbing.

"Yup. He's been following me around and I finally got to confront him."

"You're being followed? Emily, I don't like this. Does Jack know? Should we call the police?" My mother looked around, presumably for a phone.

"Wait, Mom." I held up a hand. "Calm down. It's okay. A little freaky, but okay."

"What happened?"

After making her promise she wouldn't tell Jack, I told her about the conversation with Templeton, noting he'd been at the restaurant on my birthday and at *The Green Bean* yesterday. I omitted the part about the café door incident.

"Emily, this bothers me."

"You and me both."

"And he said he knew your father?" Her head tilted to the side.

"I asked him if they worked together, and he said Dad was a salesman. No kidding! But he didn't give me any more information than that. He told me to go to the library." I waved my hand at my mother's puzzled expression. "Don't focus on that."

"Okay, well. Go on."

"Anyhow, he knew I had The Book. He made it sound like he had a hand in delivering it. Then said he was following me to keep me out of trouble." I made a face.

"This is all so strange."

"Tell me about it! Mom, what's the delivery service you used the other day?"

"Oh Emily," she said. "I didn't have much to do with your father's work. In fact, I had nothing to do with it. He was very private. He couldn't discuss most of it. Things were confidential."

"And?"

"And," she sipped her tea, "if I needed to get a message to your father while he was traveling, I would ring up this service and they would deliver the message. Packages too, if necessary."

"So, you would just call and ask them to come pick it up?"

"For packages, yes. If it was a message, I could simply tell them over the phone."

"Where are they located?"

"I have no idea."

"What do you mean you have no idea?"

She shrugged. "I only needed to call the number."

"What about billing? Isn't there a return address on the bill?"

"Bill for what, dear?"

My right eye started to throb. Oh yes, we would visit Tara today. She'd provide a nice little buffer. "A bill for the delivery charge, Mom."

"I'm not charged anything."

I wasn't sure I understood. "What do you mean? It's free?"

My mother nodded.

"Why is it free?" I asked.

"I suppose it's a leftover benefit. Maybe they felt guilty that he died when working. I never asked." Mom ran her fingertip around the rim of the teacup. "Quite useful, though. I don't abuse the service. I only use it on rare occasions."

"I see." That might explain why Templeton was involved. If he knew my father, and this delivery service was part of my father's old work world, then it would be easy for him to find me.

The letter my mother brought lay on the table. Picking it up, I took a butter knife and sliced open the envelope. Inside was a card, with gold letters embossed on the front. A large 'S' was pressed into the center with the words 'You Are Invited" in smaller letters underneath. I opened it. Inside, in black decorative ink, was an address.

Nothing else.

CHAPTER 8

"What does it say?" Mom asked.

"Nothing. It's just an address." I showed her the inside of the invitation. "Twelve twenty-one Northgate Way. I don't know anyone at this address."

"Do you know where it is?"

"I think so. Northgate Way is north of the city, but not in McMansion land. It's a pretty nice area. The homes are older. A lot of brick houses with big yards."

"Shall we go? I'm up for a little adventure."

I looked up from the invitation to find my mother smiling. "I don't think so," I said.

"It would be safer if we went together."

"It's safer if we don't go at all."

"What are you going to do?"

"I'm going to think about it for now. This is too coincidental, and until I get a better handle on Templeton and The Book, I'm setting this aside." I was lying to my mother, but there was no way I was taking her with me.

"So, what will we do for the afternoon?"

"We're going to take The Book to Tara and see what she thinks. We'll pick up lunch for us all on the way."

✻ ✻ ✻

"Why did you wait all this time to give me The Book?" I asked. We were back in the car after stopping at *The Green Bean* for salads-to-go. I didn't see Templeton while we waited for our food, but my mother started a bit of a ruckus at the counter. After making a casual comment to a fellow customer about his lovely speaking voice, an impromptu serenade was performed for the ladies in line. The man said my mother just inspired him.

"You turned thirty, dear." She dug through her bag mumbling about a pretty pen she wanted to give to Tara.

"Right. And you couldn't give it to me before?"

"That's correct."

"Why?" I navigated our way through the downtown traffic. My car was finally warm. The heater kicked on after Mom tapped the dash. She told me I needed to hit it in the right spot.

"I don't know why I wasn't supposed to, but that was the rule."

"Mom, you're killing me here." I started to look for a parking spot. We were about a block from Tara's store.

"Do you remember when that man brought us your father's hat pin?"

"Actually, I don't. I don't remember those details."

"You were so sad." My mother gave a heavy sigh. "There was no light in your eyes, and I couldn't put it back."

I glanced over at my mother's profile and for a moment, I saw an old woman sitting beside me. It startled me and I turned back to the traffic.

"That's okay, Mom," I said. "You've always done your best and really, it's fine. I'm okay."

"Thank you. It's hard to know what to do sometimes."

"I know." I had to get her back on track. "So, the man who brought Dad's hat pin to us, did you know who he was?"

"No, but he worked with your father. He was a salesman too. Oh, he was miserable. I'm sure the trip was not a pleasant one for him."

"I'm sure. Do you remember his name?" I wondered if it was Templeton, but I doubted it.

Mom thought about it. "I think he said his name was Mr. Havers. Yes, that was it. Kind man. He gave me The Book, but told me not to give it to you until you were older. He said you wouldn't be ready until you turned thirty."

I found a parking spot and pulled my car up to the curb. I put it into park and turned toward my mother. "You didn't think it was important enough to give it to me right away?" I didn't want to be angry.

"On the contrary, Emily, I thought it was too

important to give to you back then. You may think I am flighty –"

"I do... not."

"– but I loved your father very, very much. His work was extremely important to him, and if one of his colleagues said I needed to wait to give it to you, then I was going to stick to those instructions. Emily, I didn't know much about his work. I needed to trust someone who did – the salesman who gave me The Book. Who knows what I would've set in motion if I'd ignored him and simply handed it over to you then? Why should I take that risk, or maybe even put you at risk?"

I stared through windshield watching as the flakes melted on the glass. I didn't know if my mother was right to wait, but the fact was she made a conscious, thoughtful choice. This wasn't my mother giving into whimsy.

"Alright, you have a point," I said.

"I'm sorry if you're angry."

"I'm not angry." I blew out a breath. "The man who delivered The Book, this Havers guy, did you ever see him again?"

"No. I've never seen another salesman since."

"Really?"

"Really. Emily, I told you, your father's work was very private. He kept his home life and work life completely separate. He said it was better that way. After he died, well, there was even less of a reason for another salesman to visit, wasn't there?" She raised her eyebrows at me.

"I guess. Just one more question and we can go in. I called Aunt Sadie because she had a Purse from Anwat, which is something Dad listed in The Book."

"And what did she say?"

"She told me a little bit about the purse. I think it's sort of like a good-luck money charm. She said I should talk to another salesman to learn more about Dad's work."

"I think that's a good idea."

"Can you help me find a salesman?"

Mom nodded. "I would say that Templeton fellow is a good place to start, wouldn't you?"

❋ ❋ ❋

Tara was thrilled to see my mother. After a big squeal and a little tackle that left both of them laughing and hugging, I managed to peel her off my mother. We took our lunch out back to Tara's office.

"Lydia! It's so wonderful to see you! How are you? How is the painting? Are you still painting? You should see how much I've written since you were last here. I'm almost finished with the first draft and I'm ready to edit my manuscript. It's so exciting! I'm so excited!"

Tara babbled and beamed as she took my mother's coat.

"You look beautiful, my dear. My goodness, your eyes are shining, your cheeks have pink in them – oh!" My mother stopped and laughed. "And what's his name?"

"What's in a name?" Tara fluttered her fingers at my mother. "Seriously. No one special, Lydia. I'm just glad to see you."

My mother looked unconvinced, but she didn't press. I passed out our salads and we all pulled up chairs to the table. At first the conversation was the usual catching up, with Mom asking Tara all kinds of questions about her writing and if any interesting books had made their way onto the store's bookshelves.

"Speaking of books," I said to Tara. "I brought The Book for you to look over." I set my Dad's old journal on the table.

"Great. I've been dying to see this." Tara got up and washed her hands, drying them before pulling over a little cart with her examination tools. She put on a pair of soft gloves.

Positioning a small video recorder over the cart, Tara looked at me, her eyebrows raised in question. I nodded. She pressed the 'On' button and began her review. "Review by Tara Parker-Jones, manager of *Pages and Pens*. Book brought in by client Emily Swift. Book was passed down to Emily from her late father, Daniel Swift, via her mother, Lydia Swift, on December 1. The book appears to be a journal of sorts, most likely a record of work-related travel and sales. Rough guess is that it's over twenty years old, probably closer to thirty." She picked up a ruler. "The book is five and a half inches by seven inches and three inches thick."

Tara ran her fingers across the cover of the book. "Worn blue cover, fabric, with a gold embossed 'S' – probably for Swift." Lifting the book, she looked at the spine. "No marks on spine. No other embossment or lettering on the outside of book." She turned her attention to the lock. "The book is sealed shut by a small brass lock. Lock is very old and tarnished, but seems to be sturdy."

"Here's the key," I said, handing her the hat pin.

"The key to the lock is Daniel Swift's hat pin." She picked up the ruler. "The pin itself is just under two inches in length, with an antique globe attached to one end. The pin's stem is gold and results in a tiny S-shaped point." She touched it. "The point is still sharp."

Tara inserted the pin into the lock, turning the key. She lifted the cover and opened The Book to the first page. "Blank pages in beginning of book. No publisher or copyright information. As expected, the book appears to be a journal. The pages are aged, some yellowing – nothing appreciable. They are not brittle. Pages appear to be made from cotton fibers." She turned the pages, fascinated. She paused the video recording and looked up. "Em, I don't know if this book would be worth anything to a dealer or collector, but this is priceless for you."

I nodded.

Tara returned her attention to Dad's journal, again turning on the recorder. "The handwriting appears to be the same throughout and has been identified as Daniel Swift's. Ink is black. There are hand-drawn maps, notes, strings of numbers, and sketches." She pressed pause again. "Before recording any pages or text in greater detail, I want your permission."

I looked at my mother, who nodded. "A few pages might be okay," she said.

"How about the map I told you about?" I took The Book and turned to the correct page. "You've already been asking around about it."

Tara recorded as she read the locations and pointed to each spot on the map. "Any other pages you think might be helpful?"

I mentally ran through several passages before I flipped to the portion regarding the Eve of Silence. "Here's something."

When in Matar, look for
Anne Lace. Her special-ty
helps people see.
May have knowledge
regarding Eve of Silence.

Will need Rabbit's help.
Contact prior to
Solstice.
Avoid Walled Zone.

Again Tara read out loud as she filmed. She nodded at me and I turned next to the portion about Templeton:

Templeton.
Not in Matar during EoS?
Friend?

"Templeton. Got it." Tara turned off the camera and lowered her voice. "That reminds me, any more encounters with Top Hat?"

"Not since Barnes & Noble. And I had a chance to run some things by my mother." I glanced over my shoulder. Mom had moved on to browsing some of the private shelves in Tara's office where some of the more valuable books were stored. She was far enough away and couldn't hear me. "She doesn't know Templeton, but agrees he's hiding something. She thinks he's the one who can give me answers."

"But will he?"

"I think yes. Maybe, if it serves him. He likes playing games, so I'll be careful about taking anything he says to heart. But right now I'm wondering about this." I pulled the strange invitation from my bag and showed it to Tara.

"Where did this come from?"

"Delivered to my mother's house this week. I

guess there's a benefit leftover from my father's work. Someone used the delivery service to send it. It's the same one Mom used to send me The Book on my birthday."

"But you don't know who sent it?"

"I'm guessing whoever lives at this address."

"Northgate Way is in a wealthy section of town."

I nodded. "I don't want to take my Mom."

"You want me to go with you?" Tara was hopeful.

What is it with these two? I shook my head. "No, I want you to provide cover."

"Oh boy."

"You owe me."

Tara snorted. "What? I do not."

"How about last spring when you needed me to interrupt two separate dates so you could keep all three you scheduled for one night?"

"But all three were only in town for that night! What were the odds? What was I going to do?"

"All I want you to do is call me tomorrow and ask me to come and help you at the shop if I can't get out of the house on my own. No need to concern Jack with this. I'll text you so you know when to call. Mom plans to leave around noon."

"So you can go alone? No way!"

"Tara, if I've learned anything so far it's that I have better luck getting answers when I'm by myself."

"You don't even know whose house this is!" Her mouth hung open.

"True, but you'll know where I'll be, and I'll check in right after. This little investigation probably won't even take an hour." I smiled. "I'm getting good at this. Trust me."

Tara still wasn't convinced. "I have no idea why I should agree to any of this."

I lifted my hand to my ear and pretended to make a call. "Um, yes, Tara? Big emergency. Sorry to interrupt your first date of the night, but you need to come back to the store."

She threw up her hands. "Fine!"

"What's fine?" my mother asked.

"Your daughter drives me nuts," Tara answered, but she didn't spill the beans.

Mom laughed as she put her arm around my shoulders. "Takes after her mother."

✻ ✻ ✻

Tara promised to share the recording of The Book with a select group of sellers to find out if anything seemed familiar to anyone. I knew I could count on her to be discreet. Mom and I said our goodbyes and spent the rest of the afternoon doing a little holiday shopping. Although Templeton was never far from my thoughts – in fact I kept a lookout for his top hat

– I was ready for a break from The Book madness. I replaced it with holiday shopping madness. It felt good to be normal. Well, as normal as one can be when shopping with my mother. At one point, when passing an outside Santa Station, the reindeer kicked up quite a ruckus when Mom stopped to pet the lead. I hurried her into yet another gift shop.

By the time we returned home, it was close to five. Nothing new from Templeton, no mystery deliveries, and no wrong turns through doors. A couple of times I felt like I was being watched, but I knew my paranoia was at an all-time high, so I pretended otherwise.

Over dinner Jack told Mom about his latest academic endeavor and plans for the winter break. He's not the most animated of characters, but around my mother Jack becomes chatty. It's amusing.

"So what I want to do next," he said waving his fork in the air, "is work with students who plan to go into elementary teaching. Take the pilot project into the public school system and allow enrolled kids to read whatever they want – sports bios, sci-fi, graphic novels, you name it. The college students could count the project toward their internship requirements, plus get the experience of designing a program to encourage reading. I'm taking it to the department chair after the New Year. I'd like to launch it at the elementary level next September." He took a big bite of his apple pie. He looked at his plate. "This is amazing."

Mom nodded and gave Jack a wink. "I always add a little something special when baking pies for you, Jack."

"I'll take it. It's great." Jack refilled the wine glasses. "So, what did you ladies do today?"

I looked at my mother.

"We visited Tara and then went shopping. The day flew by!" My mother stood and began to clear the table. "No more wine for me, Jack. It will keep me up all night."

"No Book-inspired weirdness?" Jack took a sip of his wine.

"Well," Mom paused, "we showed it to Tara so if there's anything useful, I'm sure she'll tell us." With that, my mother carried the dishes into the kitchen and began to clean up. William, Mystery, and Mischief followed her.

"Mischief never follows me," I said.

"She's even purring," Jack noted.

"I know."

"So, really? Nothing new about The Book?" He leaned forward and captured my hand in his. Jack smiled. I smiled. He raised his eyebrows. I looked out the window at the blowing snow.

"Um, nope."

"Em?"

"Well," I searched for something to say. What

could he know? I decided to go with as much of the truth as I could without making Jack concerned – or making him mad. "Mom told me about getting The Book after Dad died. I guess the delivery service she used the other morning is a leftover benefit from his work."

I went on to tell Jack about lunch at Tara's store, adding that I should probably try to contact someone my father used to work with. I shrugged off the last little bit. I never mentioned Templeton.

Jack eyed me before giving my hand a gentle squeeze. "Just don't do anything without talking to me about it first. I want you to be careful." He let go of my hand.

"I know," I said. Jack meant well, but playing it safe wasn't going to get me any answers.

"I'm going to help your mother clean up the kitchen. It's the least I can do after she made that pie." He didn't fool me. He was heading for another piece.

I picked up my wine and moved into the living room, curling up on the couch with The Book. The invitation to twelve twenty-one Northgate Way poked out from in between the pages. I pulled it out, tracing the 'S' on the front. I read the words out loud softly, "You Are Invited."

Damn right.

* * *

I drank a bit more wine than I should have before going to bed. In my dream, I walked through an old house I didn't recognize. The furniture was polished to a high shine and arranged deliberately, creating a winding pathway leading from room to room. I carried the invitation in my hand. I felt tired. I didn't know where I was going or why I was even there. I wanted a good night's sleep.

I wandered into a large room where full bookshelves lined the walls from floor to ceiling. I recognized it as the same library from my earlier dream. I turned looking for Templeton, but he wasn't there. I knew he could be hiding. My hand tingled and I looked down. The 'S' on the invitation seemed to flicker, then glow. I remembered what Templeton said in Barnes & Noble.

"You just need an invitation to find the right door."

The dream ended as I sat up. It was the middle of the night, but I was wide awake and oh-so-very-excited. I knew exactly where to find the library.

Twelve twenty-one Northgate Way.

CHAPTER 9

It was shortly after one in the afternoon before my mother waved from her car and skidded out onto the wintry road. I clenched my teeth and Jack shook his head as she rounded the corner and slid out of view. I held my breath, but no crash sounds followed.

Jack was gearing up for a day of reviewing student papers. "Which client project are you working on today?" he asked.

I looked up from my texting. "Um, I'm not sure." My phone rang. I looked at my hand.

"Who is it?"

"Ah, huh. Tara." I answered the call. "Hey."

"Imagine this, I need you to come help me at the store," Tara sighed into the phone.

"You need help?" I looked at Jack and shrugged. Gee, what do you know? "Sure, I can come help you, Tara. Do you want me to come over now?"

"Yeah, now. Let's get this over with." I had a feeling I was going to pay for this even though she owed me. Three dates in one night, for the love of Pete.

"Okay, I'll leave here in a few." I disconnected the call.

"Tara?"

"Yeah, she said she needed me to help out at the store."

"Hmm. That's unusual." Jack cocked his head to the side. "Because of the holiday?"

"That's probably it. Listen, I better get going. I'll be back in a couple of hours. Then maybe we can go out for coffee? You can take a break from grading papers." I hoped I didn't sound as guilty as I felt.

"I'll probably need it by then. Go. Drive carefully. Tell Tara hello for me."

"Will do." I gave him a kiss on the cheek and was out the door before he could ask any more questions. In my shoulder bag I carried The Book and the invitation to twelve twenty-one Northgate Way.

❉ ❉ ❉

Yesterday I told Tara I wouldn't be more than an hour following this lead. I had no idea what to expect, but I didn't know what else to do about The Book. Finding out the story behind the invitation seemed like the best next step.

I drove up and into the older neighborhood. The roads were still a little slippery, but the plows kept up for the most part. The address belonged to one of the old two-story brick houses set back far from the road. There was a large, wrought iron gate left open at the entrance. It wasn't exactly top-notch security, but closed it might deter unwelcome visitors. I turned into the drive. All was quiet and I didn't see any vehicles or footprints leading to or from the front door. I couldn't tell if anyone was home. I parked my car and left it unlocked in case I needed to leave in a hurry.

A couple inches of new snow covered the sidewalk. I climbed the front steps and rang the doorbell before shoving my hands in my pockets to keep them warm. The chime was soft, a perfect complement to the stillness. While I waited, I turned and took in the view. A short brick wall ran from the gated entrance, spanned the edge of the yard, and then moved past the house, presumably into the back. Two maples stood in the yard. Leafless limbs were outlined in white. Snow-covered hedges lined the front of the house, their rectangles placed evenly under dark windows. Whoever lived here had a lot of money.

A few minutes passed before I heard the lock turn. A woman dressed in a pair of jeans and a black sweater opened the door. She was about my height, with plain features and dark hair. She wasn't wearing any makeup. She could have been thirty, or she could have been fifty – I couldn't tell.

"May I help you?" she asked.

"I hope so." I put on my best smile. "I received

this in the mail the other day and it's basically an invitation to come here, except it's missing a date and time. I don't know what it's for, and I don't know who lives here." I showed the invitation to her. "Twelve twenty-one Northgate Way."

"You have the right place," she said.

I waited. She waited. I let the silence hang between us for a few seconds before I spoke. "Is now a good time?"

"Follow me."

I stepped inside. She waited while I stomped the loose snow from my boots before turning to lead me through the house. We passed rooms filled with polished tables, leather chairs, and assorted antiques – at least they looked old enough to be antiques. No one else appeared to be home.

As I walked, I thought about my dream. I couldn't say it was the house I wandered through while sleeping. I shook my head. Life had become strange in the last few days. I hoped to find some answers here.

We reached a set of stairs leading down into a lower level. I had a sense we were heading underground. The temperature was chillier.

The bottom of the stairs opened into a wide den, with several small desks and chairs on wheels. I noticed a couple of monitors which provided some outside shots of the property.

Security cameras, I realized. However, no one was watching them.

The woman motioned to a leather couch along the wall. "He'll be right with you."

"Who?"

"Mr. Blackstone." She disappeared back up the stairs.

"Who is Mr. Blackstone?" I called after her.

"I am." I jumped as a voice spoke from the doorway across the room. An older man, probably in his late sixties, stood smiling. In a brown corduroy blazer with patches on the elbows he looked like any of the aging professors working with Jack. "Please, Emily, won't you come in?" He stood to the side and I could see a library behind him.

"How do you know my name?" I asked. Mr. Blackstone held out his hand and I shook it.

"I'm guessing you have a lot of questions."

"You have no idea."

"I think I might." I followed him into the old library. It reminded me of the one from my dream. This had to be the right place. Shelves were placed as low as my ankles and also as high as a foot from the ceiling. The ceiling itself was a good fifteen feet above the floor. Every shelf I could see was full. Some spines looked ancient. Tara would be in heaven.

Mr. Blackstone sat down behind a large desk and gestured to a seat across from him. I was aware of the time and wondered how fast he could answer my questions. I didn't want to be rude, but I only had this short window of opportunity.

"I'm very happy to meet you, Emily," he began. "I know you just turned thirty, and I hoped it would be soon, but one never knows."

"Was there a public announcement? Why is everyone so concerned with my birthday?"

"I wouldn't say there was a recent announcement," Mr. Blackstone said. "But yes, there are a few of your father's colleagues who were anticipating your birthday."

He shuffled some papers on his desk. "Let's see. Here we are." He read:

"Emily Swift, daughter to Daniel Swift, Salesman, and Lydia McKay Swift, born on December 1. Emily is the first child for both parents. Mother and daughter are doing well, and the baby is reported to be of a pleasant nature with a full head of hair."

He handed it to me. "An announcement was made, as you can see, but if you look at the top right-hand corner of the page, you'll note it was dated thirty years ago."

I held the paper in my hands. It was handwritten, but it wasn't my father's. The words flowed across the page in black ink and the sheet was decorated with intricate scrollwork along the sides. The scrollwork continued across the top and I noted a sketch of a top hat tucked into the left-hand corner. It was beautiful. It was a piece of art.

"Who made this?" I asked.

"Probably someone in the Empire's official records department when you were born. They still send out announcements for births, marriages, and deaths. Occasionally there's some other newsworthy event to share, but generally by the time the announcement is created and delivered, everyone already knows." He shrugged.

"So you knew my father, then?" This was almost too good to be true.

"Knew of him, yes. But no, he and I never met. I'm sorry for your loss, Emily." Mr. Blackstone reached over and patted my hand.

"Thank you. May I keep this?"

"Of course. I have another copy in the archives."

"Thank you," I said again as I tucked the paper into my bag. I let my fingers graze the cover of The Book, but left it inside. "Mr. Blackstone, I don't want to be rude, but I have a lot of questions, and the past four days have been crazy. Out of nowhere, a book shows up on my doorstep at six in the morning on my birthday. It turns out it's my father's journal from work. Then I find out my mother's been holding onto it for almost two decades because some salesman told her not to give it to me until I turned thirty. When she sends it to me, she uses some weird delivery service she says is a leftover 'benefit' from my father's job. I start to go through The Book and nothing makes sense. Most places he refers to don't even exist. To top it all off, I find out I'm being followed. Before I can catch up with him, he catches up with me. He says his name is Templeton and that he knew my father."

Mr. Blackstone patiently waited, nodding as I spoke. The moment I said Templeton's name, he held up his hand and motioned for me to stop.

"Templeton?" he asked.

"Yes, Templeton. He said he was the one who delivered my father's book to me. And I know he followed me to at least three places since Wednesday. I tried to follow him yesterday, but he keeps disappearing."

"Disappearing," Mr. Blackstone said.

"Right, disappearing. Running out of the room and –" I snapped my fingers "– poof, he's gone."

"Tell me exactly what happened." It was Mr. Blackstone's turn to sit forward.

"Well, the first time I tried to follow him, he, um," I hesitated. Oh hell, this couldn't get any weirder. "The first time I chased him was at *The Green Bean*. It's a café downtown. Anyhow, he ran into the ladies' room and I followed him."

"Then what happened?" He put a hand to his

bearded chin.

I shifted in my chair. "I ended up in the café's kitchen."

Mr. Blackstone blew out a breath as he sat back, throwing up his hands. "It has to be Templeton. You must have caught some sort of energy trail when he door traveled and it shoved you through the next closest one."

Door traveled? I had no idea what he meant, but I was more concerned with his reaction. He wasn't happy. "Anyhow, I finally got to speak to him when he showed up at Barnes & Noble. That's when he told me he knew my father and that he delivered The Book to my house. I asked him why he was following me and he basically said he wanted to 'keep me out of trouble,' but I have no idea what he is talking about." I shook my head. "He's also the person who told me to come here."

"Here?"

"Well, not explicitly," I said. "I told him I dreamed about a library. It's a long story. He said maybe I should go find it. He told me I would get an invitation to the right door, and the next thing I know, this shows up." I set the invitation down in front of Mr. Blackstone. "So you see, I have a lot of questions, and I'm not getting many answers. I don't have a lot of time today, so if you just could tell me why you sent this and what you know about my father and

Templeton, I'd really appreciate it."

Mr. Blackstone had seemed to recover from the news about Templeton. "I understand. I'll tell you as much as I can today, but you'll need to come back when you have more time. Then I can tell everything you need to know about the Empire and being a Salesman."

I started to nod, but stopped. This was the second time he mentioned an empire. "Wait, did you say empire?"

"The Empire is where the Salesmen are headquartered. It's more of a... a concept than a place, but it still contains people, cities, and towns just like any other world. You can go there." Mr. Blackstone stood. He began to pace back and forth behind his desk, collecting his thoughts. "Your father was a Salesman. He was well-respected by his peers. The journal your mother gave you contains important information about your father's travels, and Emily, it is imperative that you keep tight hold of it. Do not let it out of your sight." He looked at me.

"I won't," I promised. What in the hell was going on?

"Good." He resumed pacing, his hands clasped behind his lower back, a professor delivering a well-practiced lecture. "A long time ago, before you were born, trouble slipped into the ranks of the Salesmen. Some of the stronger, more influential members and leaders, like your father, were able to suppress most of it. However, as is often the case, the more you push down on something in an effort to stomp it out, some parts move to the outside edge, to the fringe, which is what happened back then. The further to the extreme edge some members moved, the less control the Salesmen leadership had of the group as a whole. Still, the initial action of the core Salesmen had some effect. Things seemed to die down for a while. Below the surface, there were rumblings of trouble, but for the most part nothing was made of it."

"That all changed about a year before your father was killed." Mr. Blackstone faced me. "He was assassinated."

His words punched me in the chest. "What do you mean assassinated? He died in an accident. It was a train wreck."

"Yes, and there was a bomb planted on that train. That is what caused the wreck. That is why your father died, Emily. He was targeted and murdered."

Sudden dizziness made me tip forward. Mr. Blackstone hurried around the desk and put his hands on my shoulders. "I'm sorry. Are you okay? Would you like some water?"

"Yes." I closed my eyes. The nausea hit next. My mouth flooded with acid and I stayed as still as I could. A minute later Mr. Blackstone pressed a cool glass into my hand. He also handed me a damp rag.

"For your head," he explained.

I took a sip of water and pressed the cold rag to my face. "Sorry."

"No, I'm sorry. I didn't mean to be so blunt. It's just, with you turning thirty and now Templeton appears? It concerns me. I don't know what to make of it."

"That makes two of us." I dabbed my face with the cloth. The dizziness was lessening. "Does my mother know? Does she know there was a bomb on the train?"

"As far as I know she does not. Only a few Salesmen 'officially' know. Of course, information like that is hard to keep secret. Before long people outside of the Salesman ranks found out too."

"Who did it?"

Mr. Blackstone sighed. "An investigation was made, but they were unable to establish any hard evidence linking to a specific person."

"But they did have an idea of who did it, even if they couldn't prove it?"

"Most people assume one of the extreme factions put the bomb on the train. You see, a week before the explosion many of your father's colleagues were violently attacked."

"Do they know who was behind that?"

"Only a few people were named. Most keep any affiliation to the violence a secret. Some of these men and women began calling themselves 'the Fringe.' Emily, you need to know that Templeton has been linked to some of the more vocal members of this group in the past."

"Did Templeton have anything to do with the bomb?" My stomach grew queasy again.

"No one knows. But rumor has it Templeton was seen on the train prior to the explosion."

"And yet he wasn't on the train when the bomb went off?" I already knew the answer.

"He was not."

"And the investigation is closed?"

"At this point, yes. This is all I can tell you now. I can check to see if there is any information that the Empire would be willing to share with you since you are Swift's daughter."

I blew out a breath. "Okay, alright. Well, let me ask you this. What's the big deal with me turning thirty? Why does this keep coming up?"

"That's the age when Salesmen typically enter the trade, although there have been a few unique situations." Mr. Blackstone sat back down behind his desk. His mouth twisted to the side before finishing. "Templeton, for example. He was the youngest. He was barely nineteen when he became a Salesman."

"And that's unusual why?"

"It's an early age to develop such accurate traveling abilities. Plus, a new Salesman needs to be trained on how to travel safely. Templeton already had the skill and the knowledge when he was admitted into the ranks. No one needed to teach him."

"Templeton is ahead of the curve, hmm?" I sipped at my water. That explained some of his cockiness.

"You might say that. He ended up displaying some rather extraordinary abilities as well."

"Such as?"

Mr. Blackstone hesitated, putting his hands together as if in prayer and touching his lips. "A lot of the items Salesmen carry are not physically handled by any of the Salesmen themselves. Templeton, however, never had any difficulties."

"I don't understand what you're saying, Mr. Blackstone. You mean like hazardous materials or something?"

"Not in the sense that you mean. I know I'll need to explain this in more detail. And I will, Emily, I will. Templeton showing up now has caught me off guard. He hasn't surfaced in a long time. I certainly didn't expect him to show up in Kincaid. I want to check with my colleagues to make sure I haven't missed any important information. It's too much of a coincidence with you turning thirty."

I thought about our conversation in Barnes & Noble. "It seems Templeton doesn't inspire warm and fuzzy feelings in many people."

"This is true."

"But Templeton did know my father personally, right?" I wanted to know if Templeton was at least telling the truth about that.

"He did. In fact, they traveled together. It was a condition of his early approval into the ranks. Your father recognized Templeton's mastery of door travel. He would have made an incredible ally or a powerful enemy."

"My father wrote about him in his journal. He wondered if Templeton was a friend or not."

"Most would say no, they weren't friends," Mr. Blackstone said. "But, unlike your father's peers, he was not willing to write Templeton off. Daniel knew he was young, but I think he could see the potential for great things with Templeton. He was one of his only advocates. But..." His voice trailed off and he waved his hand in an empty gesture.

"I see. What else can you tell me? You said you didn't know my father, but you seem to know a lot about him. Are you a salesman too?"

"Me? No, I'm a Record Keeper, Emily. I catalog the items Salesmen carry, as well as assist in recording the history of the Empire. I help with training and research, too."

"Oh." I didn't understand.

"Think of me as a resource for the Salesmen."

"Works for me." I checked the time on my phone. Yikes! I was pushing it. "So, you're the one who sent me the invitation though, right?"

"Yes. Part of my job is to make sure you're prepared to present yourself to the Salesman Court."

"The what?"

"The Salesman Court." He began to flip through a desk calendar. "I'll set it up so you can travel with another Salesman, of course. And I want to schedule some time with you beforehand so you'll know what you need to do in advance."

"Okay, wait." I waved my palms at Mr. Blackstone. "Slow down. Why do I need to go to some court?"

"Because you're a Salesman."

"No, Mr. Blackstone, my father was a salesman. I have my own business."

He cocked his head to the side. "But Emily, you are Daniel Swift's only daughter. His firstborn. Don't you understand? You were born a Salesman."

It was in this moment I realized Mr. Blackstone was just as confused about me as I was confused by everything I'd experienced since my birthday. Before we could take the conversation any further, the phone on his desk rang. Mr. Blackstone apologized and answered it. He listened quietly for a moment.

"Thank you, Elsa." He replaced the receiver to its cradle before looking up. "A Mr. Jack Greene is here."

I was going to kill Tara.

※ ※ ※

Before I walked out into the foyer, Mr. Blackstone pressed a business card into my hand. On it was his name and phone number. He told me to call and schedule some time for us to finish our conversation. He also told me to avoid Templeton until he had more information on why he was here in Kincaid. I told him I would try.

Jack is the epitome of appropriate behavior in public. He smiled politely as Mr. Blackstone shook his hand and apologized for taking up my time on a Saturday. He helped me into my coat and said goodbye to Elsa before walking me to my car.

I was in so much trouble.

"See you back at the house," he said.

"Do you want to go out for coffee now?" I gave him a big smile and reached for his arm.

"See you back at the house, Emily." He turned away and walked to his car.

Damn. I got into mine and maneuvered back down the driveway to Northgate Way. Fishing my phone out of my purse, I called Tara as I turned onto the road.

"What happened?" I demanded when she answered.

"He showed up at the store! What was I going to do? He was so upset I had to tell him where you went. And now he's mad at me too!"

"It'll blow over." I glanced in my rearview mirror. I could feel Jack's stare coming from the car behind me. "What exactly did you tell him?"

"I told him you got a letter inviting you to Northgate, and that you wanted to go check it out by yourself. I said I was watching your back by phone. I don't think he was impressed."

"Did you tell him about Templeton?"

"No way. I don't want any part of that."

"Good."

"So what happened? Is everything okay?"

"You won't believe the half of it. But listen, I'll have to fill you in later. In the meantime, if you find out anything about The Book, please-please-please let me know. And if you see Templeton, absolutely stay away from him."

"Is he dangerous?"

"Very."

CHAPTER 10

When Jack gets angry, he doesn't talk. By the time we faced off in the kitchen, I was sure his tongue had left the building.

"I know you're mad," I said. "But I needed to find out what this was all about." I waved the invitation at him.

Silence.

"Jack, I told Tara where I was going. She would've put up the bat signal if I didn't call her when I left Blackstone's house."

More silence.

"Please don't be mad at me. If you knew what I found out from Blackstone, you'd understand."

Jack snorted and walked out of the room. A few minutes later I heard the front door slam, followed by his car starting.

Great. I reached into my jeans pocket and pulled out the card with Blackstone's number. I thumbed the numbers into my phone.

"Mr. Blackstone," he answered.

"Hi, Mr. Blackstone. It's Emily Swift."

"I'm glad you called. I hope Jack wasn't too upset that you came to the house?"

"Actually, he's furious, but I can't do much about it now." I wiped my hand across my forehead. "Anyhow, I want to finish our conversation. I need to know more about this Court."

"Of course. Could you come by on Monday? How about in the afternoon, say at two?"

"That'll work."

"Good," he said. "In the meantime, if anything strange happens, you can call this number day or night."

"Strange?"

"Yes, like going through the ladies' room door and ending up in a kitchen."

"That kind of strange. Got it." We said our goodbyes and I hung up.

The afternoon left me with even more questions. I didn't know what to believe. Blackstone's story had rattled me. I hauled The Book out of my bag. It was time for more research.

I took a hot cup of tea upstairs to my office. It would be two days before I could ask Blackstone my questions. I wondered if anything he said today could be verified by The Book. I made a new list:

Mr. Blackstone is a record keeper for the salesmen.

Apparently, one is born a salesman – whatever that means.

There's something called the Salesman Court.

Templeton did know my father and traveled with him.

Templeton is powerful and probably dangerous.

I paused, tapping the end of the pen against my

lower lip. I added:
There was a bomb on my father's train.
Templeton was there too.

Hot tears filled my eyes when I thought about my father. There was nothing I could do to change what happened. Now Jack was mad and I needed to talk to him. I needed to tell him what really happened to my father. I rubbed at my eyes with the back of my hand. I didn't want to cry. I clenched my jaw, blowing a breath out my nose.

I grabbed The Book and began to flip through the pages. The more I thought about it, the angrier I became – at everyone! My mother for keeping secrets, Jack for not speaking to me, Blackstone for talking in circles, myself for not understanding more, Templeton for being… Templeton!

"What am I supposed to do with this? What good is this book to me? And I'm not a salesman. I don't want to sell anything. I don't want to leave my home and deliver things!" I slammed The Book back down on the desk. I was being childish, but I didn't care. I picked up my pen and scribbled on one of The Book's blank pages:

Emily Swift is NOT a salesman.

The regret was immediate. I hadn't planned on writing in my father's journal. My shoulders dropped as I stared at what I'd done. Just then my phone beeped. I snatched it up, hoping it was Jack.

I didn't recognize the number, but the text message read:

Actually, Emily, you ARE a Salesman. And that's Salesman with a capital 'S.'

My skin crawled. I sent back a text.

Who is this?

The response was fast.

You found the library? We should travel together soon.

"Holy hell," I breathed before texting:

Templeton?

There was no reply. I looked at The Book, then back to my phone. Somehow I had to make Jack understand. Something scary was triggered on my birthday, and this was one train I could not climb off. I had to find out who killed my father.

If Templeton was involved, I was going to make sure he got what was coming to him.

* * *

Jack didn't come home until after eight. I sat by the window watching the snow fall, Mystery curled up by my side. I didn't speak when he came in, but watched as he hung his coat and placed his shoes in the tray. He sat down on the couch and resumed staring at me.

"I'm sorry," I shrugged, "and I can't change what I did."

"You lied to me."

I winced. "I did. I know. And I'm sorry. I shouldn't have."

"Emily, I'm worried about you. I mean, I'm afraid of what you might do next. I don't know what is happening out there," he gestured toward the window. "But I need to know what's happening in this house, with you. Do you understand that?"

I nodded. "I don't think you'll believe most of what I've found out."

"Try me."

So I did. I moved to the couch and told him everything. Everything – from the grocery store debacle, to the Barnes & Noble faceoff with Templeton, right down to the story from Blackstone about how a bomb was planted on my father's train. I even told him about the text from Templeton while he was out. Jack sat listening, never speaking until I mentioned the text message.

"Give me the phone." He held out his hand. I passed it to him and watched as he pulled up the text. The next thing I knew, he was calling the number, the phone to his ear.

"What are you doing?" I made an unsuccessful grab for the phone.

"This number has been disconnected," Jack told me. "The number the text came from – it's not working."

I threw my hands up and sat back into the couch cushions. "Why am I not surprised?"

Jack tossed the phone onto the coffee table. "When are you going back to Northgate?"

"Monday. Two in the afternoon."

"Call Blackstone and reschedule for the evening. I'm coming with you."

"Jack, I don't know if that's the way it works," I said.

"To hell with the way it works. Your mother might've been fine living in the dark about your father's work. I'm not. This is a different world, Emily, and if you're going to start digging around in your father's past, I'm coming along. If your father's train was blown up by a bomb, you might be in danger too. Have you thought about that?"

I had. I nodded.

"Don't think I'm not still mad though."

"I know."

"No more secrets."

"I know."

"Okay." Jack ran his hand over the top of his head. "You eat?"

"No." My stomach growled.

"Pizza it is." He patted my knee before heading into the kitchen to call in the order. I walked to the window and looked out into the night. A moment later the streetlight went out, putting everything into a cold darkness. I shivered.

No matter what Jack wanted, I knew there were a lot of secrets out there.

✼ ✼ ✼

In the morning, I woke up to Jack kissing my belly. For a moment I froze and wondered if I was dreaming. I did a mind-body check. Nope. This was real. And good. Real good. I smiled.

"What are you doing?" I lifted the covers.

"You need to ask?" Jack mumbled into my bellybutton.

"Well, I'm not complaining."

"Good. Now shut up."

An hour later, I walked into the kitchen to make coffee. The Furious Furballs followed. I hummed a holiday tune as I put down bowls of cat food. Even Mischief seemed content to eat in the kitchen this morning.

Sunday mornings spent in bed have a way of making everything seem so much better. I was walking on air. I could do anything. My mind felt perfectly clear. I would get more information from Blackstone and find other Salesmen who could help me. I would find out who put the bomb on the train. I would make sure Templeton was brought to justice. And maybe I would make something sweet for breakfast.

I pursed my lips. I remembered a box of pastry mix in the pantry with *'Just add water!'* baking instructions. It couldn't get any easier than that.

I floated to the pantry, riding high on my newfound confidence. My hand landed on the doorknob and a sharp crack filled the air. I jumped, pushing my hip into the door as I started to turn around. My body was sucked into the pantry before the door jerked out of my hand and slammed shut behind me. I stood in the bathroom under the stairs. I spun around, my heart racing, every goosebump on my skin listening.

Nothing.

Silence. The bathroom was in perfect order. Nothing was out of place. I looked in the mirror. A very frightened Emily looked back.

With a shaking hand, I turned the bathroom doorknob and peeked out. No one was in the hall. I stepped through the doorway, easing my foot out, half expecting to end up in my bedroom. Nothing happened. I closed the bathroom door behind me, starting at the sound of the soft click.

Again with the doors! This is what happened at *The Green Bean*. This was what Blackstone was worried about. What did he say? Something about Templeton and catching his energy trail? Something about being pushed through the next closest door? I drew in a sharp breath. Did this mean Templeton was here in my house? Now?

Keeping my panic down to an internal roar, I checked the living room and kitchen. Clear. The pantry door was shut. Placing my ear against it, I listened. I couldn't hear anything inside. I turned the knob and opened the door an inch. Putting my eye to the crack, I saw nothing but canned goods and groceries. No one was in there.

I closed it again and mentally ran through what happened. I could've flaked out, high on a buzz from the morning's lovefest. Instead of going to the pantry, I walked to the bathroom.

Right. Who was I kidding?

I glanced at the stairs. Jack was still in bed. The noise – real or imagined – went unnoticed. I hesitated. I didn't want to set him off again. I'd tell Blackstone tomorrow.

But I knew I wouldn't be able to shake off the incident right away. I'd lost the urge to bake. Instead, I took my coffee up to my office. I turned to the page in The Book where I wrote in it the day before. Templeton's text came through right after I wrote *Emily Swift is NOT a salesman*. Maybe it would work again. I added to the page:

Were you just in my house Templeton?

I watched my phone. I knew it was absurd, but I tried again.

I went through a door and ended up in the wrong place again.

The phone remained silent.

Mr. Blackstone thinks I ended up in the wrong place because of you.

I wondered if Templeton knew Blackstone was the person who lived on Northgate. A moment later, I got a new text message and an answer.

Blackstone is a fool.

I didn't know what I expected, but it certainly wasn't that. Was Blackstone a fool? I didn't think so and right now he was the only one with information who'd answer my questions. I wrote again in The Book.

I know you were on the train with my father.

I waited for several minutes, but no response came. I looked at the clock. It was after eleven in the morning and for some reason I didn't think Blackstone was the church type. I called his number.

"Mr. Blackstone," he answered.

"Hi, it's Emily again. I hope I'm not calling too early on a Sunday?" I tapped his business card on my desk.

"Not at all. Is everything okay?"

I thought about the morning's door episode, but I didn't want to go into it over the phone. "Things are fine – I mean as fine as they can be. Look, Mr. Blackstone, Jack wants to come with me tomorrow. I need to move our meeting until the evening if that works for you."

"I can certainly see you in the evening," Mr.

Blackstone said. "Jack is more than welcome to wait for you in the study."

"I don't think that will work," I told him.

"Oh?"

"No. Jack wants to be in on the meeting. Actually, I want him there with me. All of this affects him too."

"This is unusual, Emily."

Tell me about it. "Well, Mr. Blackstone, what can I say? I'm an unusual kind of girl."

"I guess there's no harm. Jack will join us then. Are you able to be here at seven?"

"We'll be there. Thanks."

We disconnected and I decided to check on Jack. The bedroom was empty. I found him in the kitchen, stirring his coffee while he checked email on his phone. I spend a lot of time talking to the top of Jack's head. His nose often points toward a handheld gadget.

"I called Blackstone and rescheduled for tomorrow night at seven."

"Good," Jack answered. He frowned at his phone. "This is not good."

"What?"

"I must have missed an email. They're working on an electrical problem in my building. All access will be closed from today at noon until tomorrow at three." He looked up. "I have files I need to pick up."

"They're doing this on a Sunday?"

"Better than starting on a weekday, I guess." Jack shrugged. "Damn. I've got to go to campus. Want to ride with me?"

I thought about the way the morning was going between the doors and Templeton's text. This definitely fell in the category of things-Jack-wants-me-to-tell-him-and-not-hide-until-he-finds-out-and-gets-mad. I wasn't ready to ruin the morning's good vibes between us. Plus, it had been a couple of days since I studied The Book. Maybe I could do a little research – stay home and stay out of trouble. Maybe I could call Tara. Maybe I could get Templeton to tell me more through text messaging. I just needed to ask the right questions. No problem.

"You know what? I'm going to stay here. I'll be here when you get back. We'll have lunch."

Jack lifted his eyebrows. "You promise you'll stay put?"

"I have no plans to go anywhere. I swear."

❊ ❊ ❊

I called Tara after Jack left.

"I wanted to call you," Tara said, "but I was afraid of interrupting you and Jack. How mad is he?"

"Not so much now. He was pretty ticked off last night. But he's speaking to me again. I told him about everything." Except for this morning's little incident. Scratch that. Incidents.

"Everything? Even about Templeton at Barnes & Noble?"

"Yup."

"How did he take it?"

"True to form. He didn't say much except that from now on, he's to be told everything. He also insisted on going back to Northgate with me tomorrow. Turns out the address is for a Mr. Blackstone. He's the man I met with yesterday. I think he might be a book collector of sorts too." I fished his business card out of my pocket. "Rene Blackstone. Can you look him up? His office is pretty much a library in itself. He gave me some more information about my father. And, it turns out he knows Templeton."

"What did he say?"

I didn't want to talk about the bomb on my father's train just yet. In fact, until I knew more, I decided to keep some things under wraps. But I did want Tara to be wary of Templeton.

"Templeton and my father knew each other. They traveled together for work."

"You have got to be kidding me?"

"Nope. And Templeton doesn't seem to have a big fan club either. The fact that he's here in Kincaid rattled Blackstone."

"So why is he here?"

"Blackstone doesn't know any more than I do. But I guess turning thirty is a big deal. I think that has a lot to do with it."

"Why?"

"Supposedly you become some sort of official salesman then." I paused, chewing the inside of my cheek. "Blackstone says I was born to be a Salesman. Tara, do me a favor. Can you tap your people in-the-know again and ask them if they ever heard of a secret society of Salesmen? That's Salesmen with a capital 'S,' by the way."

"A secret society of Salesmen? Really, Em?"

"I know it sounds odd, but just try it. And if anything comes up, see if there was any weirdness going on with the group about twenty or thirty years ago. Or seventeen years ago." I thought about the bomb on my father's train.

"There's weirdness going on now."

"Ha ha," I said. "But seriously, can you check?"

"Of course I will! Anything else?"

"Did you hear anything on the video we made of The Book?"

"I sent clips to several colleagues right after you and Lydia left. You remember the friend of a friend who knew a man who said he'd heard of Matar? He'd said that there was a civil war or something? Well, guess what? He's M.I.A. Someone forwarded the video clip to his email and it bounced right back – and before you think it had to do with file size, it didn't. Then they called his office and the phone's disconnected. They tried his house and found out he never came home Friday night."

"You're kidding?" I didn't like the sound of that. It was too coincidental. "Do you think something bad happened to him?"

"Possibly. Maybe he was planning on disappearing. Who knows? People take off all the time," Tara said.

"I guess so." I wasn't as optimistic as my friend. Then again, she didn't know about bombings and a violent fringe group.

"I'll let you know if I hear more, okay?"

"Thanks. I don't know what I'd do without you."

"No prob. I'm racking up the favors you'll owe me."

"Great. Good to know you're operating from the kindness of your heart." I imagined her grinning. "Hey, remember if you see Templeton, stay far away from him and call me A.S.A.P. Okay?"

"I will. You're freaking me out, though."

"I know. I'm sorry."

"It's okay. But keep your calendar free. I have a two-date night planned for New Year's Eve and I'll need you to cover."

CHAPTER 11

I didn't have any desire to wander through another wrong door, so I stuck to rooms that were already open. After making some cocoa, I curled up in the living room with my laptop, phone at my side. The Book and my notepad sat on the coffee table.

I decided not to tell my mother about the bomb on the train. It wouldn't do any good at this point. It was better to wait until I had more answers. I knew Blackstone could give me some, and I was sure Templeton could answer everything.

What did Templeton have to gain? I wasn't an expert, but assuming a person wasn't a psychopath, I supposed the top reasons were money, power, and revenge. If he worked with the Fringe, it could be for money. He already seemed to have a lot of power.

What would it take to make me hurt someone? Self-defense? Maybe to protect someone I loved? I shook my head. I didn't want to go there.

I picked up The Book. It might be the twenty-first century, but there was something unexplainable going on. The portal doors were one thing – writing messages to Templeton in The

Book and having him reply to my phone was another. It was like magic.

Did I believe in magic? A part of me wanted to believe it existed. When I was little, I used to pretend I had all sorts of magical powers, like shooting beams of energy out my fingertips. I accomplished this by tying a hose to my arm and turning it on full blast, marching around my yard. I don't believe anyone was impressed. Growing up, I read fantasy-type novels, like *A Wrinkle in Time*. I loved creepy shows like the classic *The X-Files* and watched old *Buffy, The Vampire Slayer* reruns. Jack and I liked to check out older French movies; *Amelie* was a favorite. I love the idea of a whole secret world living right alongside ours.

Now it seemed like I'd found one, this Empire. If I wanted to find out more about it and my father, I'd have to keep an open mind. I'd have to believe in the unbelievable.

Was The Book magic too? Was it a way to send messages? What if I asked The Book a question? Was that even possible?

I turned to the page where I'd been sending Templeton messages. I thought for a moment, then wrote:

Can I talk to someone other than Templeton?

My phone remained silent. Maybe The Book was like a toy Magic Eight Ball. I closed it again and held The Book up with both hands. I concentrated on my question.

"Book, can I talk to someone other than Templeton?" I was glad Jack wasn't home to see this.

I pretended The Book could hear me and wanted to give me the answer. I waited for a few moments, and then opened it to a random page. I looked at my father's handwriting.

When in Matar, look for
Anne Lace. Her special-ty
helps people see.
May have knowledge
regarding Eve of Silence.
Will need Rabbit's help.
Contact prior to
Solstice.
Avoid Walled Zone.

This passage wasn't new to me. Anne Lace. Whoever she was, my father left a note to get in touch with her. Was the note for him, or was it written for me? It didn't matter. I'd asked The Book a question and it gave me an answer. Magic or coincidence? Again, it didn't matter. I had a place to start.

Would Anne Lace be easy to find? If she lived in Matar... Well, I hadn't even found Matar yet. I'd definitely need to ask Blackstone about that. In the meantime, it couldn't hurt to see if I could find her online.

I tapped away, using all sorts of search terms:

anne lace, anne lace matar, anne lace salesman, anne lace new york – and so on. Nothing came up. Well, at least nothing not involving a flower called Queen Anne's Lace.

I wondered if I should bother Tara with yet another request, but decided against it. I didn't want to try to get this information from Templeton. It would be a good idea for me to keep some things up my sleeve. I could call Blackstone, but didn't want to be a pest. Still, he said to call any time. I hemmed and hawed for about thirty seconds before I talked myself into it. I picked up my phone.

His phone rang several times, but no one answered. No voice came on the line asking me to leave a message. Who doesn't have some sort of answering service or voice mail? This was annoying. What if I drove over and asked this one quick question?

Bad idea! What in the world was I thinking? Jack would have a fit. My phone rang. It was Tara.

"Hey," I answered. "What's up?"

"Guess what I just found out about Blackstone?"

I sat forward. "What?"

"About three years ago he was the Head of the Rare Book Collection for one of the Smithsonian Institution Libraries based in New York City. He was fired for stealing a rare book, but get this: no charges were ever filed against him."

"No way!"

"There's more. He never returned the book he stole."

"What do you mean? I don't get it." I stood up and began to pace my living room. "How do you know this?"

"Fellow book collector. No reason to lie or make up a story."

"But how do they know?"

"I didn't ask. Emily, a lot of these collectors are loaded. They're powerful people. They're not typically willing to share private information. I'm lucky to have good working relationships with some of them. I also know that if they say something is true, it is."

So, Blackstone has some secrets, does he? What book would he have stolen? And why?

"I think we should go talk to Blackstone," I said.

"We?"

"Yes 'we.' If I go by myself, Jack will kill me."

"Hey, I'm willing to tag along. You should've taken me the first time. But considering what you know now, do you think it's safe?"

"I do. Blackstone's been more than willing to help. Let's go find out what he has to say. There must be more to the story. A reason for what he did. Come pick me up. My heater's still on the fritz."

"What about Jack?"
"I'll leave a note."
"Oh, boy. Okay. I'm on my way."

※ ※ ※

At least I was honest. In the note I wrote how Tara had turned up some information about Blackstone's work – well, at least about his former employment – and that she went with me to ask him some questions. I added that we would be back home in a couple of hours, and to feel free to text me. I drew a smiley face and a heart.

I doubted the note was going to save my neck, but I couldn't seem to stop myself. I had to find out what was going on. I had to know who I could trust.

I also planned to ask Blackstone about Anne Lace's whereabouts. Maybe if she lived local, Tara and I could visit her after leaving Blackstone's.

The roads had collected a lot of snow and slush, so it took a little longer than planned. Tara drove up the driveway for twelve twenty-one Northgate Way and parked. We sat looking at the house.

"Why is the front door wide open?" she asked.

A gust of wind sent flakes flying all around the car. We squinted, trying to see through the snow. I picked up my phone and called Blackstone's office. Again, no answer.

"Okay," I said, "this is what we're going to do. I'm going to dial your number, and if I need you to call or go for help, I'll hit the button. You wait here and keep the car locked."

Tara's eyes narrowed as she turned toward me. She scowled. "I really don't like this idea. Let's just call the police now."

"Look, it may not be any big deal. Let me go and poke my head in. If there's something wrong, I'll call. Don't worry." I was worried enough for the both of us.

Tara's jaw clenched. "If you are not out of there in five minutes – make that two – I am calling the police. I'm not kidding, Emily. I don't like this."

"I know, I know. Just wait for me. I'll be right back. Promise." I climbed from the car and put my gloves in my pocket. I queued up Tara's number on my phone. I held it up so she could see. She rolled her eyes from the other side of the window.

I picked my way through the snow and up the walk. Like before, I didn't see any footprints. I crept up to the open door and peered in. It was quiet and nothing I could see seemed out of place. Nothing knocked over or broken. I turned back to Tara's car. Her face was plastered to the windshield as she watched. I lifted my arms in an I-have-no-idea shrug before going into Blackstone's home.

With the door left open, the house was cold. I decided to leave it that way in case I needed to make a fast escape. I walked from the foyer and deeper into the house.

"Elsa? Mr. Blackstone?" I called out softly. My voice echoed in the lonely rooms. "Anyone home?"

No one answered. I tiptoed along, taking the same path as I had with Elsa. When I reached the stairs leading down to Blackstone's office, I felt a creepy little shiver run down my spine. Nothing like going underground alone when you're looking for missing people.

I walked down the stairs taking care to remain as quiet as possible. At the bottom, I was once again in the room with all the monitors. My eyes flitted to the screens. They didn't show anything out of place in the areas being watched. So where was Blackstone? I moved deeper into the room. My heart was hammering against my chest so hard I could feel it in my temples.

A thud sounded from behind the door leading into Blackstone's office, making me jump. I gripped my phone. What do I do? My eyes darted around the room. I shifted from foot-to-foot before summoning the courage to move closer to the door. I reached out, touching the doorknob with my fingertips. As my fingers slid forward and my palm pressed against the knob, I thought of how this would be a bad time to end up in the wrong place. Then again, maybe not. Wincing, I turned the knob and pushed the door open.

"Mr. Blackstone?" I whispered as I entered the room. It was dark except for a lamp on a side table. The shadows were thick. I wasn't alone. My fingertips scraped the wall behind me as I searched for a light switch. I found one and flipped it. Several lamps came on at once and the room was flooded with light.

The shadows were gone. Templeton stood in their place. Blackstone lay at his feet, unconscious.

"No!" My phone dropped to the floor as I pressed my back against the wall.

Templeton froze, lip curling into a sneer. Bravery fueled by some primal instinct must've kicked in because before I had time to think about running out, I grabbed a floor lamp. I brandished it like a club and moved in to protect Blackstone.

"Get away from him!" I took a swing at Templeton. The base of the lamp came close to making contact. He jumped back and the lines in his face hardened.

"Put that down!"

"The hell I will! Get away from him!" I took another swing.

"You have no idea what is going on," he snarled. "You have many enemies in the Empire, Emily. You better start watching your back."

I had to get to my phone. I needed to call Tara and yell for help. Keeping the lamp between Templeton and myself, I went for my phone. He took the opportunity to put some distance between us. As I grabbed the phone, Templeton turned and yanked open a door buried in one of the book-lined walls. He slipped through, slamming it behind him.

"Wait!" I dropped the lamp and hit connect with my thumb.

"Emily!" Tara yelled from my phone.

"Call the police and get an ambulance! Blackstone's been attacked. He's on the floor in his office!" I couldn't let Templeton get away. Taking one last look at Blackstone, I rushed to the door.

"Ohmigod! Are you okay?"

"I'm okay, Tara, I'm okay. But it was Templeton! He was here! He ran away. I'm going after him. Call the –" The minute I ran through the door, the connection cut out. I stumbled, my feet trying to find themselves in the snow as I slid into a row of garbage cans. I tumbled, falling ass-over-tin-cup and just as quickly scrambled back to my feet. I was outside. The door in Blackstone's office led to the outside.

I spun around looking for Templeton. He was gone. I stopped, realizing then that I had no idea where in the hell I was. One thing I did know: I was no longer at twelve twenty-one Northgate Way.

❊ ❊ ❊

The door I came through was locked tight behind me. No no no! I gripped the knob and yanked on the door as hard as I could, wrenching my shoulder in the process. Fine time to have a door episode! Damn Templeton! This had to be his fault. I kicked the door hard and hurt my big toe. Great. Now my butt and my toe hurt. I blew out an angry breath.

I had landed in a narrow alleyway. I limped along, trying a couple of random doors as I went. All were locked. When I reached the sidewalk, I didn't recognize the street. I sighed. I hoped I wasn't too far from home. Or Tara.

Tara! My phone was still in my hand. I tried to call her. No signal.

"Figures," I said, jamming my phone into my pocket. I began walking.

This had to be an older part of Kincaid, with its cobblestone and brick streets. I passed a bakery, a jeweler, a couple of salons, and several upscale gift stores as I walked down the lane. The neighborhood was decked out for the holidays.

Funny though, I didn't recognize anything.

Traffic was light and only a few shoppers passed by. The snow was falling much lighter here, but with bigger flakes. It was like walking inside a snow globe. I needed to find out exactly where I was and I had to find a phone that worked. My eyes were drawn to a sign jutting out over a well-worn entrance. *The Daily Brew*. Perfect.

I climbed up the two stone steps and pushed open a heavy door. A strand of India bells hanging on the back tinkled, announcing my entrance. A table for two hugged the front window, and a small order counter sat opposite the door. A hall on the right led to the back and presumably more seating.

Well-worn wood floors creaked out a welcome as I walked to the counter. Along with the old-fashioned cash register, credit card machine, and a small stack of menus, I noticed a tip jar that read: *Instead of leaving a tip for us, how about a donation for The Rabbits?* Several glass domes sheltered scones, breads, and other assorted pastries.

"Hello?" A female voice called from the back. "I'll be right out!"

"No problem," I answered. Moments later a slender woman appeared, wiping her hands on a blue apron that stopped right above her knees. She was probably in her fifties, with snow white hair cropped short in a pixie cut. Her green eyes were striking, and the corners crinkled as she smiled. She was tall, but she was also wearing heeled boots. She strutted up to the counter.

"What would you like today?" she asked. "I have a delicious leek potato soup with warm bread fresh from the oven."

"Um, I just stopped in to ask if I could use your phone." Embarrassed, I rushed to explain. "I kind of got stranded in this neighborhood. I need to call for a ride. My phone died out of nowhere, so now I'm stuck. But as soon as my ride comes, I'll get a couple of coffees to go."

She chuckled as she reached under the counter and came back with a phone. "No worries, hon. It happens sometimes."

It did? Well, I supposed it did. "Thanks, I appreciate it." I picked up the receiver. "Um, I promise I'm not nuts, but..."

She raised a perfectly white, winged brow at me. "Yes?"

"I'm not sure which part of Kincaid I'm in."

"Kincaid?"

Oh boy. This didn't bode well. "Kincaid. Kincaid, New York?"

"Hon, I don't know where you think you are, but you're not in Kincaid."

Oh boy again. "Okay. So, I'm where?" My voice hiked up a few notches. Don't freak out, don't freak out, I chanted inside my head.

"You're in Matar." She answered. "Exactly how did you get here?"

"Matar," I repeated. "I'm in Matar?"

"Matar," she confirmed, studying me. "You look familiar. Have we met before?"

"I don't think so." I set the phone back down on the counter. No sense in calling for a ride. I had to figure out how to get back to Blackstone's by myself. Maybe I should return to the alley and try the door again.

"What's your name?" the woman asked.

I hesitated. The woman seemed friendly enough, but I was in a place that didn't seem to be real until now. What did I really know about Matar? Who could I trust? I felt like Dorothy and this wasn't tornado-land. I shuddered. Was it only a matter of minutes before the flying monkeys showed up?

The woman waited for an answer, tilting her head to the side. I went with the truth. What else could happen, right?

"Emily. Emily... ah, just Emily."

"Well, just Emily," she held out her hand smiling, "I'm Anne Lace."

My jaw dropped open. Her hand hung in the air, untouched. Stunned, I stared.

"My father was Daniel Swift," I blurted out. "I'm his daughter, Emily Swift."

Now it was Anne's turn to look shocked. Her own mouth popped open in surprise. Her hand drifted to her chest, long fingers splaying across her heart. "Emily," she breathed. "Emily Swift."

I nodded before shifting into high gear. "I think I need your help. I followed Templeton here, but I didn't know I was coming here. I thought I was chasing him through Blackstone's house." I mentally slapped my forehead. Oh crap, Mr. Blackstone and Tara! "I need to get some help. Templeton attacked Blackstone and I left my friend Tara behind to call the police, but I don't know how to get back there! I didn't even think Matar existed!" My voice grew louder as I rambled.

"Emily Swift," Anne said again. She was still dazed. "You're here in Matar?"

"It looks that way! What do I do now?"

Anne put her palms to her cheeks and shook her head. "Okay," she said placing her hands back on the countertop. "Tell me exactly what happened. How did you get here?"

I started from when Tara and I arrived at Blackstone's house. I explained how I saw Templeton standing over Blackstone, and how I followed him through a door in the library. Anne listened without interrupting, a deep, vertical line growing between her eyebrows.

"And I saw your café and here I am," I finished. "What do I do? I don't know how to get back!"

"Emily, I think you came through the North Door. I don't know Blackstone, but he must be the door's keeper – all four directional doors have them. The North Door leads into Matar. But it's a one-way door. Except during the Winter Solstice. Then you can travel from Matar to the other side."

"The Solstice? Isn't that, like, on the twenty-first? Today's only the fifth!"

"Can't you just take another door to your home?" she asked.

"I have no idea how to do that," I said. "I haven't gone through a lot of doors on purpose. I just met Blackstone yesterday." I stopped. Something occurred to me. "Wait a minute, you don't know Blackstone, but you didn't say anything about Templeton. Do you know him?"

She nodded. "Everyone knows who Templeton is."

"When's the last time you saw him?"

"As far as I know, it's been years since anyone has seen him. The fact that you were chasing him today," she pressed her lips together before continuing. "Emily, you've got to get back to this Blackstone's house. You need to make sure he's alive and find out what happened."

"But I don't know how!" The India bells tinkled behind me. Anne's gaze drifted over my shoulder. She put on a tight little smile and started to come out from behind the counter.

"Can I help you?" Her voice was too cheerful. I glanced over my shoulder. Two men stood in the doorway. Each was dressed in black from head to toe, with crimson-colored collars poking up from under their coats. Both men wore unfriendly faces. Both held top hats in their hands. As Anne stepped past me to put herself in front of them, she leaned close and whispered into my ear:

"Back door. Run."

CHAPTER 12

I began a mad dash down the hall and nearly tumbled over a table, cracking my shin on a chair. I shoved it out of the way and scurried for a door marked 'Exit.' Yelling and crashing behind me sounded as if Anne had done her best to block the men. I hoped like hell they didn't hurt her.

Once out the back door, I raced down the alley behind the café. I headed for the street. I didn't stop on the sidewalk, but rushed through the traffic, shooting out in front of a car and causing it to slam on its brakes as it slid to a stop. More yelling came from behind. I hoped it was the driver and not the two men with top hats. I didn't stop to look.

I ran as fast as I could, my hands balled into fists, my elbows pumping up and down. Foot traffic had picked up some. I shouted apologies as I pushed past shoppers. I could hear the growing commotion behind me. I had to assume I was still being chased. Ahead, I saw a footbridge leading into a park. I made a beeline for it, hoping I could find a place to hide. Before I reached the bridge, my mind's eye told me to look to the left. I skidded to a stop, the sidewalk slop splashing around me.

Across the street stood Templeton. He was leaning against a streetlight. I looked behind me. The two men in black were only a block away. I turned back to Templeton. His gaze flicked to the men pursuing me and he raised his eyebrows. His eyes once again met mine and he smiled.

The footbridge now seemed very far away. Behind me, a small side street opened up into a winding corridor. It was closer – I went for it.

The sound of feet gaining on me echoed in the narrow space as I sprinted on the wet stone. They were going to catch up in no time! The head start Anne gave me was the only reason why I'd made it this far.

I slipped, stumbled, fell, jumped up, ran, and repeated several times. I was soaked from slush. The wind that kicked up ran right through my clothes as the corridor thinned even more. My palms were scraped and bleeding. I panted as I ran. My vision was blurry. I was crying.

I just want to go home! I sobbed as I rounded yet another sharp corner and slammed into a closed door. Fumbling for a handle, I wrenched it open, hurtling myself inside. I tripped and fell again. *Hard.*

I landed on my kitchen floor.

Jack stood there, eating a piece of apple pie, his fork suspended halfway between his plate and open mouth.

He cleared his throat. "I thought you were with Tara. Did you get my text? What's going on?"

"Has Tara called?" I climbed to my feet and dug into my pocket for my phone. I took in a shuddering breath. I was still crying.

"No, why?" Jack's gaze roamed over my wet clothes. I was covered head-to-toe in winter slop. His jaw clenched and his cheek twitched. "Emily, what's going on?"

My hands were shaking as I called Tara. It started to ring. "Come on, come on," I begged.

Tara answered. "Emily? Where are you?"

I leaned against the counter, all the air rushing out of me. I pressed my palm against my forehead. "I'm here – home. Where are you?"

"You're home? I'm still at Blackstone's house. The police and ambulance are here. Blackstone's okay. He was hit over the head with something."

"Is he conscious?"

"He is now. He told the police there was an intruder. He says he doesn't know who it was."

"Tara, it was Templeton, I saw him!" I glanced at Jack. He set his plate on the table.

"Emily?" he said.

"Wait, Emily, there's more," Tara's voice was strained. "They found Elsa."

My stomach churned at Tara's words. "What do you mean, they 'found' Elsa?"

"I mean, they found her. In the kitchen. No one is telling me anything, of course. But, Emily, she's dead."

I stumbled away from the counter and sat down at the table. "Oh my god."

Jack came to me, putting his hand on my shoulder. "Emily, look at me. What is going on?"

I looked up, my eyes filling with tears. "Somebody killed Elsa. They found her inside Blackstone's house. There was an 'intruder' at Blackstone's house."

"Does Blackstone know Templeton? Would he recognize him?" Tara asked into my ear.

"I don't know. Did he mention me to the police?" This was not going to be good.

"Well, he kind of had to. The police wondered why I was here." Tara lowered her voice. "And since you're M.I.A, they've been looking around the house for you."

"Oh great." My eyes cut back to Jack.

"Blackstone told them you probably ran off after the intruder. What should I do now?"

"Come over here. I need to tell you and Jack what happened."

"Okay, but Emily, you need to talk to the police."

"I know. If you can, tell Blackstone that I'll see him tomorrow. If you can get away without having to say anything to the police, that would be good. But if you do get stuck, tell them I called you and I'm home. They can find me here."

"This isn't good, you know. It looks bad that you were here and now you are not."

"I'll think of something."

"Fine. I'm on my way. But I'm being eyeballed by one of the detectives. I'm sure he's very interested in who I'm talking to." Tara ended the call.

Jack sat down at the table and stared at me.

"I left a note," I told him.

"Yes."

"I was with Tara – I didn't go alone!"

"You were supposed to wait for me. Emily, you just told me that someone killed a woman at Blackstone's! Don't even try to offer an excuse for going there by yourself!"

"This couldn't wait!" I had enough of arguing with Jack, even though in this case, he was right. "Damn it, Jack! Whether or not you believe I should've gone, the fact is, Blackstone had been attacked! We got there right after it happened and called for help." Well, eventually.

"You could have been attacked too," he shouted. I sat back, startled. Jack didn't yell, even when he was angry.

"I know, but I wasn't. Jack, it was Templeton – he was standing over Blackstone!"

Jack became quiet as his gaze moved to the pantry door. I spun around, half afraid that I'd see the men who chased me in Matar.

"What? Did you hear something?" My poor heart began to pound again.

"You were in the pantry." His frown deepened.

I walked over to the pantry door and listened for a moment. I couldn't hear anything coming from the other side. I opened it, peering around the door as I looked inside. Nothing but canned goods. I closed it with a sigh of relief.

"Emily, you were in the pantry," Jack repeated.

"Not quite." I rubbed my face with dirty hands. The cuts and scratches needed a swipe of peroxide. So what had happened? I had wanted to go home with every fiber of my being. So did Dorothy. She had Ruby Slippers. Apparently, I had doors.

Alright then. I have doors. I nodded to myself.

"You're going to have to give me a little bit more than that, Emily."

"Yeah, I know, I know. Tara's coming over. Probably the police, too." I took a breath. "Jack, I'm freezing, beat to hell, and filthy, so I'm going to take a shower first. Then I'll tell you everything."

✸ ✸ ✸

After showering I sat at the kitchen table wrapped in a big, bulky sweater, my hands wrapped around a mug of hot chocolate. Jack was silent as he sipped his coffee. He stared out the window while we waited.

I decided it was to my advantage – and probably the best thing for my relationship – if I didn't say anything to Jack until Tara arrived. I used the time to gather my thoughts. Well, mostly I chased them around my brain while I tried to figure out what the hell had happened. Or more to the point: how it happened.

I was in Matar. And I had met Anne Lace. Okay, so I didn't get anywhere with Anne, but now I knew how to find her. Now I knew how to get to Matar. Of course returning from Matar like that was an experience I didn't want to repeat. There had to be an easier way. Maybe Blackstone could tell me.

Then there was Templeton, laughing as his henchmen chased me through the streets. Well, maybe he wasn't laughing, but he had that little smirk on his face again. I wanted to slap it off. I hated him.

The two men chasing me had to be part of the group Blackstone talked about: the Fringe. Anne must've known who they were too, or at least she knew they weren't friends of mine. I sighed and took a sip of my hot chocolate. Jack turned in his chair and shot me another black look.

"Not you," I said.

He looked back out the kitchen window.

Anne clearly knew who I was. She was shocked

to see me, but she definitely knew me. Templeton and Blackstone both knew me too. I hadn't heard of any of these people until The Book showed up. But it wasn't The Book making this happen. The Book was only pointing to a story. My father's story.

The doorbell startled both of us and Jack followed me to the front door. He cut in front of me and peered through the window.

"It's the police. I see Tara's car parked outside. She's standing by her car."

"You better open the door," I answered. How in the world was I going to explain what had happened?

A tall man dressed in a brown suit stood in the doorway. He looked past Jack to me. "Emily Swift? I'm Detective O'Connell. I need to talk to you about the afternoon events at twelve twenty-one Northgate Way." He turned to Jack. "We'd like to come in."

Jack moved to the side. "She's pretty shaken. Is this going to take long?"

"That depends." Detective O'Connell stepped inside, a uniformed officer joining him. O'Connell's eyes swept the living room, presumably taking in every little detail. He turned to Jack. "And you are?"

"Jack Greene. I'm Emily's boyfriend. We both live here." Jack moved a step closer to me. "Should I call our lawyer?"

"I don't think that's necessary," Detective O'Connell answered. "But you are free to do so if you think you should, if Emily needs legal representation as a result of her activities this afternoon."

"I don't," I replied. I certainly didn't need to add more people to the mix.

"Ms. Swift, I need you to start at the beginning and tell me why you were at the house on Northgate, what happened, what you saw, and," here Detective O'Connell paused and looked directly at me, "and you need to tell me why you left and came home."

I moved to the couch and sunk into the cushions. I shook my head no before realizing what I was doing.

"No?" O'Connell asked.

I looked up. "It's a blur."

"Start at the beginning. Why were you at the house on Northgate?"

I certainly did not want to lie to the police, but there was so much that I could not explain. There was so much I had to find out, and I could not have the police getting involved before I had the answers I needed.

Still, if I could just keep it simple without lying, I might be able to buy some time. I had to get back to Matar.

"I received an invitation to meet with Mr. Blackstone. He works for the same company my father used to work for before he died. I think he wanted to give me some old papers." There. That should do it.

"And what company is this?"

Well, maybe not quite.

I shrugged. "I think you'll have to get that information from Blackstone. I always thought my father was an independent contractor."

Detective O'Connell didn't look convinced, but he jotted down a few lines into his notepad. He looked up. "You were there today because Blackstone invited you?"

He knew something was up. "Well, he didn't technically invite me there today. I was going to meet with him on Monday, but I couldn't wait."

"And when you got there with –" O'Connell flipped back several pages. "– with Tara Parker-Jones, what happened?"

At least this part I could describe without worrying about lying to the police. "Tara and I pulled up to the house and the front door was wide open. We couldn't see anyone or any reason for the door to be left like that, so I decided to go see what was going on."

"You what?" Jack interrupted, his voice uncharacteristically loud.

Detective O'Connell put up a hand. "Mr. Greene, I need to know exactly what happened today. We have an assault and a murder on our hands, and Emily needs to explain her role in both."

"My role?" Now my voice went up an octave.

"Yes, you were there. You have information we need for this investigation." He glanced down at his notepad. "Please continue. The door was open to the house."

I told O'Connell how I went in and made my way to the lower level, that I had visited Blackstone before and knew the way. I described how I found him in the library, unconscious with a man leaning over him.

"Did you recognize him, this man?"

"Um, yes. I'd seen him before." Stick to the truth Emily, I told myself. "He was in a restaurant we ate at last week. I might have seen him in a few other places. But I don't know him." Well, not really.

"Do you believe he was following you in these other places?"

"I can't be sure." Okay, the truth was getting harder to stick to.

Detective O'Connell spent a long minute looking at me without speaking. Finally he said, "Tell me what happened when you saw him standing in the library."

"I yelled at him to get away. I tried to hit him with a lamp stand." I pressed my lips together at the memory before continuing. "But I missed."

Jack made a sound indicating that he was well beyond any line of patience with the whole mess. I avoided looking his way.

"Anyhow, the guy ran out of the library. There was a door in one of the walls. I tried to follow him, but he was gone."

"Gone?"

"Gone." I didn't even try to look the detective in the eye.

"And you were where?"

"Outside."

"Ms. Swift, we did not find any doors leading outside from the library." Of course they didn't.

"It was a blur, my adrenalin was kicking in, I was running. I don't know which door I went through." Lie, lie, lie. I was so going to jail.

"Ms. Swift," O'Connell paused. He looked at Jack once before directing his attention back to me. "Why did you leave your friend Tara at Blackstone's and come home?"

It wasn't quite the question I expected and there was no truth I could tell him that he would believe. I met his gaze and elevated my lying to a fake cowardly confession. "I was scared so I came home."

It was easy to see that he didn't believe me, but he continued. "How did you get home?"

"I walked."

"What route did you take?"

"I don't remember. Everything became a blur." This was bad. I truly was going to need a lawyer, not because I was guilty, but because I was stupid and would need a whole lot of legal help to get out of this hole.

"Ms. Swift, I don't believe you. I do believe, however, that you will tell me the truth." He pulled a card from his pocket and handed it to Jack. "Call me when her memory returns. The sooner the better for her."

Detective O'Connell turned and made his way out the front door, the uniformed officer following. He paused on the steps and spoke to Tara briefly. She nodded and he held the door for her as she rushed inside.

"Thank god you're okay!" Tara hugged me as she tumbled in. "It was horrible. I was so afraid for you!"

I could feel Jack's stare burning into the back of my head. I cleared my throat. "Well, let's not dwell on it."

"Not dwell on it? God, Emily, I was really scared!" Tara was not helping. I decided to get everyone back in the kitchen and go from there.

"I know, I was too, but let me tell you what happened." I took her coat and hung it on the hall tree. She pulled off her knit cap and her fine hair floated around her head in a halo of static electricity. "Jack, can you make Tara some hot chocolate?"

"Don't let her out of your sight," he told my friend.

"Oh, he's mad." Tara watched Jack disappear

into the kitchen.

"Understatement."

"What happened? Where did you go?"

"Matar."

"Get out! What are you talking about?"

"Come sit down. I've got a long story to tell."

❋ ❋ ❋

First, I had to catch Tara up on some details I'd left out earlier. She about fell out of her chair when I told her the train wreck that killed my father was caused by a bomb. The color left her face when I told her Templeton had been on that train before the explosion.

Both Tara and Jack sat unmoving while I told them about finding Blackstone and following Templeton. Jack's expression remained the same when I explained how I landed in Matar. Tara's eyes got wider as my story unfolded. I told them about meeting Anne Lace at the café before the men in black showed up, and how she ran interference so I could get away. The twitch in Jack's jaw returned when I described running through the streets. I finished by telling them about Templeton watching me, and then how I ran into – literally – the door that brought me home.

"And you ended up in the kitchen?" Tara held her mug in both hands. Her eyes were glassy. She looked even more worried than when she first arrived.

"Bam. Right on the kitchen floor." I held up my hands to show her my scuffed palms. "I'm pathetic. I did a lot of falling today. You should see my knees. Black and blue."

Tara looked at Jack. Jack took his empty mug to the sink.

"So, um. Yeah. Okay, this is like the wardrobe-thing in *The Lion, the Witch, and the Wardrobe*, right?" Tara asked. "Head through a door, end up in Matar? Maybe time travel a bit?"

Great. It's one thing to sound crazy, but it's worse when people think you are. I pressed on. "Kind of. But I don't think there's any time difference. I think Matar is on the same clock as we are."

"Unbelievable." Tara shook her head and looked down at her mug. She chewed her lower lip. A moment later her expression changed from disbelief, to acceptance. The business-savvy game-face appeared. "Okay, Em, next steps. What are you planning to do? How do we do this?"

"I think the next step is going back to Blackstone's tomorrow night."

"Good. He wants to see you," Tara said. "And I'm coming with you. I think you owe me after today."

"I'd think you'd want to avoid all of this."

"No way. I'm in it with you." Tara pointed at the man with the storm cloud hovering over his head. "We both are, right Jack?"

Jack didn't share Tara's enthusiasm, but he nodded. "Until we figure out what the hell is going on, you will not leave my sight, do you understand?"

"Trust me," I said. "I'm not looking for a repeat of today."

"That's it, guys. I'm going." Tara stood and clapped her hands once. "Thanks for the hot chocolate. Thanks for the afternoon heart attack." She headed for her coat. We followed her to the front door.

"Come over early," I said. "We'll eat before we go."

"Sure." Tara turned back to Jack. "I know you're mad, but be nice to her. A lot of bad things happened today. No matter what you might think, everything would've happened in some way even if we didn't go to Blackstone's."

Jack didn't argue. It seemed as if there were bigger forces at work.

"I'll make sure nothing happens between now and tomorrow night," he said.

※ ※ ※

Jack was my shadow from the moment Tara left. Detective O'Connell called later that evening to verify a 'few more points.' Thankfully, Blackstone had confirmed that I was a friend and not the person who attacked him, that he could not see how I could have had any part of the attack. However, I was told it would be better for me to stay local and not engage in any travels until arrests had been made. I was also 'encouraged' to call O'Connell when my memory of the events following the attack on Blackstone became clearer. And again, it would be advantageous if that was sooner rather than later.

Sure.

Jack was quiet, but didn't seem to be angry anymore. Exhausted from the day, we went to bed early that night. Jack pulled me to him, holding me close, saying nothing. I fell asleep right after feeling his lips brush the top of my head and his voice whisper 'I love you.'

※ ※ ※

I was so tired from day's drama that I anticipated an uneventful night's sleep. But there I was, standing in Blackstone's library, wearing my PJs. I didn't see Blackstone, and the lamp on the desk was the only light on in the room. I heard a clock ticking in the distance. I began to worry I wasn't alone. My stomach started to churn. Stop it! It's only a stupid dream, I reminded myself.

"Yes, yes, Emily. It's just a dream. How many times will we need to go through this?" Templeton stepped out from the shadows.

"You!" My voice shook. "You attacked Blackstone." I backed away.

Templeton strolled through the room, weaving in and out of the lamplight. "Is that what you think? Maybe I was here to find something he's hiding from everyone. Maybe Blackstone was already on the floor unconscious when I arrived."

"I don't believe you."

He shrugged and picked up a book from the floor. He thumbed through a few pages. "Why don't you ask Blackstone?"

"I will," I told him. I could smell the dusty books lining Blackstone's shelves. The carpet felt thick under my bare feet. I was afraid. I watched as Templeton walked closer, his eyes scanning the pages in the book as he flipped through. "And you can keep your goons away from me," I added.

"My 'goons'?" Templeton glanced up. He stopped, only a few short steps away. "Those men chasing you today? Trust me, Emily, if I want to catch you," he leaned in closer, "I'll chase you myself."

I shivered. This felt too real to be a dream. I took a hard look at Templeton. He stared back, his upper lip curling, mocking me. "This is real, isn't it?" I whispered.

I jumped when Templeton slammed the book shut and tossed it on Blackstone's desk. "It's all real, Emily. Get used to it." With that he turned and strode toward the door to Matar.

"What did you take from Blackstone, Templeton?"

"Nothing. But you might want to ask him if he's missing anything." He didn't look back as he opened the door. And then he was gone.

I didn't follow. I didn't want to get stuck in Matar again. I was too afraid to leave the library and go looking for Blackstone, or even for Elsa. Instead, I backed up until my calves bumped into a little couch set against the book-lined wall. I curled up on the cold leather and tried to stop trembling until I finally fell asleep – still worrying that Templeton might come back.

❊ ❊ ❊

I woke up the next morning cuddled comfortably against Jack. He was awake, watching me sleep.

"Good morning." I yawned.

"Big day ahead of you," he said.

"I promise I'll wait until you come home," I began.

"I'm not going into the office. I'm working from home. I was serious about not letting you out of my sight."

"You can't do that forever."

"No, but I can do it today. Then tonight, we'll talk to Blackstone and find out what we can do to stop this mess from getting any worse."

"I don't know if that's possible."

"Anything is possible."

"Remember that." I looked at the clock. Whoa! It was already eight. I rolled out of bed and headed for the kitchen.

"Where are you going?" Jack called after me.

"Coffee. I had a bizarre dream I need to shake off and it's going to be a long day of waiting to see Blackstone."

✻ ✻ ✻

Jack reminded me over morning coffee that I needed to earn a paycheck, so I started to put together an email to send out to past clients. Then I went through a pile of paperwork and looked at monthly invoicing. Drat. No one new to invoice. No new money.

Although The Book, Templeton, and Matar were never far from my thoughts, I made myself focus on being normal for the morning. I stuck to a typical weekday routine. I paid bills. I cleaned the litter boxes. I busted a few yoga moves. At noon, Jack made us lunch and we both avoided talking about our plans with

Blackstone. It was the proverbial elephant in the room, but it was a tolerable pachyderm at this point, so it wasn't too bad.

In the afternoon, I let myself think about Anne Lace. I hoped she wasn't too worried about me. I hoped she was alright. I didn't know what I'd do if she'd been hurt by the two men in black. I decided the delivery service my mother used might come in handy now. I called Mom and asked her for the phone number she used. At first she peppered me with questions about what I was up to, but I pacified her curiosity by telling her I had a meeting scheduled with someone who could help us learn more about Dad's journal. I promised to fill her in later. I wrote the number down and made the call.

"Hello. May I help you?" A crisp voice asked. I couldn't get a bead on whether I was talking to a male or a female.

"Um, hi. I need to send a message to someone?"

"Very good. And to where should the message be sent?"

I cleared my throat. "To Matar?"

"Very good. And what is the name of the recipient?"

"Anne Lace."

"And the address for Ms. Lace?"

I hesitated. "Well, I'm not sure of the street address, but can it be delivered to her café? It's called *The Daily Brew*."

"That's fine. We'll confirm the physical address for you. And may I have the message please?"

"Um, how about just say I'm home and okay, and I'll be in touch as soon as I can. Can you add that I hope she's okay too? That I'm sorry for any trouble?"

"Yes. Very good. When do you want this message delivered?"

"Can it be sent right away?"

"Of course. And do you want to include your name with this message?"

I wasn't sure if I should give my name, but thought it best to at least give Anne some clue – in case I wasn't the only person in Matar running from two scary guys dressed in black.

"You can sign the message with an 'E.' She'll know who it is." I hoped.

"Very good. Will that be all?"

"There's no charge, is that right?" No matter what Mom had said, I had to find out for myself.

The voice paused before answering. "There is no charge. Will that be all for today?"

Well, there you have it. "Yes, that's all."

"Very good. Have a nice day." And the voice was gone.

I looked at my phone. I'd have to trust that Anne would get the message and I'd get to talk to her again soon.

CHAPTER 13

Tara arrived right on time. I didn't feel like cooking, so we ordered subs for takeout and talked about our so-called plan of action.

"I think you should confront him about the book he took from the Cooper-Hewitt Library in New York." Tara devoured her Italian sub, adding more dressing as she went along. That skinny girl could pack it in.

I looked at Jack and grinned. He watched Tara with an amused smile.

"I will. First, I want to know what happened with Templeton. I need to clarify if Blackstone ever met him. He knows a lot about him, but would he recognize him? I want to know if he saw Templeton's face when he was attacked." I took a bite of my turkey sub, mentally running through the questions I wanted to ask. I swallowed. "And I want to know if something is missing. I think Templeton took something. I want to find out if Blackstone knows what was stolen and why. I think it's time Blackstone told me everything."

"Told us everything," Jack corrected.

"The three Musketeers," Tara said around a mouthful.

* * *

A new woman let the three of us into Blackstone's home promptly at seven. Like Elsa, she was plain and quiet. When Jack asked how she was doing, she shrugged and motioned for us to follow her. I made mental note to ask Blackstone where he found his help. I didn't trust many people these days.

"Emily." Blackstone stood as we were led into his library office. "I'm extremely glad to see you. Are you okay?"

"I'm fine, but what about you?" I pointed to the bandage on his temple.

"Much better, but I still have a dull headache." He looked at Tara. "And this is the lovely woman from yesterday who helped rescue me. I'm not sure if I properly thanked you."

"Glad to have helped," Tara replied as they shook hands. Blackstone shook Jack's next.

"Please sit down." He gestured to several chairs as he took his seat behind the desk.

I didn't wait for him to begin. "Mr. Blackstone, what happened? I saw Templeton standing over you when I came in. And Elsa. She…" I shook my head, unsure of what to say. "I don't even know how she was killed."

"She was hit in the head as well. The blow knocked her into the edge of a table. The medical examiner will report on which event actually killed her. I don't suppose that detail matters as much." He sighed. "She was in the kitchen. I didn't hear any commotion."

"Where were you?" I asked.

"Presumably I was coming from my room upstairs on my way to the library to do a little work," he said. "I saw nothing on the monitors as I walked by them. But, when I walked into the library, I knew something was wrong."

"How so?"

"The North Door was open."

I looked at the door that took me to Matar yesterday. In one of The Book's passages, my father instructed me to enter through the North Door. This was it. "I'm guessing it shouldn't be left open?"

"It should not. When I started to walk toward it, I heard a noise behind me and then nothing! I was hit over the head and knocked unconscious."

I winced. "Would you recognize Templeton if you came face-to-face with him?"

"I would," Blackstone answered. "But I saw no one. I heard the sound of scraping and then there was nothing but darkness. The next thing I remember is you –" he motioned to Tara, "– standing over me and telling me the ambulance was on its way."

I let out a breath. "So, it might not have been

Templeton who hit you."

"That's true, although I don't know who would do such a thing."

"What about burglars?" Tara chimed in.

"Nothing is missing," Blackstone told her.

I thought about what Templeton said in the last dream. "Mr. Blackstone, are you sure? I had a dream about Templeton last night and he said he was here looking for something. Are you sure nothing is missing?"

"That was just a dream, Emily," Jack interrupted.

Blackstone ignored Jack's comment and leaned forward. "Emily, has Templeton been talking to you while you're dreaming?"

"Sometimes," I nodded. "Last night's dream took place here in your office. It was creepier than usual."

"I see. Well, Templeton is rumored to have many unique talents. Pulling people into his dreams is one," said Blackstone.

"Wait, pulling me into his dreams? Not coming into mine?"

"Exactly. That's something very different. But he can bring your sleeping consciousness into his."

"Um, excuse me," Tara said. "But the whole dream thing seems pretty impossible period."

"Go with it for now." I glanced in her direction. "This isn't the craziest thing I've heard in the past few days." I turned back to Blackstone. "You said you heard a scraping sound before you were hit over the head. Can you think about that? Can you imagine what it could've been?"

Blackstone sat with his hands folded, his two index fingers pointed toward the ceiling as he tapped his lips. A moment passed before realization flickered across his face. "It was a ladder."

"A ladder?" I asked.

"Yes." He gestured toward several sliding ladders placed along each book-lined wall. "These ladders are very old and when you slide them, they make a scraping sound."

"I think you need to look for something Templeton might've wanted to steal from you. Make sure it's still here," I told him.

Blackstone's gaze drifted across the room. A little prickle ran down my back. This wasn't going to be good. Blackstone stood and walked over to one of the bookshelves in the corner. The three of us followed, shooting each other worried looks. Sliding a ladder produced the scraping noise Blackstone described. He nodded before climbing up to retrieve a large book from a shelf near the top. He brought it down to us and placed the old book on a table. When he opened it to the middle pages, he made a garbled sound. "It's gone!"

I leaned in. The book had been hollowed out

on the inside, creating a secret space. And it was empty. "What was hidden in this book?"

Blackstone cleared his throat before answering. "Ultimately? The power to take over the entire Salesman Empire."

"What do you mean the power to take over the Empire? What was in there?"

Blackstone collapsed into a nearby chair. He shrugged, defeated. "It's a book of children's fairytales, Emily. It contains a legend about an elemental gem called the Crimson Stone, with incredible magic embedded inside it. Buried in the legend are clues to where the real stone is hidden. I believe it's somewhere in the Empire."

"How did you get the book?" I asked.

"I took it from the Cooper-Hewitt Library's Rare Book Collection. It was a new acquisition. Word hadn't yet spread that it was there. I had access to it, so I was able to take it and hide it here."

"That's why you were fired," Tara stated. Blackstone nodded.

"Why weren't you made to give it back?" I asked.

"Two things worked in my favor." Blackstone stood. He picked up the fake book and began to climb the ladder so he could put it back. "First, it's a handwritten book of fairytales and labeled as a children's book. It was a unique find, but it wasn't a priority review piece. Secondly, none of the experts at Cooper-Hewitt had any idea as to what the book contained. I did."

"That doesn't seem like a good reason to let you keep the book. You stole it, and yet they didn't press charges? That's a tough one to swallow," I said.

Blackstone sighed. "Several so-called accidents happened after I took the book. One person died under mysterious circumstances. The Board was persuaded not to pursue legal action and advised to forget about the book. A large endowment was made as compensation."

Persuaded, huh?

Jack was quiet throughout the conversation. I looked at him and raised my eyebrows. He watched Blackstone descend. Finally, he spoke. "Why didn't you check to see if the book of fairytales was missing after you were attacked? If it's so important, why isn't that the first thing you did?"

Good question.

"Only a few people knew I had it," he said. "And it was protected. There are systems in place to keep it from being stolen."

"They didn't work," Jack replied.

"No. No, they did not." Blackstone walked back to his desk. "I had no idea. I didn't think the attack had anything to do with that book."

"Wait a minute, Mr. Blackstone. We found out on our own that you took the book from the library in New York. We didn't know the reason, or what the book was about, but someone out there knows something. That's how we found out. Word made it back to Tara from one of her colleagues."

Tara nodded. "It's not common knowledge, but some people in my professional circles knew you stole something."

"I suppose I have been naïve," he said. "I believed the book was safe with me. If Templeton has that book, and the Fringe gets a hold of it, the entire Empire is in danger. They might be able to determine where the Crimson Stone is hidden based upon clues in the legend."

"What happens if they find it?" I asked.

Blackstone turned tired eyes toward me. "They'd have absolute power to rule any world they wanted to. Nothing could stop them."

"What can we do?" I had a feeling I wasn't going to like the answer.

"Someone needs to go after Templeton. Someone needs to get the book back."

❊ ❊ ❊

"Absolutely not," Jack said. We'd stepped out into the hall after I told Blackstone I'd go after Templeton and bring back the book of fairytales. I didn't mention I'd also take any opportunity I could to get the truth from him about my father and the train explosion. No surprise, Jack was not at all in support of me chasing after Templeton.

"I understand how you feel," I told Jack, "but someone has to go after him and it looks like I'm the only one who can."

"Blackstone can go."

"No Jack, he can't. He can't travel through doors like I can."

"You're not exactly a crack shot at it either," he pointed out.

"But this door, the North Door is a guaranteed portal. It always goes to Matar. There are four doors like this throughout the world – one for each direction."

"Emily, it's a one-way door."

"Not on the Winter Solstice. It reverses and I can get back guaranteed. I might even find a way to get back before then. That's my plan, anyway. Blackstone is going to ask around and see if someone can help me."

"Why do you want to do this?"

"For a whole host of reasons! Jack, I want to make sure Anne Lace is safe, and I want to get the book back for Blackstone. I need to find out what Templeton knows about my father's train being bombed. I've got to find out if he was there or not."

"Do you believe he'll tell you anything?"

That was a good question. "I don't know. But

in the past few days I've learned that anything is possible."

Jack took my face between his two hands and kissed me hard. I could feel his fear in the kiss and it scared me. He was never afraid. He tilted my head forward and pressed his lips to my forehead. "Is there any way I can go with you?" he whispered. "I'll go with you."

"I don't think you can." I closed my eyes for a moment. My heart twisted as I felt Jack's love for me, his fear for me, reach into my very being. But I could do this. I could definitely do this. "I'll be fine. Really. Blackstone is going to make sure another Salesman travels with me. He said we could check on Anne Lace first. I'll see what I can find out from her, then we'll go to the Salesman Court. Blackstone said they'll be expecting me."

The trip to Court was a double mission. I'd present myself before the bench and ask for recognition as a Salesman. I'd also be carrying a letter for a Justice named Beverly Spell. Blackstone told us that Spell knew about the book of fairytales. Since he'd deciphered a few of the clues from it, he had an idea of where the Crimson Stone might be hidden. Spell would be the one to trust. If we couldn't get the book back, she might be able to help us find the magical gem and hide it again.

I squeezed Jack's arm. "I'm going to trust

Blackstone on this one."

"I don't trust him."

"He's the only one in this mess who has given me any real information, Jack. And he was attacked. I don't think he's out to get me."

"Just be careful, Emily. You don't know any of these people."

I touched Jack's cheek with my fingertips. "I'll be careful."

❋ ❋ ❋

The three of us left Blackstone's house a little before nine. Tara made arrangements to meet with him in the next couple of days about the stolen book. Her contacts might be able to shed some light on its origins. She'd also keep her ear to the ground and would let us know if it showed up on the Black Market. Jack all but threatened Blackstone's life if something happened to me. He insisted on meeting the Salesman I'd be traveling with and giving his approval before I went anywhere. Blackstone assured Jack he would have the Empire's delivery service at his disposal to keep in contact with me. Phones from our world wouldn't work in the Empire. I told Blackstone about my experience of losing the connection to Tara the last time I went through the door. According to Blackstone the reason was simple: no phone towers in the Empire.

Blackstone originally planned to spend time preparing me for the Salesman Court. He wanted to give me the history of the Salesmen line, but Templeton had thrown a real monkey wrench into the mix. After pressing him, he gave me a brief explanation on why I was required to appear before the Court.

Even though I could travel through doors now, albeit not very successfully, I was not authorized to do so. I'd have to be approved by the Court. It was a way to monitor Salesmen traffic. The items carried by Salesmen were often valuable and sometimes even dangerous. It was important to make sure the system ran smoothly. It was also a way to determine where the Fringe might be traveling and trafficking stolen items.

After receiving approval from the Court, I'd receive a Salesman stipend – which I'd need since not many places in the Empire took foreign currency. Blackstone cautioned against carrying too much cash. Although I could probably use a credit card, there was the risk of leaving a paper trail and we didn't want the Fringe to know where I was traveling. We decided I should leave the card at home and limit any cash I carried to about two-hundred dollars. The stipend would carry me through until I returned.

I was kind of excited to learn I'd receive my own 'official' top hat. It acted as some sort of badge for door travel. To travel through a door now without one would alert the Court. Offenders could be punished, or even expelled from the Empire. Blackstone told us my unauthorized travel had already reached the Court's ears, but he was confident I'd only be scolded due to the fact I knew nothing before traveling. He did suggest it was Templeton's energy trail pushing and pulling me through doors, but when I told him about how I left Matar, he didn't know what to say.

The top hat itself was more than a badge. Approved hats tapped into a well-traveled web of doors all over the Empire, and even the world in which I already knew. Hats acted as sort of a unique GPS – a mysterious global positioning system which allowed Salesmen to more easily tune into the door and destination they wanted. They were valuable Salesman tools. Blackstone suggested they helped one focus power and gave a special 'oomph' when traveling.

I tried very hard to ignore the looks of disbelief Jack shot Blackstone during this explanation.

We decided I'd leave the next morning. We figured I'd have two weeks at most to present myself to the court, give Justice Spell the letter, find Templeton, get Blackstone's book back, and make Templeton come clean on his involvement in my father's assassination. Okay, so I added the last part. Blackstone told me I'd have to return to the North Door on December twenty-first so I could get back home without any trouble. A part of me wondered if I could get back home on my own, but Blackstone cautioned me not to take the risk again. Plus, I wasn't authorized by the Court for door travel as of yet.

I asked Blackstone about the men who chased me the last time I was in Matar. He guessed they were members of the Fringe, but he couldn't be sure. He seemed evasive, and Jack was none-too-happy about it. Blackstone said maybe Anne Lace could explain once I arrived.

Blackstone also told me I could travel by train once I made it to Matar. Finding Templeton would have to wait until I presented myself at Court. Afterwards, I needed to find someone named Rabbit. He might have information on where Templeton had gone. I thought about my father's Book:

If a Rabbit has no tale, can he still tell a story?

I would find out.

※ ※ ※

That night I curled into Jack's body and hung on. I was scared, but I didn't want to voice my fears. I knew Jack had his. William, Mystery, and even Mischief settled in around us. It was as if everyone was worried and by tucking in together, we could find comfort.

I didn't know what the next few days would bring, but I was anxious to get going. I had a feeling I would finally get some answers, and maybe even find a little justice for my father.

❋ ❋ ❋

"This is Alfred Havers, Emily," said Blackstone. "Luckily he was traveling through Matar when I put in a request for an escort. He can accompany you through the North Door and then on to the Salesman Court." I was allowed to door travel as long as I was with an approved Salesman and it was for an official purpose – such as going to Court.

"Nice to meet you." I held out my hand. Havers was a pleasant-looking man of about fifty-five. He was average in height and probably on his way to a perfect pear shape. His hair was graying and thinning.

"Emily Swift," he smiled. "It's so nice to meet you. I had the pleasure of working and traveling with your father. He was a good Salesman."

"Thank you." I paused. Why was the name Havers familiar to me? Is this the man my mother had mentioned as bringing her The Book after my father died? We shook hands before Blackstone pulled Havers aside. I would have to ask him what he knew about the explosion on the train and my father's murder.

I adjusted my winter coat and tried to be patient. I'd packed light with only one bag. The Book was stashed safely inside; the hatpin stored in a little wooden box and zipped into a pocket. I didn't plan to stay in Matar long even though I wasn't approved for door travel yet. I decided that right after I visited Anne Lace, I'd get the Court's approval and set out to find Templeton. I wasn't going to waste any time.

Jack was quiet, but restless. I held out my hand and we walked to a corner of the room for privacy.

"You know I don't want you to go," he told me.

"I know, but I'm going to do this. I have no idea what will happen if I don't take some sort of preventative action. I'm still trying to wrap my head around all of this too, you know."

"I don't think Blackstone is telling you everything."

"I don't think he is either, but I don't believe he's a bad person. We've discussed this Jack. We'll just have to trust him on all of this." I took a deep breath. "And I need to count on you to run interference with my mother. I don't want her to worry." We slightly altered the story and told my mother that I needed to introduce myself to a panel of my father's colleagues, but we omitted anything about Templeton and the attack at Blackstone's house. We emphasized that I was just taking a routine trip.

"Lydia is flighty, but far from stupid," Jack said.

"Just do your best."

Jack's gaze traveled across the room and settled on Blackstone. "I'm holding him responsible for anything that happens to you."

"I don't think Blackstone has that kind of power. I think right now he's doing the best he can too."

As if on cue, Blackstone cleared his throat and motioned to the North Door. "Emily, it's time to go."

I nodded. Jack walked with me. Cupping my face in his hands, he kissed me. My eyes grew wet and I held on, for a second torn between tracking Templeton down and hiding at home with Jack. When he released me, I saw that his eyes were watery too.

"She'll be back before you know it." Havers did his best to reassure Jack. He gave us a big smile. "No trouble at all! As soon as I take her to Court, she'll be approved and one step closer to coming home to you."

"I'll be back soon." I squeezed Jack's hand. "Promise. You won't even have time to miss me."

"Too late."

I took a deep breath and let go. Slinging my bag over my shoulder, I nodded again to Blackstone before turning to Havers. "Okay Mr. Havers, I did this before, but apparently not the easy way. What do I do?"

"It's very easy, my dear." Havers, travel case in hand, stepped forward. He placed a dapper top hat on his head and looked like quite the Dickens character, with his shiny red vest. He held out his left hand and I took it with my right.

"What we'll do is stand in front of the door and think of Matar. Don't just picture it; focus on feeling where you want to go. Feel what it's like to visit your friend's café. Do this until you sense a little hum, or a vibration of sorts, coming from the door. As soon as you do, give my hand a little squeeze and I'll open it. As soon as the door is open, we'll walk right on through. We don't have to run. Just take a step inside. Keep hold of my hand until we're in Matar. It should only take a moment, but sometimes a few more. Don't be alarmed."

"Okay, I got it. I'm ready." I could feel Jack watching us from behind. It made my heart ache. I had to let go of my thoughts about him. Instead, I concentrated on going to Matar – feeling Matar. Feeling the coziness of Anne's café. Picturing her smile and how happy she was to meet me. I remembered how excited I was to find her. I pulled the feeling up and expanded it across my chest.

"Think about traveling with ease, flowing from one world into the next. Fluid movement. There's nothing to it." Havers stepped closer to the door and began to reach for the handle. "Just be open–"

"I hear it," I said. The door was definitely starting to hum.

"Are you sure?" He looked at me in surprise.

The door was beginning to rattle. It sounded as if it was going to shake off its own hinges. "Oh, I'm sure."

Havers touched the doorknob and before we knew what was happening, the door flew open and pulled us in by an unseen force. Wind howled in my ears. There was no such thing as fluid movement in this travel. We were flung into Matar. I held onto Havers hand for dear life.

CHAPTER 14

As we tumbled through the door into a familiar alley, both of us landed on the cold ground. Havers on his padded behind; me sliding on my knees across the cold brick. I let go of his hand and scurried to my feet. The poor man looked like he was in shock. I picked up his top hat and handed it to him.

"What in the name of the Empire was that?" he demanded. I helped him to his feet.

"I'm guessing that's not normal?" I asked as Havers put his top hat back on his head. He brushed the snow off of his coat. Thankfully, we hadn't landed in any slop. The snow on the ground had recently fallen and was still fluffy and light.

"That was anything but normal, Emily." Shrewd eyes evaluated me. "Was it like that for you before?"

"Sometimes. It always feels a little shocking. This time was pretty brutal though. Maybe it was because there were two of us?"

Havers shook his head. "I've escorted others to Court, other new Salesmen. It has never been like that."

"Well, maybe the Court will know." I didn't like how Havers was reacting. I decided to press forward with our plan. "Listen, Anne Lace's café is not far from here. Let's go make sure she's okay and find out if there's anything we should know before we go to Court. We'll get you some hot tea. You'll feel better."

"Yes, I suppose we should just get on with it." He was grumpy now. I supposed landing on your butt could rattle even the most seasoned traveler.

We picked up our bags and walked out of the alley to the street. Everything looked just as picturesque and ready for the holidays as it did the other day. We walked along, Havers occasionally nodding to a passerby. He scowled every time he looked at me. So much for his cheerful disposition.

Anne Lace's café was a welcome sight. We climbed the stairs to *The Daily Brew* and the little India bells signaled our arrival. A second later, an anxious Anne Lace appeared from the kitchen. She wore a blue apron around a cream sweater.

"Emily! Thank god you're okay. I was so worried about you!" She rushed from behind the counter and hugged me.

"I'm fine. Didn't you get my message?" I asked hugging her back. She smelled like holiday spices. It was comforting.

"I did, but ever since those men were here..." Anne' eyes strayed to Havers.

"Anne, this is Mr. Havers. He brought me back to Matar and we're going to the Salesman Court as soon as we leave here. He's a friend."

Anne nodded, placing her hand on my escort's arm. "It's nice to meet you. Quite the nippy day out there – would you like some hot tea, Mr. Havers?"

"Yes. Thank you." He set his travel case down on a table and sighed as he sunk into a chair beside it. Anne raised her eyebrows and looked at me.

"It was a rough trip," I told her.

"I see. Let me get that tea."

✽ ✽ ✽

After Havers was set up comfortably with a hot pot of tea, Anne and I sat down at another table to talk. She had flipped her 'Open' sign to 'Closed' and locked the door. Even though my last visit to *The Daily Brew* wasn't a great experience, I felt safe with Anne now.

"What happened when I ran out the back door?"

"I tackled one of the men!" Anne laughed. "I completely caught him by surprise. I managed to slide a few tables in front of them too. I knew I couldn't stop them, but I could slow them down."

"You did! But Anne, you really could've gotten

hurt."

"Nonsense! I've been in hairier situations." She winked at me.

"Well, thank you," I said. "Really. Thank you. You didn't have to help me, but you did anyway."

Anne took a sip from her own teacup and glanced over at Havers as a snore reached us. She shook her head. "He'll probably be out for a while. We can talk freely."

I looked at Havers. His head tilted back against the wall and he slid down into his chair. His mouth was slightly open. I looked at Anne. She didn't exactly look guilty, but I caught a bit of mischievousness in her smile.

"What did you give him?" I asked.

"Oh, just a little of this, and a little of that. Mostly chamomile tea. Makes one sleepy, you know."

I wondered what a 'little of this, and a little of that' was, but decided it was better I didn't ask. I turned my focus back to our conversation.

"Do you know who those men in black were?"

Anne nodded. "They were Salesmen, of course. I'm guessing part of the Fringe. How they knew you were here is beyond me, but I'm sure they've been watching for you, waiting for you to show up in the Empire."

"But why would the Fringe be after me?" My first trip to Matar was certainly unplanned and I hadn't known then about the book of fairytales stolen from Blackstone.

Anne frowned. "Because you're Emily Swift."

I took a deep breath. Everyone assumed I knew what was going on just because I was Daniel Swift's daughter. "Okay, how about this: pretend I'm not Emily Swift. Pretend I know nothing. Tell me everything. Tell me about my father, the other Salesmen, the Fringe, door travel, anything you can think of."

"I can do that, but didn't your father tell you anything?"

"No. Anne, really. No one has told me anything. Well, Blackstone's told me some things, but it's definitely on a need-to-know basis. We haven't spent a lot of quality time together. He's had a lot going on."

"That's right. You said he was hit over the head the last time you were here. Is he okay now?"

"He is, but his housekeeper was also attacked. She didn't survive. He's more focused on getting me to Court right now than anything else. So, if you have any answers, anything at all. Start at the beginning. My father didn't tell me about his life as a Salesman."

Anne sat back in her chair, cocking her head to the side. "Perhaps Daniel did that on purpose. Maybe he was worried about what could happen, although I question the wisdom of that decision, considering."

"Then tell me now. The longer I don't know everything, the more things get out of control."

* * *

"As you've probably heard by now, your father was an exceptional Salesman. He was also a good man who sat on the Court as a justice. He cared deeply about the Empire. Many Salesmen did, but as often the case, there were a few ambitious men and women who wanted even more power. They believed with their ability to door travel to other places, that they should have more power in the Empire than they already did. This group became disruptive and eventually succeeded in recruiting others to their cause."

"How big is the Empire?"

"Believe it or not, no one really knows for sure. It keeps expanding. It might be as big as the universe itself. Salesmen map new places when they find them." Anne paused as I pulled The Book from my bag. I turned to the map showing Matar, Anwat, Vue, and all the other places my father referenced.

"This is the map I have. Are there more than these cities?" I showed her the page.

"Yes, but these are the primary cities of this particular region – most people live in Matar or Anwat. Others live in Vue, but it's definitely a smaller city. It tends to attract a more artsy or eclectic crowd. Is this the only map you've found?"

"So far. The Book seems to have an endless supply of pages. I feel like I'm on a treadmill. I keep going forward, but the end never seems to show up."

Anne gave a sly smile. "Sounds pretty typical of a Salesman journal."

"How do you know so much about Salesmen? Is it because you knew my father?"

"My mother was a Salesman." Anne shrugged. "I'm not the firstborn so I'm not one. Only the firstborn have the ability to door travel."

"Firstborn or not, I'm not particularly good at it. Plus, I don't have a top hat and Blackstone says that'll give me an extra boost when I travel."

"From what I understand, successful door travel is simply raising your level of feeling. Your feelings for a place, or your desires to go somewhere in particular, are what take you from one spot to another. The most adept Salesmen are experts at taking a feeling and escalating it high and fast. That feeling is what tunes them into the doors they can travel through. The top hat is helpful, I'm sure, but not necessary," Anne finished.

"Is it any door?" I glanced at Havers. He hadn't moved since the last time I looked at him.

"Not quite. It's supposedly the 'right' door. You've door traveled a little. Think about it. Were you really emotional when it happened?"

I thought back over the past few days. I was terrified when running from the Fringe. I wanted to go home. And I did, without even knowing what I was doing. Before that, I desperately wanted to catch Templeton at *The Green Bean* and ended up running into the kitchen. Then there was Sunday morning. I was feeling pretty euphoric after Jack and I had our little romantic interlude, but who knows how I ended up in the downstairs bathroom.

"Can one door take different people to different places?" I asked.

"As far as I know, yes. But you need to get that kind of information from Blackstone or another senior Salesman."

I thought about what she said. "Is it magic?"

She shrugged. "Maybe. Or maybe we all can do it, but we believe only Salesmen can. Emily, what is magic? It's what we can't explain, right? Some people are simply better at doing the unexplainable." She gave me a smile.

"You sound like my mother," I said. Oh. Mom. I missed her. "Do you know her?"

"No, I never met Lydia. She's never come to Matar, of course. But your father adored her. He adored you too."

"Have you ever been, um, to our world?" That

was one of the most bizarre questions I'd ever asked.

"Of course!" Anne laughed.

"Oh, I mean since you're not a Salesman, I wasn't sure how you get through the doors."

"There are other ways to travel, Emily. The trains, for one. Some people drive. When I was in my late teens, I hiked around what is now known as the Walled Zone to visit friends in Massachusetts."

"You can get here without going through a door?" This was news to me. Why hadn't Blackstone given up that information? Did he keep it to himself so Jack wouldn't try to come with me?

"You can. It's a long journey, but it's not impossible."

I nodded. "Okay, tell me more. I'm sorry to be a pain, but I need to know everything."

※ ※ ※

The Salesman world was huge. There was no written record of when the Empire came to be, but it was clearly older than the many countries, kingdoms, and nations I'd learned about in my world history class. The Salesman line went back thousands of years. Change rarely came and tradition was the key to keeping the world running smoothly. Not that everything was perfect, but all in all, the Empire operated well century after century.

Not only Salesmen lived in the Empire. People like Anne – small business owners, trades people, artists, average Janes and Joes – lived here just like people live in any other city or country. There were schools, stores, restaurants, and sporting events. Crime levels were low, but a police force was available to handle the petty incidents that came up. They were known as the Empire guards.

Life was generally good for everyone; however, just over thirty years ago, there was trouble in the Salesman ranks. A new generation of Salesmen entered the force after a population explosion of sorts. Anne likened it to the 'baby boomers' generation of the U.S. after World War II. Many of these new men and women didn't assimilate well into the Salesman Empire.

In the beginning it wasn't a big problem – in fact the new generation brought with it fresh approaches to the Empire and how things were run. There was a small Renaissance of creative ideas in the Salesman world. The old way and the new way tried to blend.

It may have worked, but some of the older Salesmen were unwilling to consider making changes to the way it always had been. On the other side, some of the younger Salesmen were frustrated at their lack of power and what they saw as an outdated bureaucracy dictating the way the Empire was run. Salesmen like my father worked hard to bridge the gap – and often did. But the newest generation of Salesmen wasn't ready to buckle under the older rulers of the Empire. While some worked within the system to create change, others decided to work outside of the Empire, rejecting tradition as they sought to build their own power. They began to ignore basic rules developed for the safety of the Empire and for those who called it home. They broke laws and over time, became increasingly violent.

These rogue Salesmen eventually became the Fringe.

Salesmen and non-Salesmen alike were afraid. This uprising was unprecedented, at least in the Empire's written history. Still, the Fringe was a relatively small group and initially the stronger Empire Salesmen were successful in cutting its power. Some members of the Fringe were expelled from the Salesman ranks and even barred from entering the Empire. Some Salesmen avoided being associated with the Fringe and retained their official titles. They walked a fine line between working with the Empire and working against it. In the end, the traditional Empire carried on as always, and Salesmen like my father kept a sharp eye out for those who would disrupt the system.

In the years that followed, however, what was left of the Fringe worked hard at gaining support throughout the ranks of Salesmen. Some members were bought; others were blackmailed. Sporadic outbursts colored the decade, and then someone extraordinary appeared on the scene.

Templeton. John Templeton, actually.

He was only nineteen when he entered the Empire with his mother, a Salesman herself. She brought him to Court to ask for recognition so he could door travel.

At first the Court dismissed the request since Templeton was so young. But what emerged was his incredible skill at traveling. He'd never been trained, yet his abilities were effortless. It was almost as if he didn't need to do much more than pull up a thought and step through a door to his destination. Any door, as a matter of fact. His mother sought early recognition for him so he wouldn't be punished or expelled for unauthorized travel.

The majority of the Salesman Court didn't want to approve Templeton. With the Fringe activities in the background and the changes to the culture, they were already skittish. It was my father, Justice Daniel Swift, who recognized the potential of Templeton's natural talent. He advocated for his approval.

Templeton was admitted into the Salesmen ranks. The caveat being he was to work alongside my father – who would be responsible for Templeton's character and behavior.

And so it was. Templeton traveled with my father, and during that year, several significant events occurred. The Fringe resurfaced and made no secret about wanting to bring Templeton into their fold. A young man with his talent would bring them an incredible advantage. And in fact, there were reports of Templeton visiting with members of the Fringe, but nothing was ever proven. Fringe activity was heating up and there were several attacks on prominent officials' homes and workplaces. Some of the more vocal, traditionally-inclined Salesmen were killed during the violence.

It was against this turbulent background that Templeton's 'unusual' gifts were revealed.

"What do you mean he had 'unusual' gifts?" I interrupted.

Anne lifted her white eyebrows. "It turned out Templeton could do things other Salesmen could not."

"Such as?"

"Templeton can actually handle items carried by Salesmen. I'm not talking about tea leaves or trinkets, Emily. Templeton can handle magical items. He can touch and use the items he's only supposed to transport."

"I don't get it," I said. "What do you mean, magical items?"

"Emily, in the past few days you've seen things you never believed possible. You've traveled to the Empire through a door. It shouldn't be too hard for you to stretch your imagination a little further and understand there are literally magical items used by people all over the world for a whole host of reasons."

I thought about the Crimson Stone. "Okay, I get it. But what kind of magical items are we talking about?"

"Well, let's say you wanted a potion to gain someone's affection, or maybe a pair of Whispering Flowers to gather information. If you could locate these items, a Salesman would be engaged to safely deliver them to you, wherever you are."

Anne continued her story. Apparently there were people all over the world, not just in the Empire, who created, passed down, used, bartered, and sold magical items. And apparently there were people who searched for and used them. It wasn't a 'black market' – it was the Magic Market.

Obviously there was great risk involved when shipping magical items all over the world. Many of the pieces were unstable and had to be carefully transported. Theft was always a possibility. Also, compensation had to be sent through a safe and reliable service. Secrecy was an absolute necessity. Traveling through doors reduced the risk of accidents, theft, and brought transactions to swift completion. Using the doors allowed Salesmen to slip from place to place outside the Empire without alerting any regulatory authorities in the world in which I lived.

The Salesmen were unique in what they could do. It was a perfect fit.

More than magical items were transported this way. Official documents, correspondence, general supplies – all were part of the Salesman service. They were a mix of governmental regulators, traffic controllers, and businessmen.

But even with their supreme abilities, Salesmen are not practitioners of magic. They can't physically handle some of the more powerful pieces. Smaller items like Door Dust, yes. But an amulet, or cursed jewelry? No way! Magical items were safely packed by the owner before the delivery ever touched Salesman hands.

"Until Templeton," Anne finished.

"And Templeton can use magical items."

"Yes. He can use them, and if we believe the rumors, Templeton has quite a bit of power without any magical item. He's an adept practitioner of magic, Emily."

"He can't be the only Salesman who can do this. I mean, what would be the odds?"

"Well, there hasn't been any other. And like I said, the Empire realized this during that critical year. The timing was strange."

"I bet the Fringe couldn't wait to pull him right in." Just thinking about it made me angry.

"Oh, well, it's hard to make Templeton do anything." Anne chuckled.

"What happened?"

"As you guessed, the Fringe nearly turned itself inside out trying to persuade Templeton to become a part of their cause. But he was a smart young man. He realized the power he had without them. He didn't need the Fringe. And, he realized the Empire, although they didn't know what to do with him, probably wanted to keep him in their control to use his talents, maybe even as a weapon to use against the Fringe. Your father was probably best positioned to keep him under control. To my knowledge, he never worked against Templeton. He tried to help him understand his abilities and how they could serve the greater good. How they could one day lead and serve the Empire."

"But Templeton didn't get with the program?" This was a lot to process.

"Well, by all appearances Templeton continued to work alongside your father. But he was also seen meeting with members of the Fringe, and regardless of what he was actually doing, it looked bad."

"Was he really working with them?" I thought about the explosion on the train and my stomach gave a turn.

"No one knows for certain." Anne paused, considering a thought before she spoke again. "Emily, just so you know, I don't believe Templeton put the bomb on your father's train. Oh the Fringe was definitely behind it, but I'd bet on my life Templeton was not the one who killed your father."

"Why do you believe it wasn't him?"

She shook her head. "It's just my own intuition. I don't believe Templeton is to be completely trusted by any means, but I don't believe he would have let your father die either."

I thought about what Anne was saying. I had no reason to believe in Templeton's innocence, but I had no proof of his guilt either.

"I want to show you something my father wrote," I told her. I turned to the passage with her name and handed it to Anne.

When in Matar, look for
Anne Lace. Her special-ty
helps people see.
May have knowledge
regarding Eve of Silence.
Will need Rabbit's help.
Contact prior to
Solstice.
Avoid Walled Zone.

Anne read it silently. I waited then asked, "Do you understand what he's saying here?"

"Yes," she nodded, looking up from The Book. "The Eve of Silence, as it came to be called, happened about a week before your father was killed. Like I said, the Fringe was becoming more and more aggressive. The Salesman Court was pressured to act. They planned to vote on a ruling approving yearly review and broadening the scope of 'reasonable expulsion.' The night before it would have passed there was a mass slaughter of Salesmen who influenced or sat on the Court. The next day, when Court reopened, there was no one on the bench. The Court had been effectively silenced, hence the name, Eve of Silence. Your father was one of three justices who survived the attack. He wasn't in Matar that night."

"Who were the other two Salesmen?" This kind of violence terrified me.

"Beverly Spell, who still sits on the Court. She's a good Salesman. Sharp as a tack and works hard for the Empire. The other is Tahl Petrovich. He's also still sitting on the bench."

I noted Anne didn't have much to say about him. I went back to the passage in The Book. "So, did my father reach you? Were you able to give him information he needed?"

Anne smiled. "Emily, I think that message is for you. Your father wanted you to come here."

"Because he knew I was going to get The Book and he wanted me to talk to you?"

Anne touched her finger to her nose indicating that I'd gotten it.

I went back to The Book and turned to the first reference I had found about Templeton.

Templeton.
Not in Matar during EoS?
Friend?

Anne read the three lines and nodded. "Templeton was not in Matar during the Eve of Silence. Is he a friend? Well, truthfully I don't think Templeton keeps any friends. But he traveled with your father. If he were to have a friend back then, it would have been Daniel."

"Okay, well, who is Rabbit?"

"Rabbit is... hmm." Anne tapped her chin, thinking. "Rabbit is not necessarily one person, although I do know who your father is referring to."

"I need you to tell me a little more here." I waved my hand at her. "Rabbit is not one person?"

"The best way to describe the Rabbits, well, they're sort of a group of informal dealers in information. They're unusual like the Salesmen are unusual. But there's no central structure, and they end up being quite the nomadic creatures. Not quite gypsies, and incredibly well-connected to one another. They are also notoriously hard to find unless they want to be found."

My tea had gone cold in its cup. Anne noticed and stood to heat up some more water. I remembered the first time I'd come to her café. There was a tip jar on the counter. It was still there. The sign attached to it said:

Instead of leaving a tip for us, how about a donation for The Rabbits?

"A donation for 'The Rabbits'?" I asked. "Are those the same Rabbits?"

"Rabbits are also notoriously short on cash. Once in a while one will travel through here. Lunch is always on the house." Anne walked toward the kitchen.

"This is a strange world you live in, Anne."

"Yes it is."

❊ ❊ ❊

"So why should I contact Rabbit – or, a Rabbit?" I asked when she sat back down.

"Rabbit. I'm not sure. Maybe you'll know by the time you get to Court. Remember, Rabbits deal in information, so maybe you'll need to find out something at that point. Your father wrote to do it prior to Solstice, and that's right around the corner."

"Okay, what about the rest of the passage here?" I pointed to the page again.

"The Walled Zone is further north. It's mostly

mountains. Brutal weather too. The Fringe used the region to hide during some of the more fierce battles, but I don't think they have a huge presence there. It's a rough place to live."

"And what's your 'specialty'? How can you help me see?"

Anne laughed, shaking her head. "Your father," she began then paused. "I think your father is referring to my 'special tea' – as in tea." Anne tapped the tea pot between us. "I'm guessing he tried to use some sort of code here. Not very clever though."

"But what does it mean?" I looked over at Havers. He was still out, sleeping soundly.

"I tend to brew a little." Anne shrugged.

"Brew a little?" I thought about the café's name, *The Daily Brew.* I looked back at Anne and she winked at me. "Brew? As in, tea and coffee? Or as in double double, toil and trouble?"

"The latter." Her green eyes sparkled.

"Okay. So, what's the tea?"

"It's a hallucinogenic brew, actually. And one I don't make often. It's dangerous, but some believe it helps them tap into a source, a higher knowing. As a result, they 'see' more."

"Do you believe this is true?"

"I make the tea, don't I?"

"Is it legal?"

"Not in your world."

"And here in Matar?"

"I probably wouldn't talk about it with just anyone."

"Got it." I rubbed my face. Rabbits dealing in information, hallucinogenic teas, mass slaughter of Salesmen on the Eve of Silence, Templeton – *Templeton!* I almost missed it. "Wait, how do you know Templeton was not in Matar on the Eve of Silence?"

Anne stood, picking up the teacups.

"Because he was with me."

CHAPTER 15

I didn't expect Anne to say that. I knew so much more than I had just hours ago, but I needed to know more about my father's assassination and Templeton's role in it, even if she didn't believe he'd played a part.

"I know you're confused, but there is a legitimate explanation," she said. "I was in Anwat picking up supplies the week before the Eve of Silence. Templeton was also there. I knew him through your father and he was curious to learn more about my practices."

I lifted my eyebrows.

"Anyhow, we spent time together that week and were together the evening of that horrible night. In fact, we had just finished dinner and Templeton was walking me back to my room when we heard the news." She shook her head. "I was shocked. Even Templeton seemed affected, and he's always in perfect control. We continued on to my room and before he left, he told me to stay in Anwat until it was safe to return to Matar. He said it was possible that more than Salesmen could be in danger and I should stay put until things were sorted out. I agreed."

"Then what happened?"

"Then he thanked me for sharing the evening

with him and said good night. I closed the door and realized I was still holding a list of items I wanted him to have. I went back out into the hall just in time to see Templeton step into a broom closet."

This sounded familiar. "Let me guess. He was not in the broom closet when you opened the door."

"I knew he wouldn't be there," she said, nodding. "But, curiosity is a strong motivator."

"So, he could have gone back to Matar then."

"I suppose, but he certainly was not there when the others were killed."

"When was this again?" I asked.

"A week before your father's death, Emily."

"But the Fringe got him in the end too," I said. My anger warred with my grief.

"Yes. Daniel worked hard to pull all the non-Fringe Salesmen together the week between the Eve of Silence and the train explosion. Many were very afraid after the attacks and looked to him for leadership. He was liked by a lot of people on both sides of the Split, so many were willing to listen. They were coming together."

"The 'Split.' Wait, I've seen references to it in The Book. What is it?"

"The Split is a fancy way of describing the separation between the older, more traditional Salesmen of the Empire, and the newer Salesmen who wanted to make sweeping changes.

It's significant because they did not usually work together. The division weakened the Salesmen. If your father could have bridged the gap between the two sides, things might have turned out very differently."

"But then, the train."

"I think the bomb was a message and your father was the target. But your father was so powerful in life, that in death, he became a martyr for the Empire, Emily. The Fringe didn't count on that. Daniel became a symbol for all of those who had stood to the side – on both sides of the Split, by the way. After his death they were almost fanatical when rooting out anyone even thought to be associated with the Fringe. They went too far sometimes. I'm sure there were innocent Salesmen expelled during this time. Or worse."

"Or worse?"

"Executed."

"Oh." I shuddered. "And what about Templeton? Wasn't he on the train?"

"He was seen on the train. Supposedly."

"Supposedly?"

"They couldn't prove he was there. It's also highly unlikely if he was on the train, that he could've gotten off before the explosion."

"Why?"

"If he were to go through a door on a train that's moving, it's virtually impossible to end up where you intended to go. The door is essentially a moving target."

"I see." I thought about Anne's words. "Virtually impossible, but not impossible, right?"

"Well," Anne shook her head. "Well, no. Not impossible I guess."

"What happened after the explosion?"

"There was an investigation. They could never prove exactly who did it. Of course many members of the Fringe were caught and punished. Most believe the guilty were dealt with in the end."

"And Templeton? What about how he was seen with members of the Fringe? Why wasn't he taken down?"

"He's too powerful. And he's smart. He aligned himself with the two Salesmen who escaped during the Eve of Silence: Beverly Spell and Tahl Petrovich."

"Why did they allow that?"

"I don't know, really. He's certainly done well for himself over the years. He's wealthy and he's exercised quite a bit of power and influence. Several years ago, he seemed to have disappeared. Every now and again there were rumors that he'd been seen, but most were just stories."

"Do you know where he went?"

"No. I didn't know he was back until you told me you saw him standing over Blackstone."

"But the Fringe are definitely back? Right?

Those two men who chased me were from the Fringe."

Anne nodded. "Things were quiet for a long, long time after your father's assassination. But the hunger for power is too much for some people. As new Salesmen come in, many have been misled and quietly recruited to the Fringe. Still others choose to believe the worst is over. Because of their apathy, the Fringe has been popping up over the Empire for several years now. Nothing's been at the level like when your father was alive, but many are not fooled. I'm not fooled."

"And now I'm thirty and I'm here." I was starting to understand.

"Indeed. Daniel Swift's daughter has entered the Empire. For some, this is a celebration, a homecoming of the martyr's daughter. For those who have been in hiding for over two decades, it's the beginning of a new battle."

* * *

Havers stirred in the chair as Anne gently nudged his shoulder. "Wake up Sleeping Beauty," she teased.

"What –? Wait, what time is it?" Havers sat up, looking around. "What happened?"

"You dozed for a few minutes. We thought since you have such a big day of traveling ahead of you, we'd let you take a little cat nap." Anne smiled.

"Oh, well, yes. I've been traveling quite a bit, and well, yes. You know a high level of activity is expected, and... Yes." Havers head bobbed up and down. I looked over at Anne. She raised an eyebrow and winked.

"Mr. Havers, I'm going to stop in the ladies' room and I'll be right back. We can go to the Court if you're ready." I gestured to his traveling case.

"Good. We really should be going."

Anne directed me to the bathroom and after freshening up, I made sure I had the letter for Beverly Spell in my jeans pocket. I was a little worried about passing the letter over to her, since Anne mentioned Templeton had aligned himself with Spell and Petrovich, but I would have to trust that Blackstone knew what he was doing. Plus, Anne had spoken favorably of her.

I was just about to round the corner to the front of the café when the entrance was smashed open by a big man with dark hair and even darker eyes. His shoulders were broad and in his hand he held a gun. He was followed by another man of similar size and ugliness. Both wore top hats. The Fringe. My voice caught in the back of my throat as I tried to call out a warning.

Havers spun around when the men crashed

into the café. Without hesitating, he raised his cane and swung at the first man. He was surprisingly fast for his portly shape. The cane bounced off of the side of the gun-carrying Salesman and knocked him to the floor. The second man lunged at Havers, who squatted and spun again, his foot catching the second man's legs and causing him to fall backward. I stood there, unable to move, watching the scene unfold.

"Emily, you have to get out of here now!" Anne shouted as she tossed my bag across the room. It landed at my feet. "Go! Go! I'm right behind you!"

I picked up my bag and turned toward Havers. He was still fending off the two men with his cane. The first man had been knocked down a second time – a gash in his forehead dripped blood onto the floor. As Havers swung his travel bag into the gut of the second man, the man on the floor raised his hand and pointed the gun.

"Look out!" I yelled as I found my feet and lurched forward.

"No Emily, no!" Anne grabbed my arm and pulled me toward the kitchen. "You have to leave now!"

The gunman's finger barely moved and the gun fired. Havers flew backwards and I screamed. Anne's fingers dug into my flesh as she pulled me through the kitchen and pushed me toward the exit. As we ran, she grabbed a large butcher knife. Stopping for a second, she slit open a fifty-pound bag of white flour. She ripped at the tear spilling the white dust.

"Emily, I said run!" Anne's hand smacked alongside the wall, catching a switch. A huge fan kicked on and flour filled the air. I couldn't see behind me. A cloud of flour filled the room, moving toward us both. Anne grabbed my arm again and pushed me through the door onto a small side street. Behind me, she grabbed a pack of matches from a shelf and sent a lit one over her shoulder as she ran outside. The air in the kitchen flashed and a small explosion rocked the little café.

"Havers! Havers!" I shouted.

"It's too late, Emily. We've got to get out of here. This way!" Anne pulled me down the lane. I gripped my shoulder bag.

"Which way do we go?" I spun around looking for an escape.

"Can't you find a door to go through?"

I looked at her. "I'm not leaving you."

"You can't let them catch you!"

"They won't," I said, "but we've got to keep moving." We ran across the road and dodged between some of the slower moving cars. This was like my first trip to Matar. Again I was running from two of the Fringe's bad guys. Again I was running and slipping in the snow and slop. Only this time, Anne was with me.

"We need to get you to the Salesman Court," Anne puffed out as we ran.

"Can we make it on foot?"

"No, we'll have to take the train. It's like a subway, but it's not underground. There's a stop not far from here. Come on." Anne did a quick shuffle and we crossed a busier street, avoiding a city bus and one angry cabbie, who swore at me in a language I had never heard before.

I couldn't believe we made it to the sidewalk alive.

"Just a few more blocks. I think we can stop running." Anne took a deep breath and glanced over her shoulder as she pulled a slim wallet from her pocket. She looked at my bag. "Do you have anything warm we can put on? Do you have a hat? We should try to disguise you."

"No hat, but I have other stuff in here." I dug into my bag and pulled out a sweater for Anne and a hooded sweatshirt for me. Our coats were left behind in the chaos. I looked back. No men chasing us. No Havers. I looked at Anne. "Havers," I began.

"Was shot. There was nothing we could do, Emily. We'll tell the Court and have someone go back to my café. They'll send the Empire guards."

"What if he was only wounded? What if he is waiting for help?" My throat felt tight. What if he really was waiting there for us to help him? The thought was unbearable.

"I don't think so," Anne said gently. "Come along. Let's get you to Court and to safety. That's so much more important right now."

* * *

The trains whipped in and out of the station. Anne was right. It was very much like a subway, but above ground and without graffiti. It was packed with men and women and bored teens. A few mothers dragged younger children along, hurrying as they climbed on and off the trains. We didn't need to pay a toll to ride. City taxes paid for the service.

"The next one will be here in five minutes," Anne noted as she nodded to the departure and arrival screens. They were updated every few minutes.

"I don't see those men." I looked at the faces passing by.

"I think we lost them."

"But they've found me twice already." We looked at each other nervously.

"That's a good point," Anne finally said. "We'll just have to keep on our toes."

The train taking us to the Salesman Court roared in and we jostled with the other passengers to climb aboard. Quickly finding two seats, we crammed in with our backs to the wall. We kept a lookout for anyone who might be following us.

"I don't see any Salesmen," I whispered to Anne.

She gave me a smile. "How do you know?"

"No top hats."

"Did your father always wear a top hat?"

"When he traveled, yes."

"But he didn't have to wear one all the time, just when he chose to, or needed to. There may very well be Salesmen on the train and you wouldn't know it."

I supposed that was true. I nodded and looked out the window. I thought about everything Anne told me about my father, Templeton, the Fringe, how people had been killed. And for what? Power mostly. Those who had it wanted to keep it. Those who didn't have it wanted to get it. It seemed like the only people dying were the ones who wanted to protect the Empire, like my father.

And what about Templeton? How did he fit into all of this? Even if Anne was right and Templeton didn't play a role in the Eve of Silence or the train bombing, there was still something about him. I couldn't trust him. It didn't matter if Templeton wasn't on any particular side. He had his own agenda, and to me, that made him just as dangerous.

Where had he been in the past several years? Why hadn't anyone seen him? He definitely knew where to find me. And he knew when it was my thirtieth birthday. I chewed my lip. Why did he play with me though? What was his game?

Maybe it was some sort of test. Maybe Templeton wanted to see what I could do. No, that was silly. Besides stumbling through a few wrong doors, I wasn't very good Salesman material. I thought about what he said in Barnes & Noble. He wanted to make sure I 'stayed out of trouble.' And then what did he say at Blackstone's? My memory was foggy. I pictured the scene in my head, recreating Templeton in Blackstone's office.

'Things have been set in motion. You have many enemies in the Empire.'

His words bounced around in my head. Templeton was right about that. If I could only figure out what he was doing in the mix. Maybe he would talk to me if I stayed with Anne.

Anne interrupted my thoughts. "We get off at the next stop."

I focused on the view outside the window. It looked like we moved to the heart of the city.

* * *

Stretching out for an entire city block, the

courthouse sat heavily under ornate stone. Carvings, statues, and winter birds watched over us as we climbed the steps. Once inside at the security checkpoint, Anne asked one of the guards where new Salesmen should sign in to be introduced to the Court. We followed his directions and wound ourselves down a long hall to a window where a pleasant but tired-looking woman asked for my name.

I told her my name was Emily Swift. She nodded, and for once, someone associated with this world did not seem to care I was the daughter of Daniel Swift. It was kind of nice.

"Here's your docket number. You'll be called in at around eleven. The exact time cannot be guaranteed. It's Court, after all."

"I understand." We had about an hour. Anne and I sat in a small, private waiting room. I was grateful we didn't have to stay in the general waiting area. I'd had enough of the criminal element during the past few days.

Only twenty minutes passed before the door to our room opened and a uniformed man with big eyeglasses poked his head in. He swiveled his head back and forth on his neck like a praying mantis.

"Emily Swift?" He looked at me.

"Yes?"

"Come with me. You've been called by the Court."

I glanced over at Anne.

"Looks like you got moved to the top. Remember, you're Daniel Swift's daughter. I'm sure the Court is eager to meet you."

I turned back to the bug-like head. "This is my friend, Anne. She can come with me, right?"

He blinked once. "She can sit in the gallery with the others."

Anne took my hand and we followed the man down a narrow hall to a door leading into the Salesman Court.

The courtroom was beautiful, filled with dark polished wood. Six big crystal chandeliers hung from the ceiling, and stained-glass windows placed high in the walls ran along the length of the room. It resembled a church. At the front, seven Salesmen sat on the raised bench, their eyes on me as I entered from the back. The uniformed man directed Anne to the gallery with other onlookers before escorting me to the front. He pointed to a tall podium facing the judges.

I walked forward and gripped the stand. My heart pounded as my insides quivered. I wasn't sure if I could speak.

One of the judges leaned forward. "Emily Swift, we've been expecting you." I looked at the nameplate. Beverly Spell. She didn't smile, but looked curious.

I nodded, clearing my throat. "Hello." Brilliant.

Another judge leaned forward. He was younger, probably in his mid-forties. He sat in the middle of the seven judges and his nameplate read Howard Manchester. "Emily, it's my understanding you are the daughter of the late Daniel Swift?"

I nodded.

"We need you to speak, Emily, so it will be entered correctly into the Court's record," Manchester said.

"I'm sorry, Your Honor. I'm Emily Swift. And yes, my father was Daniel Swift." My voice was low, but at least it didn't appear to be shaking.

"Good, we've established that. And your age?" Manchester seemed to have taken on the role of questioner.

"I'm thirty, Your Honor. My birthday was last week on December 1." I looked at the other judges. Which one was Tahl Petrovich? He, along with Spell, had escaped the slaughter on the Eve of Silence. The others obviously came to the bench afterward. I ran my eyes across the nameplates.

Petrovich sat to the right of Manchester. He was tall and slim, with thinning blondish hair. He sat back in his chair, his elbows balanced on the armrests. His fingertips came together as if he were praying. He was evaluating me.

"And how is it that you came to Matar?" Manchester continued.

I was unsure of what to say first. I had to tell them about Havers. Was this the right time? And the Court knew about Blackstone already. Maybe it was safe to start there. I had a feeling I should be brief and to the point.

"The Record Keeper at the North Door, Mr. Blackstone, arranged to have a Salesman named Alfred Havers escort me to Court, Your Honor." Was I supposed to keep saying Your Honor? No one told me what to do.

Manchester looked at a paper in front of him. He frowned. "I don't see that Alfred Havers is here with you." He looked up and into the gallery behind me. "Where is Havers?"

I took a deep breath. "We were attacked after we arrived in Matar. We went to my friend's café, *The Daily Brew*. Your Honor, two men broke in while we were there. They attacked Havers and he was shot." Manchester sucked in a breath as I continued. "Honestly, I don't know if he's okay. Anne and I came here as fast as we could. Your Honor, we hoped the Court would help. The men were chasing after us and we didn't dare stop. Havers never caught up."

There were murmurs throughout the courtroom following my plea. Manchester was clearly upset as he leaned to his left to speak to Beverly Spell. They whispered and finally he nodded, motioning to one of the guards. They spoke at the bench before the guard left, taking with him several other armed men.

"We are sending guards over to investigate. Do you know who these men were?" Manchester asked.

I hesitated. The truth was I didn't know. Although I thought they were members of the Fringe, I had no proof. I glanced back at Petrovich. His eyes narrowed as he pursed his thin lips. I didn't like him.

"I'm not sure. They were carrying top hats, though."

A collective gasp sounded throughout the courtroom. Only Spell and Petrovich remained still. Spell leaned forward again and spoke directly to me. "Were these men Salesmen?"

"I think so, Your Honor. But I don't know." I had to get my letter from Blackstone to Spell. I wasn't sure how to do it. I decided to wait.

Spell looked down both sides of the bench. "I think this discussion should be held in private chambers. Let's move forward with Ms. Swift's recognition so we can address this new issue. Are we in agreement?"

The other judges responded in the affirmative – except for Petrovich. When he spoke, his voice was sharp and precise. "Ms. Swift, is this your first visit to Matar?"

"Really Tahl," Spell interrupted. "I think we know the answer to this."

"Justice Spell, we do have procedures to adhere to in this Court. Regardless of who her father was, Ms. Swift is subject to the same rules upheld by this Court." Petrovich turned his eyes back to me. "I asked you a question, Ms. Swift."

"No, Your Honor. This is the second time I've been in Matar." This was not good.

"I see. And when was the first visit?" He looked down his nose.

"This past Sunday, Your Honor." I was getting nervous. My eyes flickered to Spell. Her face was still unreadable.

"How did you come to be in Matar, Ms. Swift?" Petrovich asked.

I cleared my throat. "Through a door, Your Honor. The North Door to be exact."

Petrovich sat back and smiled. "Unauthorized travel? You've not yet been approved by this Court. This is a punishable offense."

Spell snorted in disgust. I met Petrovich's eyes with mine. I didn't like him and I didn't understand why he was going down this road.

"Your Honor, I honestly did not know I was traveling through a door to Matar. I had no plans to come here. I was chasing Templeton. John Templeton."

If my announcement that two men in top hats attacked Havers caused quite a stir in the courtroom, mentioning Templeton's name resulted in a virtual uproar in the gallery.

Spell began banging her gavel. "Order! Order right now or I will have this courtroom cleared completely! Order!"

At first Petrovich looked surprised, but then he pointed a bony finger at me. "Emily Swift, lying to this Court will have you expelled, if not worse."

I looked over my shoulder for Anne. She was white as a ghost and standing still in the noise behind me. She nodded once, encouraging me to continue.

I turned back to Petrovich, lifting my voice over the remaining din. "I am not lying to you or this Court, Your Honor. I went to see Mr. Blackstone and found Templeton standing over him. Mr. Blackstone was on the floor, unconscious. I chased after Templeton, and he went through the North Door. I didn't know anything about the door and was shocked when I ended up here in Matar. I didn't know this place existed!"

The courtroom quieted down as onlookers behind me struggled to hear what I was saying.

"Templeton has been missing for years." Petrovich glared at me.

"Well I found him. Your Honor." *You jerk.*

"This Court does not believe you." Petrovich shrugged, dismissing my words.

"This Justice wants to hear more," Spell snapped at Petrovich. "But once again, in my private chambers! It's my understanding – and I know others on this bench have been privy to the very same information – that Ms. Swift has not had the benefit of her father's tutelage and has only recently learned of her legacy as a Salesman. This Court is also aware of door travel in Kincaid, as well as to and from Matar." She looked at me expectantly.

"Yes, Your Honor," I said.

"Considering that Ms. Swift was not aware of the rules governing the Salesman body, and the fact that when she learned she was in violation of this Court she sought to reenter Matar with a Senior Salesman, I move that the information is officially and correctly entered into the books, and that Ms. Swift is assigned another Senior Salesman to oversee her future schooling." Spell didn't miss a beat. "I further move that Emily Swift is approved for door travel so we can move on to address the other issues that have come to light during this session. How say you?" Spell addressed both sides of the bench before turning directly to Petrovich. "I only need a majority, Tahl."

Petrovich smiled, but a snake pulled a better face. He inclined his head. "As you wish, Bev."

"I vote 'aye' to approving Emily Swift as a Salesman with the aforementioned caveats. How say you?" Spell looked at Manchester.

He nodded. "Aye."

Three other 'ayes' were heard. The justice sitting the furthest to the right watched me carefully throughout the process. I guessed him to be in his late sixties, with a balding head and a mustache. He tapped his fingers on the bench behind a nameplate that read Norford Smith.

"Ms. Swift, I am voting 'nay.' Yes, we all have the same information about your recent travels, and yes, I am concerned that two men attacked you. I was not on the Court when your father was alive, but I knew him very well and I respected him. Today I ask myself if Daniel Swift would vote 'aye' if he were in my shoes. The answer is no. He would want to know more about what is going on around you before giving this Court's approval." Smith shook his head. "It will not make a difference if I vote against you, as you already have the support of five justices, but I could not vote to approve you in good conscience."

I nodded. "I understand, Your Honor."

"Tahl?" Spell prompted.

Petrovich scowled. "Nay."

Spell raised her gavel along with her voice as she made the proclamation. "This Court counts five 'ayes' and two 'nays' in the ruling to approve Emily Swift as an official Salesman recognized by the Salesman Court and authorized for travel in and outside of the Empire. If anyone present at Court has additional information that might affect this Court's decision let him come forward now and object, otherwise he shall hold his tongue and it shall be."

Spell paused for the customary moment. Then, as the gavel descended, a familiar voice filled the courtroom.

"I object, Your Honor."

I closed my eyes and breathed deep. The courtroom fell into a dead silence.

Templeton.

CHAPTER 16

I didn't dare turn around. Spell's gavel hung in the air. She looked down from the bench at the scene unfolding in her Court. My eyes cut to Petrovich. He looked worried.

Templeton walked up behind me, standing just to my left. I didn't turn my head; I didn't acknowledge him. He leaned in, his breath on my ear as he whispered low:

"Emily, you smell... *afraid.*"

I shuddered.

"Templeton!" Spell regained her composure, but still looked wary. "As surprised as this Court is to see you, we are ruling on the approval of Emily Swift to the Salesman ranks. And you are objecting to this? I cannot fathom why. Let us hear it."

"I believe this ruling is impossible, Your Honor, since under the Birthmother Act of '31 Emily Swift does not exist." Templeton's voice was calm, measured.

"You can't be serious?" Spell slammed the palm of her hand down on the bench. Petrovich smiled while the other five justices looked confused.

"I'm quite serious, Your Honor." Templeton turned to me. "Emily."

I refused to look at him and stared at Spell. Her mouth set into a firm line.

"Emily," Templeton continued, "did your mother, Lydia McKay Swift, present you to Court any time after you were born?"

He already knew the answer. He was playing with me again. I resisted the urge to strike him.

"Wait a minute," Manchester interrupted. "First of all, Mr. Templeton, you are not here in this Court to ask questions of Ms. Swift. You will only respond to this bench."

"My apologies, Your Honor." I glanced sideways at Templeton and noticed the corners of his mouth had turned up in a barely there smirk.

"Secondly," Manchester began as he turned to Spell. "What in the name of the Empire is the Birthmother Act of '31? I've never heard of this."

"An old law. It's no longer enforced." She glared at Templeton. "The Birthmother Act is antiquated. It was only put in place during a period of history in which Salesman parentage was being questioned. It was politically motivated and hasn't been used in centuries."

"Your Honor, if the law is no longer relevant, why hasn't it been repealed?" Templeton asked. I seriously doubted he cared this much about forgotten laws.

"Because, Mr. Templeton, this Court has had

more important items to address! Applying this law now would revoke approvals made for..." Spell threw up her hands. "Would we even have an approved living Salesmen left in the Empire?"

Templeton cocked his head to the side, pursing his lips. He nodded as if he were giving Spell's words serious thought. I finally turned to face him. I caught a hint of a sinister little smile playing about his lips. Oh my god. I remembered Anne's story about Templeton being brought to Court.

"Well, my mother presented me, Your Honor. Surely others were brought before the Court as well?" He lifted his palms.

"You're a real prick," I said to him.

Templeton gave me a full, cold smile. "Justice Spell," he said, "you have made an excellent point. Applying this law retroactively would be harmful to the very Empire. I daresay all Salesmen would agree with you." He paused, feigning concern once again. "Still, this is a challenging decision the Court must make now that the law has been brought forward. Ignoring it would probably set horrible precedence. Who knows what might be used for personal gain?"

"Mr. Templeton, whatever you are hoping to gain from this better not in any way hurt the Empire – or harm Daniel Swift's daughter. Are we clear?" Spell picked up her gavel.

"Of course, Your Honor." Templeton bowed slightly toward the bench. I stood, stunned.

Spell drew in a breath. "In light of Salesman John Templeton's objection in front of this Court, I hereby delay approval of Emily Swift as a Salesman until the Birthmother Act of '31 has officially been repealed. Court will now adjourn and I want to see Emily Swift and John Templeton in my private chambers. *Immediately.*"

The gavel slammed down as the room erupted in frantic chaos. A swarm of men in black flooded the courtroom and two shots were fired. The justices fled to the sides of the bench as Empire guards moved across the room in defense. Those in the gallery either tried to escape or dove under the courtroom's common pews. I couldn't see Anne.

Templeton spun around, his long coat billowing out behind him. He snarled at the commotion behind us before moving toward a side door to escape. I lunged after him, grabbing his sleeve. He tried to shake me free, but I hung on for dear life.

"Not this time! You're not getting away!" I yelled at him. Templeton pried my fingers from his coat and swung me around, forcing me against the courtroom wall with his body. He put his nose to mine. His eyes were cold but bright. I swallowed.

"This was set in motion long before you were

born, Emily. There's nothing you can do now," he growled, holding my wrists to the wall.

"Did you kill my father?" I shouted at him. The noise in the room was deafening. More shots were fired and I heard screaming. "Did you put the bomb on that train?"

Templeton didn't answer. He didn't blink. I could feel my heart slamming in my chest; I wondered if he could feel it too. Things were out of control. People were being attacked. Havers was dead. People were counting on me and I didn't know what to do. I thought about the letter for Beverly Spell. How would I get it to her now? What was I supposed to do? I felt helpless. Weak. Scared.

Much like at Barnes & Noble when I first learned that Top Hat was Templeton, the noise went away and I couldn't breathe. Again I had the sensation of falling, but this time I managed to jerk myself out of it and pull away from Templeton's gaze. But it was too late. Before I could stop him, he pulled Blackstone's letter to Spell from my pocket. I tried to grab it with my free hand, but he easily avoided my efforts. I struggled against him, but he was stronger.

Templeton put his hand to my throat, holding me to the wall. My fingers gripped his wrist. His lips touched my ear. "If I were you, I wouldn't piss the Court off by any more unauthorized travel," he hissed, "but I would find a way to go back home before you really get hurt." He pushed away from me and in a flash was through the side door. I barely had time to realize he was gone.

The courtroom was a battleground. I saw Anne swing my bag and catch one of the attackers alongside of his head. He went down and Anne kicked him in the stomach.

"Anne!" I yelled. She looked up and I caught her eye. I realized I was out in the open standing by the wall. How no one had seen me with Templeton was beyond me.

"Get out of here!" she yelled back. "I have your bag!"

And The Book, I thought. Finding my feet, I skittered around a body as one of the guards was pushed in my direction. I kept going. Adrenalin propelled me forward, and I went through the same door as Templeton. I don't know if he used it for door travel, but I simply ended up in a courthouse hallway leading to an emergency exit. I ran down the hall and out into the city.

I wasn't sure where to go, but I suspected Anne would be looking for me as soon as she could get away. I didn't see Templeton. He was long gone by now. Across the street from the courthouse was a small park. I found a bench at the far end, pulling my hood up to help cover my face. I could see the front of the courthouse. The place was crawling with Empire guards. I assumed at least some of the men who attacked the Court were also still around the building. They were probably members of the Fringe.

I'd only been waiting for a few minutes when I saw Anne hurry out of the front of the courthouse and move swiftly down the stairs. Thank god she still had my bag. Anne stood on the sidewalk, looking right and left. I was just about to pop up and try to get her attention when she spun and walked to the right. Standing in front of the sign for the train station, she pointed at it for several seconds as she continued to look up and down the street. Then she turned on her heel and walked in the opposite direction and away from me.

But I got the message. She wanted to meet at the train station.

❋ ❋ ❋

"Something strange is going on, Emily. The Fringe is getting really bold. They haven't been this active in years. It has to be you." Anne met up with me an hour later. I had paced the train station sweating bullets while I waited. Anne made a quick stop at her home and picked up money for traveling. She also brought a couple of coats and a travel bag. She was thinking ahead.

"We need to get out of Matar. They will be looking for you. Everyone will be looking for you. We'll go to the Port of North and take the ferry to Vue. I have a friend there who might know where to find Rabbit. Your father said to look for him and right now you need all the help you can get."

I nodded. Since Rabbit dealt in information, he might know where to find Templeton. My fear of him had definitely ratcheted up several levels. I could still feel his hand on my neck. I touched my throat. No matter what Anne believed, Templeton was dangerous.

Although I'd planned to send an update after arriving in Matar, I was afraid to try to get a message to Blackstone now. I didn't want to reveal where I was or where I was going. If Templeton stole the book of fairytales from Blackstone, the letter he took from me might help him find the Crimson Stone. And if Templeton found the stone... I shuddered. I worried I'd added to the disaster. But how did Templeton know about the letter? Good god, he couldn't read my thoughts, could he?

"Can Templeton read minds?" I asked Anne. I fidgeted with the strap of my bag.

"I hope not," she said, dismissing my question. "Okay, we're taking a train to Anwat now, and then one overnight to the Port of North. From there we'll take the ferry to Vue. We probably won't get into Vue until tomorrow afternoon, but this is the best we can do right now. At least we can sleep on the train tonight." Anne folded the train schedule. "We have to pay for trains going from city to city, so I'll get two tickets now."

I followed, hiking my bag up over my shoulder. The Book was still stowed safely inside.

"Too bad you weren't approved at Court today. You would've received an official top hat. Travel would have been a lot quicker for you," Anne said as we boarded the train.

"I still need a Salesman to go with me so I don't mess up."

"Seems like you can travel well enough by yourself. You just need some practice."

"With my luck I would try to go to Vue and end up in Cleveland."

Anne shook her head as she pointed toward the back of the car. "Let's get into our seats and settle in. You sit by the window and try not to attract any more attention."

I did as she suggested and after sinking into my seat, I tried to make some sense of what had happened. This Birthmother Law was a real surprise. Templeton knew about it, but some justices had no clue. How come?

"This Birthmother Law," I began, "have you ever heard of it?"

"No." Anne adjusted her coat. "But Templeton

is clever. He knew what the Court would do. But why he wants to clip your wings is a mystery to me."

"Maybe he's afraid I'll find out he did have something to do with my father's death."

Anne didn't look convinced. "I think he wants something from you, Emily."

I tilted my head back. "Do you know what?"

"Not a clue."

Anne had bought a couple of sandwiches before we left the station. She handed me a ham and cheese and we ate in silence. Afterwards, Anne drifted off to sleep and I turned my face to the window, resting my temple against the pane. The train rocked back and forth as we traveled. I closed my eyes. The experience at Court undermined my confidence. I had no idea how I was going to keep away from the Fringe and catch Templeton. I missed Jack and knew he was worried. I thought about my mother and all she didn't know and what she had lost. I wished I had more power.

❊ ❊ ❊

It was late afternoon when I opened my eyes. I guessed it was about four. Anne was still dozing so I quietly dug inside my bag and pulled out The Book. I hoped The Book would give me some direction. We were almost to Anwat and we'd need to catch the overnight train to the Port of North so we could take the ferry. I turned to the passage I found earlier that mentioned the Port.

Tickets
for travel from
Port of North
must be purchased
in Anwat.
do not pay at
the counter.

I didn't understand why we couldn't purchase the tickets at the counter, but I wasn't going to question what my father wrote. So far he hadn't led me astray. He could have added more details though.

The Book wanted to give me answers. I knew that. Whenever I focused my attention and asked it for help, it pointed me in the right direction. Or at least the right general direction.

Did my father know about the Crimson Stone and the book of fairytales? Blackstone might've only just found the book, but if it contained clues to a gemstone hidden somewhere in the Empire, surely someone here knew about it. Even if my father didn't have any direct knowledge, maybe he heard some rumors or stories. I started to page through The Book, thinking about the stone.

After thumbing through pages of numbers and

lists, I found an interesting passage:

There is a Legend
about a child
who liked to play
with pretty stones.
One Stone was
Very Special.
She had to hide it,
so she put it in
Plain Sight
after breaking it into
three pieces.

I shook my head. Okay, so The Book wasn't always helpful. I supposed the 'pretty stone' could be the Crimson Stone. I wondered about the part where she broke it into three pieces. That was strange. And who was the girl?

Blackstone could probably tell me if the passage had anything to do with the hidden gemstone. Eventually I would need to get a message to him. Anne stirred and stretched. She opened her eyes and looked over to see what I was doing.

"Finding any answers in your Dad's journal?"

"Mostly coming up with more questions. Anne, did you ever hear a legend or a story about a powerful gemstone hidden somewhere in the Empire?"

Anne gave me a funny look. "Sure. About fifty different stories about fifty different magical stones."

"No, I mean a very specific story about a gemstone called the Crimson Stone. I haven't had a lot of time to tell you everything, but Blackstone had a rare book of children's fairytales stolen the day I saw Templeton standing over him. Apparently it contained a legend with clues about where the Crimson Stone is hidden. Blackstone believes it's somewhere here in the Empire. Whoever finds it will have absolute power."

"And you think Templeton stole the book from Blackstone?"

"It looks that way. Of course someone else could've taken it too. If Templeton or the Fringe get a hold of it, I can't imagine what would happen."

"Did you know the legend? Do you have any idea where it could be?"

I shook my head. "No, but Blackstone was working on finding clues in the story. He said he had an idea of where to start. Then the book was stolen from his office." I decided to tell Anne about the letter. "He wrote about it in a letter to Beverly Spell. I was supposed to give it to her when I went to Court. But I couldn't get it to her before all hell broke loose."

"Let's look at it now. Maybe it will give us an idea of where to look," Anne said.

"Well, that's going to be a bit of a problem."

"Why?"

"Templeton stole it from me when you were mixing it up in the gallery."

"What?" Anne's eyes grew huge. "He stole it?"

I sighed. "He pinned me up against the wall and he took it out of my pocket. Then he threatened me and dashed out a door. Poof." I snapped my fingers.

"But how did he know you had it?"

"Here's the thing – he shouldn't have known. And if I wouldn't have grabbed him when he tried to leave, I'd probably still have the letter!"

"I don't get it, Emily."

"I think he read my mind."

"What?"

"I know, crazy, but that's what I'm coming up with. He held me up against the wall and stared into my eyes. I felt like I was falling. This isn't the first time I've had that sensation with him, by the way. Anyhow, I was so afraid with everything going on and I suddenly thought about the letter for Spell. I didn't know how I was going to get it to her. A few seconds later, Templeton digs into my pocket and steals it."

Anne closed her eyes and shook her head. "I suppose Templeton's powers could include mind-reading, but to be honest Emily, I don't know anyone who can do that. And I know a lot of people with a lot of special talents."

"I know. I mean, I'm getting used to the idea of

people doing things I thought were impossible. But I still don't know what's real and what I'm imagining. The truth is, he might've read my mind or he might've just gotten lucky."

"Add this to our list of questions for Rabbit." Anne shifted in her seat.

"Will he be able to answer everything?"

"Not necessarily, but I bet he'll have a lot of very good information for you."

"Am I going to have to pay for it, because I'll admit right now, I don't have a lot of money with me. Just a couple hundred dollars American."

"Rabbits don't generally give information away for free, but they don't always ask for money either. You might have something of value. In fact, you might even have information to trade."

"Maybe, but I don't want to spill my guts. That doesn't seem too wise."

"Exactly. It will be up to you to decide what is valuable and what you are willing to part with. You can negotiate. Then again, Rabbit was an ally of your father's. He might be willing to help you out because you are Emily Swift."

"I hope so." The train felt like it was slowing down. I looked out the window and noted we were entering another city after passing miles of snowy countryside. "Are we in Anwat?"

Anne leaned over and looked. "Yes, we're here.

Probably another ten minutes before we arrive at the station. We'll get off and buy tickets for the ferry."

"That reminds me." I flipped back several pages in The Book and showed Anne the passage.

Tickets
for travel from
Port of North
must be purchased
in Anwat.
do not pay at
the counter.

"That's odd," Anne said. "How are we supposed to get the tickets?"

"No idea. I'm guessing you usually buy them at the counter?"

"Of course. I don't know why he would have written that. We'll look into it when we get there."

I began to pack up and placed The Book back inside my bag. A few minutes later the train pulled into the station and we were allowed to get off.

Anwat's station was bigger and busier than Matar's. Anne explained the city was a major travel hub, so the station was usually packed with people from all of the other Empire cities and neighboring towns.

We pushed along with the rest of the throng.

When Anne purchased our train tickets in Matar, she made sure the journey included passage to Port of North. Tickets for the ferry to Vue, however, were to be purchased in Anwat. We weren't sure what to do because of my father's note, but we decided to scope out the counter anyway.

"That could explain it." Anne nodded to the counter across the room. On the other side of the crowded lobby, I noted several Empire guards standing near the ticket counter for the ferry. "I wonder if they are looking for you."

"Damn!" What should we do? I turned to Anne. "Maybe they want to help?"

"Do you want to take that chance? They could detain you."

"Good point. No, let's get out of here before they see us." We stayed close to the wall and headed for a side exit. "Maybe we should just get on the next train and hope there's another way to get on the ferry once we get to Port of North."

"I don't have a better idea," Anne said. "The train leaves in a couple of hours. It will be dark by then and easier to board. Of course they might have guards on the train too, Emily. I don't know what you want to do."

"For now let's just plan on taking the next train."

Anne nodded. "Listen, I'm going to pick us up some more sandwiches for the trip. We should keep a low profile on the train, so the dining car is probably out. I didn't book us a sleeping car either, so we'll have to keep to ourselves."

The air outside was bitterly cold. We moved away from a streetlight and into the shadows alongside the train station. I stepped up into a dark doorway of a closed diner.

"Stay here and I'll grab us something from the station's gift shop. I'll also try to find out about what happened earlier today and if people are looking for you." Anne took her wallet out of her travel bag before handing it over to me. "Hold onto this. I'll be right back."

CHAPTER 17

Anne disappeared around the corner and I did my best to blend into the dark doorway. I was cold, tired, worried, and clueless as to what we should do. I missed Jack and Tara and the Furious Furballs. I missed my Mom, too. At some point I had to get word to Blackstone, although he probably heard about the eruption in the courtroom. He probably also knew about poor Havers.

Which meant Jack knew about it too, assuming Blackstone was keeping him informed. I slumped against the door behind me. He was probably a nervous wreck. It was no use thinking about it now. I tried to clear my thoughts and focus on Templeton. No one knew where he'd been in the past few years, so finding him seemed like such a long shot without knowing what was in the book of fairytales and the letter.

Fortunately this side of the building had little traffic. But now I heard snow crunching underfoot. I straightened. Instead of Anne, a young man walked by, his head down and his hands buried in his pockets. He didn't look up and I held my breath as he passed. I listened to the sound of his footsteps as he continued down the street. Then he stopped. Keep going, keep going, I chanted inside my head. The footsteps started again. They were coming closer. I tried to shrink into the shadows.

The man reappeared and stopped in front of me. He smiled. "Everything okay?"

"Um, yes. Just waiting for a friend." Our breath ran into each other in the cold air.

He nodded. "Okay, but you look like you're hiding in there."

"Maybe a little bit," I admitted.

"Been there." He nodded again. He was dressed in a short black leather jacket, with layers of flannel shirts poking out from the bottom. He wore fitted black jeans tucked into heavy work boots. A chain ran from his belt to a wallet. His grey knit cap pushed out a few dark curls across his forehead and over his ears. He looked to be somewhere in his early twenties.

"My friend is grabbing some sandwiches and we're getting on the train. She'll be back in a minute." I hoped.

"Cool." He stepped up into the doorway and stood by me. "I'll wait with you."

I stepped to the side, wary. "That's okay. You don't have to."

"I know. But this isn't the best neighborhood at night." He shrugged. "I'll wait until your friend comes back and then I'll be on my way." He leaned against the door. "So where are you from?"

I hesitated. I didn't know how many people from outside the Empire came in, so I chose my words carefully. "I just got in from Matar."

"Matar is nice." He looked at me closely. "I make it up there once every month or so. I like it better here though. More to do."

I nodded as if I understood.

"So where are you heading?" Was it me or was he studying my face?

"Vue. See a friend." I leaned my head out of the doorway and looked down the street. Where was Anne?

"Cool." His phone buzzed. He dug it from his pocket to read the feed. I noticed he wasn't wearing gloves and his hands looked like they saw some labor. Working man. Wait a minute.

"How come your phone works?" I frowned. "I didn't think there were any towers here." Had Blackstone lied to me?

"Who needs a tower?" He tapped a message into his phone.

"Oh. Okay." I supposed I'd have to be happy with that. "So, what do you do?" Sometimes I feel the need to make conversation when I'm nervous.

He looked up from his phone. "A little of this and that. Whatever needs to be done. I travel a lot. Talk to people."

I nodded as if any of that made sense. "Traveling is nice."

He grinned and I noted what a friendly smile he had. His whole face got in on the action. "It can be. I like being on the move. So much out there to see and hear."

"It's a big wide world," I agreed.

"You're not from the Empire, are you?" He kept smiling.

I wasn't sure what to say, so I shook my head no. At that moment, Anne rounded the corner and stepped up into the doorway.

"Well, they only had vegetarian sandwiches left," she began but stopped when she saw my new friend. Her mouth opened in surprise.

"It's okay." I waved my hands hoping it really was. "This guy just stopped to make sure everything was alright while I waited for you." I looked at him. "Um, I'm sorry. I didn't get your name."

"Rabbit!" Anne's eyes were wide.

"What?" I looked at him and he nodded.

"In the flesh. A little surprised to see you here, Anne." He stopped and looked back at me. Realization filled his face. "Ah, I know. This must be the famous Emily Swift. I thought there was something fishy going on here."

"Rabbit, what's going on?" Anne leaned in. "The building is crawling with Empire guards."

"You don't need a Rabbit to know what's up. The mid-day news reported the attack on Court today. It's all over the Empire: the Fringe attacked the Court and Emily Swift is missing. The Court wants to get her back before things get out of hand. They flashed your picture too, Anne. They know you're traveling together."

"Oh no." I looked at Anne. "We've got to get a message to Blackstone that I'm safe. Somehow I've got to let Jack know I'm okay so he won't go crazy."

"Well lucky for us, we've got a Rabbit." She squeezed the young man's arm. "Do you have a place where we can talk?"

Rabbit nodded. "What about your train?"

"We were on our way to Vue to see if we could find you. We don't need to go there now."

"You still might want to keep moving, though," Rabbit told us. "Hold onto those tickets."

"We only have train tickets to the Port. I couldn't risk going to the counter to buy tickets for the ferry," Anne said.

"No worries. I'll get you ferry tickets." He dug his phone back out and punched in a message. "Two tickets will be waiting for you at the Port. Look for a Rabbit. Now, where were we?"

I didn't know what to think, so I looked to Anne. She was all smiles. "Perfect. Thanks. Can we go someplace private now? Someplace close?"

"Sure. I have an apartment about five minutes

from here."

❉ ❉ ❉

Rabbit's place was small and unsurprisingly, a bit of a mess. It wasn't dirty, but it was filled with all kinds of clutter and parts. About a dozen computers and laptops in varying states of repair were scattered around the room. Several screens blinked along one wall. From time to time, an image would flash by. They appeared to be hooked up to webcams, but I couldn't be sure.

Rabbit cleared off a couple of chairs placed next to a makeshift kitchen table. I sat down as he pulled up a stool. Anne reached into her bag and pulled out one of the sandwiches.

"Don't worry, there's no meat and it's the least we can do." She handed the sandwich to Rabbit.

"I'll take it," he said. I remembered what Anne said about Rabbits coming to the café without money for lunch. Rabbit was lean, but he didn't look like he was starving. Besides, surely the equipment I saw here was worth some coin. He could sell something if he needed to.

"Do you live here alone?" I asked.

"There's always someone passing through," he said chewing. "But right now we're the only ones here."

"So what can you tell us?" Anne pulled out the

other sandwich and gave me half. It was cold grilled red pepper and mushroom.

"The buzz is that Emily Swift went to Court today for recognition. That alone would've been big news, but add in the attack on the Court, bigger headlines." Rabbit shook his head. "You're gonna have a lot of trouble traveling unnoticed."

"Great." Being famous was getting old. "Is that all the news said?"

"Since you haven't been found, they're guessing either you've been kidnapped by the Fringe, or you're on the run. And since there was an attack at Anne's café, the official word is that Anne is with you." Rabbit took another bite of his sandwich. "The Empire is looking for you both. You can bet the Fringe is too."

"So, that's all the news is saying?" I noticed Rabbit didn't mention Templeton's appearance.

"Pretty much." Rabbit's dark eyes seemed to sparkle. "That's the official news."

Anne knew the drill. Leaning forward, her hands on her knees, she pressed him for more information. "What's the 'unofficial' news? What are they not reporting?"

Rabbit grinned. "You mean things like Templeton showing up at Court today too?"

Anne nodded. "Things exactly like that."

Rabbit finished his sandwich and stood up.

He pawed through a few boxes and came back with bits and pieces of paper. He sorted them, reading. "Looks like Templeton's been a busy guy these days. He's popped up in a few places. Mostly in Matar for the past week, but before that he was in New York State. He was definitely in the City visiting a library. I'll have to check and see if anyone's seen him since the courthouse, but I'm guessing he's way off the radar right now."

"That would be helpful," Anne said.

Rabbit looked from Anne to me. It was then I realized I'd expected Rabbit to be much older. In fact, if he knew my father, he would be a lot older by now. If he was only in his early twenties today, he would've only been a few years old when my father died.

"How old are you?" I studied his features.

"Old enough." Rabbit winked at me. But he didn't elaborate. "Anyhow, there's quite a bit of chatter going on right now. A lot of information is getting passed back and forth. Mostly rumors, so you can't trust everything you hear."

"But Rabbits have excellent hearing," Anne prompted.

"We do."

"I'm going to be honest. We don't have much to offer you, and we need a lot of help," Anne said.

"I got it." He was ready to get down to business. "But you might know more than you think. Would you be willing to share?"

I remembered what Anne had said earlier about giving information to get some. "I'll share what I know as long as it doesn't put us or the Empire in danger."

"Fair enough," Rabbit said. "Very much like your father." Rabbit glanced at the time. "Your train leaves in about an hour. I might go with you."

"We'd appreciate the escort," Anne said.

"I have a question though. Should I get in touch with the Court?" I bounced my eyes from Anne to Rabbit. "Can they help? I mean, we're on the same side here."

"Some of the chatter suggests the Empire's leadership is being influenced by the Fringe. I personally don't have any proof of it, but my resource is reliable," said Rabbit.

"I'm not surprised the Fringe is working behind the scenes." Anne folded her arms.

"Okay, I don't want to take any chances," I said. "We need to find out where Templeton is going, though. Can you help with that?"

"It'll be hard, but I'll keep my ears open. Are you chasing Templeton because of the book of fairytales?" Rabbit asked.

I'm sure I looked surprised. I stalled. "Um, what book?"

Anne laughed. "Emily." She gestured toward

Rabbit. "I'm sure he knows more than you think. He probably knows more than you know."

"Oh." Well, I thought it was a huge secret.

"I know the book was found recently, but no one knew who had it. Blackstone's never been a high-profile type of guy, so I doubt anyone thought of him. It's only by coincidence that he would be the Record Keeper at the North Door. Since you're from that area, the 'Swift' spotlight included Blackstone. More people took notice of him. They heard about his stint at the library. They heard a book was stolen. It wasn't a stretch to put two and two together."

"So the Fringe knew and so did Templeton?"

"Among others, I'm sure," Rabbit said.

"Do they know what's in the book?" I asked.

"To a point. They know the book contains a hidden message explaining where the Crimson Stone is hidden. A lot of people want to get their hands on that."

"Do you think they can figure out the location? I think it took Blackstone a long time," I told him.

"The right person, sure. My money would be on Templeton." Rabbit gave us a sly smile. "If he had the book of fairytales, of course."

That got my attention. "Are you saying Templeton doesn't have it?"

Rabbit nodded. "That's what I'm saying."

Anne and I looked at each other in surprise. I found my voice. "Who has it then?"

"In general, the Fringe. Specifically –" Rabbit stopped smiling "– the word is that someone on the inside of the Empire ordered a hit on Blackstone."

I thought about Beverly Spell, but had a hard time believing she would do something like that. Petrovich was another story, of course. Perhaps it was better I didn't give the letter to Spell. If Petrovich was dirty, the less information Spell had the better. I noticed Rabbit was watching me closely.

"Is there something you know? Something you wanna share?"

Quid pro quo. I looked at Anne and she nodded. She knew what I was thinking.

"You probably already know about this," I began, "but I had a letter from Blackstone to give to Beverly Spell. She knew about the book and the legend. After it was stolen, Blackstone wrote the letter explaining some of the clues he was able to decipher. I guess he had an idea of where the stone might be hidden and thought she could help. Maybe even beat the thief to it."

Rabbit's nose actually twitched and his dark eyes shone even brighter. "I didn't know this. And did you give it to Spell?"

I sighed. "Templeton stole it from me at Court."

To my surprise, Rabbit laughed.

"This is not a good thing," I told him.

"I know." He laughed again. "But Templeton never ceases to amaze me. And right now it's probably a good thing he has the letter. The Fringe is after you, not him."

It was an unusual way to look at it, but Rabbit had a point. "Okay," I said. "Well, will you keep this info under your hat? If the Fringe finds out Templeton has the letter, they might try to get it from him. Then they'll have the book of fairytales and a possible way to decode it."

"I won't say anything. At least not yet and not with anyone who would use this against you."

"Can you get a message to Blackstone though? Can you tell him we're okay, but that Templeton has the letter and I need to know what's in it? And make sure he knows the Fringe has the book of fairytales, and not Templeton."

"I can do that."

"Can you also ask him to make sure my boyfriend Jack knows I'm okay? That I'll get home as soon as I can and he doesn't need to worry about me?" My voice caught in the back of my throat and we all ignored it.

Rabbit smiled. "Sure, Emily. I'll get a separate message to him. No worries."

I sighed. "I appreciate it."

"No worries," he said again.

"So next step is for me to find Templeton."

Sure. Easy.

"I think so," Rabbit answered. "The Court didn't approve you for door travel yet, but you have traveled, right?"

"Yeah, although I'm not exactly an expert." Understatement.

"I think she has a lot more talent than she's giving herself credit for," Anne said. I shook my head no. Anne waved a hand. "It's true. And she's traveled without a top hat more than once, so it's raw door travel talent."

"That's cool. Do you have a top hat now so you can travel under the wire?" he asked.

"No, the Court didn't give me one. Templeton and all." I rolled my eyes.

"I have something for you," Rabbit said. "But I need to go get it. It's in storage. I have time before the train leaves, so I'll meet you at the station." He stood to leave. "You'd better get going too."

"He's right. Let's get back to the train." Anne stood and picked up her bag. "We'll be on board," she added.

"I'll see you there."

As we exited Rabbit's building, I remembered what my father wrote in The Book.

If a Rabbit has no tale, can he still tell a story?

I stopped and turned to Rabbit. "Do you have a 'tale'?"

Rabbit looked at me carefully, a curious expression shifting over his face. "As far as I know, Emily Swift, not one Rabbit has a 'tale' to tell, but our information is always reliable."

✼ ✼ ✼

Anne and I walked back to the train station with our heads bent against the wind. The snow was coming down harder now and a couple of inches had accumulated.

"You trust Rabbit, right?" I asked.

"Absolutely. He's always been honest. Your father trusted him too," she said.

"Which brings me to my next question. How old is Rabbit? I mean, he looks like he's only about twenty-three or so."

"Rabbits age very, very slowly. I don't know how old he is, but I'm guessing he's in his fifties."

"No way! I don't believe it! That's impossible."

"After everything you've been through in the past week, you're not going to believe Rabbit is in his fifties?" Anne's brows pulled together into a frown.

"Good point. But I thought you also said Rabbits were hard to find?"

"Only if they don't want to be found," Anne reminded me. "Guess Rabbit wanted you to find him."

Back at the train station, we took careful pains to stay out of sight. There were only a few guards that we could see and we avoided them. I pulled the collar up on my coat and tried to look inconspicuous.

"I think we can board over there." Anne pointed across the platform. We hurried to the car and showed the porter our tickets. He nodded and we climbed the stairs. Once again, we looked for seats in the back.

"Will Rabbit find us?"

"Without a doubt." Anne motioned for me to sit on the inside next to the window. "We'll save a seat for him." She put her coat on the bench across from us.

What were the chances of meeting Rabbit here in Anwat? I stopped and thought about The Book and my father's message. He had written 'do not pay at the counter.' Did he have some sort of foreshadowing about the guards and Rabbit? Of course I had no way of knowing.

But meeting Rabbit was the best stroke of luck second only to meeting Anne. Both were taking great risks to help me. My eyes felt wet and I wiped a tear away. I realized Anne saw me. She gave me a small smile and squeezed my arm.

"It'll be okay," she told me. "We'll figure it out."

We had to figure it out. If the Fringe had the book of fairytales, and Templeton had the letter, we were all in danger.

About five minutes before the train left the

station, Rabbit appeared at the front of the car. He spotted us quickly and made his way to the back. He carried a backpack and a medium-sized brown paper bag. He grinned when he sat down.

"Everything okay?" he asked. "Anyone see you?"

"Got right on the train with no fuss," Anne said. "What's in the bag?"

"It's a surprise for Emily." He glanced around. The car was only half full. "Wait 'til we get going."

"What is it?" I asked.

"You've heard of pulling a rabbit out of a hat, right?" he teased.

"I've been accused of that once or twice," I said.

"How about a hat out of a Rabbit?"

"What do you mean? What are you talking about?"

At that moment, the porter came through collecting tickets. I pretended to pick something off of the floor while Anne handed him ours. Rabbit passed his to the porter and the man moved on to the next car.

"So what do you mean, hat out of a rabbit?" I asked.

"I've been holding on to this for a long time. I didn't know what to do with it, but now I do." Rabbit handed me the paper bag. "This is yours."

I looked at Anne and she lifted her shoulders. "Open it," she said.

No one seemed to be paying us any attention, so I unfolded the top of the bag and looked inside.

It took a minute for me to understand what I was seeing. I looked up at Rabbit. His dark eyes had that playful, shiny look again.

"Emily, what's in the bag?" Anne whispered.

I reached inside and pulled out the worn, black top hat.

"It's my father's hat."

* * *

There was a lot of debris left over from the train wreck that killed my father. Bags, clothing, purses, shoes, luggage, packages – you name it. Rabbit traveled through the night with many others to reach the train. They knew it was the work of the Fringe. But they had no idea as to the extent of the carnage until they got there.

"It was horrible," Rabbit said, the shine in his eyes now dull. "A lot of people were killed. The Fringe are effective terrorists. You could smell the fear and hatred in the air."

"But how did you get my father's hat? How did you know it was his?"

"The word spread pretty quickly that your father was on the train. Salesmen were on the scene fast, of course, because of door travel. I was close, but it still took me several hours to get there. I traveled with a cluster, and we scoured the area looking for survivors."

"A cluster?" I asked.

"A colony of Rabbits," he answered.

"Oh." I traced my fingertips along the hat's brim. I waited for a moment. "Did you find any?"

"No, Emily. We didn't. There were a few the Salesmen found when they first got there, but we did not find anyone else."

"Did you," My voice caught in my throat. I had to stay quiet. I didn't want to draw any attention to us. "Did you see my father?"

Rabbit was so still. I lifted my eyes to his face. I knew the answer. He nodded. "Yes. He was dead."

I swallowed and gripped the hat. "They told us... They said there was... Nothing." My heart hurt so much. My insides were churning. Why did they lie to us? Why did they say there was nothing left?

"Emily." Anne spoke low into my ear. "Emily, don't do this to yourself now."

"Why did they say there was nothing left?" I whispered to the hat.

Rabbit was very pale. His face was tight, his jaw clenched. "There wasn't much left," he said through gritted teeth.

If I could have vomited, I would have. The

only thing that stopped me was the sudden appearance of a man in a top hat at the front of the car. When he turned, I could see his red shirt under his coat.

Anne saw him too. "Rabbit, we might need interference."

Rabbit was very much aware and on point. He stood up with his backpack and began to lumber up the aisle, banging the bag into people as he went. He was doing a good job of drawing attention away from our seats.

"Coming through!" he announced. "Not feeling well. Motion sickness!"

I still felt nauseated myself, but I didn't have time to give into it. Anne moved to the aisle too, and I slipped out behind her, taking my bag and my father's top hat with me as I went.

"Hide somewhere!" she hissed. I ducked and slipped into the vestibule connecting our car to the one behind it. I peeked through the window and the coast seemed to be clear. I slid the door open.

Only a few people looked up. Some were reading or typing on laptops. Most people were already beginning to doze. I hurried to the back, and then on into the next car. This one was a sleeping car and all the doors were closed. I tried one, but it was locked. The second one was too. I licked my dry lips and looked behind me. I didn't know how long I had.

I held my father's hat in my hand. I realized I could try to door travel. But what did Anne say about train doors? They were 'moving targets.' I might not end up where I planned to go. I supposed it would matter if I actually knew where to go. I couldn't go home and I had no idea if I could get to a place I'd never been. I took a deep breath and put my father's hat on. It was a bit too big and slid down over my ears. I held it on my head. Where to go, where to go? I had to find Templeton.

"I want to go to where Templeton is," I said to the empty hallway. I pictured his face the last time I'd seen him. It wasn't a pretty memory, but it gave me something to focus on, and that's what I figured I needed to do. I needed to focus on a destination and feel it. I needed to pull up how I felt when Templeton was near; I needed to dive into the emotion. I shivered.

"Templeton... Where in the hell are you?" I closed my eyes and listened. I pulled up all the fear and anger Templeton stirred up in me. I let myself feel overwhelmed with the desire to catch him, to find him, and to get the answers I needed. The sound of the train faded into the background. I could hear voices, but they were far away. I could hear my heart beating too, the sound of my blood pumping in my ears. And then faintly, I heard it. A humming sound coming from the last door in the car. Surprised,

I opened my eyes and walked toward it. The humming became a buzz and the buzz moved into a rattle. The door shook. I swallowed and held tight to my father's hat and my bag. I reached for the handle and let the power of door travel pull me through.

CHAPTER 18

The landings kept getting rougher. This time I tumbled out of a doorway and fell right into a bathtub.

Thank god it was empty.

My entrance made quite a racket, however. I heard a shout of 'What the –?' come from another room. I climbed out of the tub, grabbing my bag and top hat just as the door to the bathroom swung open. A balding man, probably in his mid-fifties, stood there in a thin, white bathrobe, gaping at me.

"What in the hell are you doing in my bathroom?" His eyes bulged out of his pudgy face as he looked at me from head to toe.

"Um," I looked around. "I was just leaving?"

"You were just leaving?" His gaze wandered to the top hat in my hand. To my surprise, he laughed. "Oh! You made a wrong turn!"

"I beg your pardon?"

"You must be new, yes?"

"Um, yes?" I tucked the top hat behind my back.

"No, it's okay," he tried to reassure me. "My brother's son had the same problem in the beginning. Once he ended up in a ladies' dressing room and had a terrible time trying to explain that one!"

Slowly it dawned on me. The man knew I was a Salesman. I kept forgetting things were different in the Empire. Traveling through doors wasn't so strange.

"Er, thanks. I mean, I'm sorry. I thought I was going to my friend's house. Where am I anyway?"

"You're in my hotel room at the Bedrest Inn."

"Oh." Bedrest Inn? "Okay then, I'm on my way. Um, perhaps I'll leave through your room door?"

"Certainly! You can go out this way." He backed out of the bathroom and pointed to the door. "By the way, I didn't catch your name?"

"Agatha." Agatha?

"Agatha! Good name! Strong." The man was a human bobble-head. "Well Agatha, good luck in your travels. Avoid those bathtubs!" He walked me to the door and held it open for me.

"Thank you. I'm sorry I disturbed you." I slipped out of the room and hurried down the hall. Agatha? Where did that come from?

I decided to take the stairs. I needed to figure out where I was. It occurred to me I might've been successful with my door travel. I only focused on going where Templeton would be. It was possible he was actually here in the hotel. The stairwell had a plaque indicating I was on the third floor. I headed for the ground floor lobby.

The hotel was rather nice and I worried I wouldn't blend in very well. My outfit and I had seen better days. I pretended I knew where I was going and stopped at one of the end tables to pick up a brochure. I looked at the address on the back.

Bedrest Inn, Vue.

No kidding? I was in Vue? I looked around. It was getting late and I'd need a place to stay. Sure, I was in a hotel, but I didn't know if they would let me pay in American dollars. Blackstone said not many places would. Besides, I didn't want to be recognized. What to do, what to do?

I decided I had three choices. I could leave and try to find another place to stay, but I would probably run up against the same problem. I could try to find an empty room to door travel into, but there was no guarantee it worked that way. With my luck the empty room would become a rented room before I had time to slip back out.

The third way was to take a chance and try to get a room here. I'd had my share of good fortune meeting Anne and Rabbit, hadn't I? Maybe that luck would continue. I might be able to get the room without being discovered. I regretted not bringing my credit card with me, but maybe they would accept foreign currency being a hotel and all. Maybe if I gave a fake name. Agatha seemed to work.

I walked up to the desk and a perfectly put together clerk looked up. She gave a well-practiced smile with precisely lined lips. "Welcome to the Bedrest Inn. May I help you?"

"Hi, yes. I don't have a reservation, but I wondered if I might be able to get a room, just for the night?"

"That's possible." Her unblinking blue eyes stayed glued to her computer screen. "How many will be staying this evening?"

"Just me."

"Non-smoking or smoking?"

"Non-smoking."

"I have a single, non-smoking room with a queen bed for one-seventy-nine."

Damn. I only had two-hundred on me. "Do you have anything cheaper?"

The blond clerk looked up, annoyed. She blinked once. Her lips thinned and she started typing again with her manicured nails. "I have another single for one-fifty-nine. Are you a senior citizen?"

"Um, yes?" God, how bad did I look?

"Then I can give you this rate. I'll need your credit card."

"Here's a question for you." I leaned in. "Do you accept American dollars? I kind of left my card in another purse."

The clerk gave an exasperated snort. "Yes, you can use your currency here. The exchange rate puts the cost up to, one moment," she said as she punched a few numbers into the computer. "One-hundred and eighty-five dollars American." She smiled. "Lucky for you you're a senior citizen."

I wanted to bang my head on the counter.

"What name will this room be under?"

"Agatha," I said. "Agatha Greene." I handed over the cash and waited for her to ask for my driver's license which identified me as Emily Swift, but the request never came. She simply pushed a sign-in book across the counter and pointed to a line. I wrote Agatha Greene with a bit of flourish. I was in.

"Room 339. Check out is at eleven in the morning. Do you need help with your bags?"

"No, thanks. I'm all set." I took the key card and headed for the elevators. I decided to skip finding something for dinner. The half veggie sandwich Anne shared with me would just have to do. Tomorrow morning I'd stop somewhere cheap for a coffee and bagel. Then I'd find out where the ferry docked. Hopefully Anne and Rabbit would be on it. I had no idea where I'd sleep tomorrow night if they didn't get here. I was down to my last fifteen dollars.

Number 339 was a functional hotel room, with little more than a bed, nightstand, television, and desk with a matching chair. The décor focused on beige, with shades of it everywhere. The carpet was dark beige. The bedspread was light beige. The walls, maybe eggshell. The artwork consisted of one large beige canvas on the wall above the bed. At least the mattress was firm.

A small window looked over the parking lot and the bathroom did not have a bathtub. There was a narrow shower stall and I'd be able to wash off the day. I sighed. At least I made it to Vue safely. I sat down and took off my sneakers.

Since I hoped to land wherever Templeton was hanging out, I wondered if it was possible to learn if he was staying at the hotel. I couldn't imagine an easy way to find out. I couldn't call the front desk and ask for his room. He might not even be using his real name. Apparently a fake name was easy enough to pull off at the Bedrest Inn.

I stripped out of my clothes and hung everything up in tiny closet. Tossing my underwear and bra into my travel bag, I hauled out a nightshirt and pajama bottoms and hung them on the back of the bathroom door. The shower spray warmed my bones. I was utterly exhausted. So much had happened in one day. Havers was dead, the Court didn't approve me, the Fringe were chasing me, and they had the book of fairytales. Oh yeah, and Templeton stole the letter from me. I was one helluva Salesman. I hung my head.

It was barely nine when I crawled into bed. I ignored my growling stomach and instead wished I was with Jack. I missed him terribly. I hoped he got Rabbit's message saying I was okay.

I tried hard not to cry.

❊ ❊ ❊

The train rocked gently from side to side. The events of the last twenty-four hours had really taken their toll. I needed to stretch. I decided to get up and walk around.

Carefully climbing over Anne, I made sure not to disturb her. She was sleeping hard. Kicking ass in the courtroom and running from the Fringe must be catching up with her. I glanced at Rabbit. He was also sleeping, his thick eyelashes dark against his fair skin. As I moved into the aisle, he opened his eyes. He frowned, his eyebrows heavy over curious eyes.

"Where are you?" he asked.

"Shh." I pointed to Anne. "Let her sleep."

I turned away and walked down the center aisle. We were the only passengers in the car, and beyond the sound of the train, it was quiet. Everything felt peaceful. I moved slowly. Things felt a little off, almost like I was dreaming.

That startled me. Yes, it felt like a dream. Before I could shake myself awake, I turned back to Anne and Rabbit. Anne was still sleeping, but Rabbit wasn't there anymore. I looked around the car, but he was definitely gone. Strange.

Unlike the other dreams I'd had lately, this one didn't have any bad energy floating through it. I realized this was my own dream. I could decide what was going to happen. I kept walking, wondering how I could make it work for me. If Templeton could pull people into his dreams, maybe I could try to pull him into mine. Maybe I could figure out exactly where he was and how to find him. He couldn't hurt me in a dream. At least, I didn't think he could.

I stopped at the front of the car where a door led to a private compartment. I turned the handle and entered the narrow, empty room. There were two bench seats facing one another. I closed the door behind me and sat down. I had no idea how to pull Templeton in. I didn't know how this dream stuff worked, but maybe it was a little like door travel. Maybe I needed to imagine him sitting across from me.

Closing my eyes, I pictured him in as much detail as I could. I focused all my energies and feelings on seeing Templeton clearly in my mind's eye. I tried to raise my feelings like I did before trying to door travel. I felt what it would be like to be in control and pull him into my dream for once. Come here Templeton, it's just a dream. I imagined pulling him through the darkness of the night and into my little world. I felt a cool blast of air slide by me.

"Really, Emily," Templeton said. I opened my eyes. He sat on the bench facing me, wearing black pants and a black sport coat. A purple silk shirt, so dark it was almost black, offered an attempt at color. The top three buttons were undone. His black shoes were perfectly polished. He didn't have his top hat, but he wore one very annoyed expression. His dark hair was tousled slightly.

I felt underdressed in my pajamas.

"Yes, really, Templeton." Holy-mother-of-pearl. I did it.

"You think you can just up and pull me into your dream? I do have more important things to do, you know. I thought our last little special time together made it clear that you should quit while you're ahead and go home."

"Gee, did I catch you on a date or something?" I shot back. I'd had enough of Templeton. "Well, too bad. Looks like you're here now."

"Are you so sure? Maybe you're making up this whole conversation." He stretched and folded his legs, balancing his right ankle on his left knee. He let his arms rest on the back of the compartment's bench. My 'date' comment was ignored.

"Maybe I am, but I'm willing to play it out." I stared at him. "You stole a letter from me and I want it back."

"That's not going to happen."

Oh yeah? "Is that so? It's sticking out of your pocket."

Templeton looked down at his chest. The letter poked up from the breast pocket of his jacket, just like a handkerchief. Before he could act, I leaned forward and snatched it from his coat.

"You can't take it with you." He flinched when I took the letter, but he kept his pose on the bench.

"I know. But I can read it here." I opened the letter and skimmed Blackstone's message to Spell. Blackstone wrote the book of fairytales had been stolen, and that he believed the Crimson Stone was hidden in Vue, somewhere in 'plain sight.' According to the legend, the only way the stone could be kept safe was to break it into three pieces. He asked Spell if she could help to recover the book of fairytales before the Fringe was able to decode the passage. He also said I would help in any way I could as the daughter of Daniel Swift. He hoped I would be approved right away so I could door travel.

"Satisfied, Emily?" he sneered.

"I know the Fringe has the book of fairytales," I told him.

"And?"

"And I need to get it back before they find the Crimson Stone."

"Why don't you let me worry about the stone?" He unfolded his legs and leaned forward. I could smell his cologne. Slight, but there. Dark and sensuous. Expensive. Maybe he really was on a date. Good grief, I'm running for my life all over the damn Empire and he's playing man about town.

"Besides," he continued, "the letter gives me enough information. I'll probably have it before tomorrow's over."

I worried that Templeton was telling the truth. "And then what? You'll sell it to the Fringe?"

"Dear, naïve Emily." Templeton shook his head. "After all we've been through, you still think I work for the Fringe?"

"Oh, right. You're a loyal servant of the Empire then?"

"I work for one person and one person only."

"Let me guess," I said.

The corners of his mouth picked up. "That's right. Sorry to disappoint Daniel Swift's precious little girl, but yes. I work for the most powerful Salesman in the Empire. Me."

"I don't get it." This was frustrating. "Why were you so hot on delivering my father's journal to me and pointing me to Blackstone?"

He waved a hand, dismissing my question. "On some level I was curious about you. Of course the book of fairytales being stolen by Blackstone was a delicious stroke of good fortune."

"But you didn't need me to find Blackstone. I don't get it." I was still confused.

"No, I didn't need you, and yes, the Fringe found the book of fairytales first. But you have been a wonderful diversion."

"Excuse me?" A diversion?

"Entering the Empire caught the attention of the Fringe, didn't it? In fact, the whole Empire has focused on you. Making sure you found Blackstone meant less attention on what I planned to do."

"But you showed up in Court – that wasn't exactly keeping under the radar."

"You surprised me. I never expected you to make it to Court. When you did, I needed to make sure you weren't approved. Slow down your travel a bit." He shrugged.

The words hung there in the air between us. "You never expected me to make it to Court? You thought the Fringe would get me first, didn't you? And you did nothing to stop that from happening?"

"Nothing personal, Emily. And besides, I can see you are quite capable of taking care of yourself. You might even be useful in the future. Look how you managed to conjure up a dream for this lovely chat."

"I've had enough." I stood up.

"That makes two of us." Templeton stood too. We were inches apart and he towered over me.

I reminded myself it was just a dream. He couldn't hurt me.

"Time to watch your back, Templeton," I warned. My heart was beating a little faster than I would have liked.

He laughed. "I wonder how much like your father you really are."

"I'm not as nice." I stepped toward the door and paused. I just couldn't resist. "Enjoy your night at the Bedrest Inn, Templeton. I know I will."

That earned me a surprised look. "You're not on the train?"

"What do you mean?" I reached for the door handle. My fingers just barely grazed it. I felt my control waning. I realized I was starting to wake up. I had overplayed my hand. I had to get out of there.

"You're not on the overnight train coming from Anwat, are you? No. You're in Vue!" Templeton actually sounded happy.

"So?" I finally managed to grip the handle, but the door was locked. I shook it. This didn't make sense. I pulled Templeton into my dream. I was the one in charge here.

"Oh, you've got a lot to learn, Emily. Someone

should teach you a lesson or two." Templeton snickered as he reached around me and put his hand over mine. I flinched as he pressed his body into my back, his lips at my ear. "Nice pajamas, by the way. Now let me help you get back to bed," he whispered. With that, he shoved me hard and I flew through to the other side – and landed on my back in the hotel bed. I scrambled to my feet and spun around in the darkness, gasping for breath as my eyes roamed the shadows.

At least he didn't follow me. I was alone.

❊ ❊ ❊

I barely slept for the rest of the night. I was hypersensitive to every little sound. Even if Templeton hadn't been part of the attack on Blackstone and poor Elsa, and even if he hadn't stolen the book of fairytales, he was still dangerous. And yet, my father traveled with him and they had some sort of a relationship. He even advocated for Templeton and wanted to help him learn how his talents and powers could be used for the good of the Empire. I didn't think my father was a fool, but maybe he was too much of an optimist where Templeton was concerned.

When I finally did relax, it was only minutes before the alarm woke me. I groaned and my stomach grumbled. I wasn't looking forward to fumbling my way through the day on an empty stomach. I'd get directions to the pier where the ferry would be arriving first thing. And then I'd find coffee. Coffee was crucial.

I pulled myself out of bed and shuffled into the bathroom. Looking back at me from the mirror was one pitiful face. Dark circles exaggerated my tired eyes. Worry wrinkles replaced laugh lines. I splashed some lukewarm water on my face and sighed.

I didn't want to forget what I learned when I read the stolen letter last night in my dream. I used some paper and a pen from the nightstand.

It had been such a strange experience. I knew I'd definitely pulled Templeton into my dream. I was certain of it. But something had gone wrong at the end. I had started to wake up. I had gotten cocky, careless. Maybe that was it. I stopped focusing on staying in control. That gave Templeton room to take over. He saw the opportunity and he took it. He was right. I still needed to learn a thing or two.

I shook off my frustration and instead pictured the letter. Blackstone wrote that the Crimson Stone was in Vue and hidden in 'plain sight.' He noted that the stone was broken into three pieces so that the power could be kept under control and safely hidden.

This sounded familiar. Pulling The Book from

my bag, I flipped to the page about the girl who liked to play with pretty stones.

There is a Legend
about a child
who liked to play
with pretty stones.
One Stone was
Very Special.
She had to hide it,
so she put it in
Plain Sight
after breaking it into
three pieces.

It didn't exactly match what Blackstone had come up with, but it was pretty damn close. According to my father, this pretty stone was hidden in 'Plain Sight.' This wasn't particularly helpful, but maybe something would be obvious after I talked to Anne and Rabbit.

The sooner I packed and left, the sooner I could catch back up with my new friends. After dressing and making sure that The Book was back in my bag, I left. This time I took the elevator to the lobby. As I stepped out, I had a strange feeling someone was watching me. I looked around for any of the usual suspects: Templeton, the Empire guards, or worse, the Fringe.

No one. The coast was clear. I hiked my bag up and made a beeline for the exit. I had just passed through the doors and stepped out onto the sidewalk when a young woman stepped in front of me and blocked my way.

She was about eighteen or nineteen, dressed in ripped blue jeans tucked into a pair of brown hiking boots. The hood of her grey sweatshirt was up over her head and pulled tight. Black curls peeked out around her face. She wore a black leather jacket over the sweatshirt. Her face was red from the cold.

"Emily Swift?" Her breath puffed out into the crisp morning air.

"Um, maybe?" Smooth.

"Rabbit sent me. He told me you would need some information." Her black eyes glittered.

"Oh, okay. Yeah, I'm Emily."

She grinned. Her face resembled Rabbit's. "I kinda figured that out by now. Here." She gave me an envelope. "Rabbit said he'd meet you at the pier when the ferry docks at noon. If you see any Empire guards, just hang back. He'll find you. This is a map of Vue. I marked a route you can walk. You have plenty of time though."

"How did he know I was here?"

"Rabbits have a good network. Information travels fast."

"Well, thanks."

"No worries." She turned and headed down the street.

"Hey, I didn't catch your name," I called after her.

She glanced over her shoulder and gave me a funny look. "It's Rabbit."

I watched her walk away. I didn't really get it, but I was getting used to not getting it. I took the map out of the envelope and looked at the route. The pier was about ten blocks away. A cold walk, but I had plenty of time. I would find a coffee shop on the way. Somewhere in Vue was a bagel and coffee with my name on it. Hopefully fifteen dollars American would cover it.

Pulling the collar up on my coat, I set off in the direction of the pier. Although the air was brisk, the sun was out. The sidewalks were relatively clear of snow and ice. I thought about the past few days as I walked, looking for details I might've missed.

I realized Blackstone didn't mention Templeton in his letter to Spell. I wondered if that meant anything. Surely he would want to tell her I saw Templeton standing over him in the library? But Blackstone didn't include it. There was no way it was an oversight.

After walking a couple of blocks, I popped into a corner diner and ordered a coffee and plain bagel at the counter. The waitress barely gave me a second look as she scribbled on her pad and turned away. I didn't dare pull out The Book, but I was anxious to go through it again. The Crimson Stone was in Vue, according to Blackstone. If that was true, I wondered if my father noted it somewhere in his journal.

The coffee was surprisingly good and the bagel was toasted to perfection with a swipe of cream cheese across both halves. I ate it slowly and stared out the window facing the street.

Now that I knew what the letter said, finding Templeton wasn't the next step. Beating him to the Crimson Stone was. Getting the book of fairytales back from the Fringe only mattered if I couldn't find the stone. If I had the opportunity to get it back, I would. Then again, I should probably avoid the Fringe altogether.

My head hurt.

CHAPTER 19

I hoped Rabbit got a message to Jack. I knew I'd only been gone for a couple of days, but so much had happened. I assumed he heard about the attacks on Havers and the Court. I hated not being able to call him and tell him myself that I was okay. Clueless, a little lost, and pretty much broke, but okay.

As I sipped my coffee, I thought the man across the street looked familiar. He emerged from a sleek, black car and stood on the sidewalk talking to another man. I studied him for a second longer before he put on a top hat. I realized it was Tahl Petrovich. What was he doing in Vue?

The two men turned and went inside the building. I was relieved they didn't head for the diner. I didn't want to push my luck, so I took one last gulp of my coffee and left several dollars on the counter beside my empty plate. I slipped out of the diner and put as much distance as I could between Petrovich and myself. It bothered me that he was here.

I had time before the ferry arrived. As I walked, I took in the different shops and studio storefronts. A couple of short blocks from the pier I passed an old antiques shop. In the window sat the usual trinkets and knickknacks, but what caught my eye was a small top hat, black with a pink ribbon and a flirty purple feather. It was definitely made for a girl. I smiled. I would wear a hat like that. Well, at least now that I was a Salesman.

I glanced at the door. An 'Open' sign hung in the window, inviting me in. I wasn't in Vue for pleasure, but the pier wasn't far and I still had time to kill.

I walked into the shop and much like Anne's café, little India bells tinkled as the door shut behind me. Inching my way around several tables stacked with odds and ends, I was careful not to knock anything over. The shop was packed with clutter. To reach the window I had to walk through a maze of haphazardly arranged furniture, racks of old coats, and wooden boxes filled with gaudy costume jewelry.

As I moved, a sleek black cat jumped up on an old desk.

"Well hello there," I said. "I didn't expect to see you popping up."

"She's good at that." A woman appeared from behind a wardrobe. She was short and wiry, with blazing red hair. The color was the result of a bottle, not genetics. "That's why I call her Trouble."

I scratched the cat under her chin as she purred, her eyes closing. "She's a pretty girl."

"What are you looking for today?" The woman smiled at me.

If it were only that simple, I thought. But I motioned to the top hat in the window. "I saw the hat and thought I'd try it on."

"Certainly! Do you need help getting it?"

"Actually," I leaned across a dresser, "I think I've got it." My fingers caught the brim and I pulled the hat from the window. It was light, but sturdy. I was surprised at how well it was made. "It's really nice."

"It is. It was made by a talented milliner decades ago. You should try it on. You have a fine-featured face. This hat wouldn't overwhelm it."

I picked my way back through the furniture. A cheval mirror sat near the checkout counter. I stepped in front of the mirror and put the hat on my head. It fit perfectly.

"Now that is very pretty," the shopkeeper said. "It was made for you!"

I had to agree, it looked good. The stack was shorter than those I'd seen worn by the other Salesmen. Then again, so far I had only seen male Salesmen in their hats. This brim seemed more feminine too. The sides curved up slightly creating the perfect shelf for the pale pink ribbon and the flamboyant purple feather on the right. A black ribbon wrapped all the way around the stack.

"I love it," I admitted. "But I'm short on cash

today. How much is it?"

"For you, let's make it an even one hundred."

"That's fair, but I'll have to come back." I handed the hat to her.

"Sure. I'll even set it aside for you."

"Oh, I appreciate it. But it might not be for a couple of days." At least.

She shrugged. "You'll be back." She pressed a business card into my hand. "So you don't forget where to find it."

I smiled and said thanks, before giving the hat one last look. That hat was definitely meant for my head. Funny, a week ago I wouldn't have been interested in trying on a top hat.

I stepped outside and glanced at the map from the female Rabbit. I was still on course. I was also going to be there in plenty of time. The sun continued to rise in the sky and it was finally getting warmer. I opened my coat as I considered my route.

Leading up to the pier was a block of tourist shops and restaurants. The pier itself was nestled in a park. The paths spiraling through appeared to be shoveled and the sun was melting away what little slush had been left behind on the stones. I hefted my bag up higher on my shoulder and crossed the street to the park. I hustled along, keeping an eye out for the Fringe and Empire guards. So far I didn't see either. Not a top hat in sight.

The snow dripped off of the evergreen branches. The park was decked out for the upcoming holiday and some trees were strung with white lights and garland. It was probably pretty at night.

The park was empty except for a few joggers. I picked my way past several benches and I could see Sight Sea. Sunlight bounced off of the surface and I shielded my eyes. No sign of the ferry yet.

Rounding a corner, I walked past a small gazebo. I wished I had a pair of sunglasses, but I hadn't thought about it when I packed. I squinted and glanced ahead.

That's when I saw my father. I froze, my breath catching in my chest.

He stood on a pedestal about three feet off of the ground. The statue was made of bronze and whoever created the sculpture captured his likeness perfectly. It looked exactly like him. I walked the path to the monument. When I reached his feet, I looked up.

The statue was larger than life, and my father towered over me. He wore his top hat, of course, and a long coat over his suit. The coat billowed out slightly behind him as if he were facing into the wind. His hands were placed on his hips. Even though his pose was still, the statue appeared to be in motion.

I studied his face, noting how the artist managed to capture every detail, from the beginnings of lines around his eyes, to the small bump along the bridge of his nose. This was my father at thirty-five.

He wasn't smiling, but the expression was kind, confident. And yet, this wasn't the father I knew as a child. This was my father as a leader in the Empire looking into the future. His eyes saw nothing at his feet, but his gaze stared out over Sight Sea.

A plaque had been set into the pedestal base. His name and dates of birth and death appeared at the top. Underneath it said:

A Respected Salesman
A Leader for the Empire
A Uniter
A Visionary
A Hero

I nodded before looking up at my Dad again. "And husband and a father."

A bench faced the statue and I sat down. As a little girl I loved my father very much, and he was wonderful when he wasn't traveling, but why hadn't we been included in his world – in this world? People here knew about us. Anne knew exactly who I was that first meeting in her café. She even knew who my mother was. Why hadn't my father told us about the Empire? Why didn't he trust us?

Maybe Blackstone could give me these answers once everything died down. Assuming it would die down, of course.

I stayed on the bench until I decided to go scope out the dock and find a place to wait for Anne and Rabbit. Any further conversation with my father's likeness would have to be put on hold. He wasn't saying much anyway.

I walked farther through the park and down toward the dock. The ferry terminal was busy with travelers and workers. I didn't see any Empire guards, but I hung back as Rabbit directed. I half-leaned, half-sat on a large stone planter off to the side and away from the main traffic. I could see where the ferry would arrive.

While I waited, I wondered if Templeton was any closer to finding the stone. The letter Blackstone wrote was pretty vague. I hoped the actual passage in the book of fairytales was even more so. I also realized that both Templeton and the Fringe might have information about where the Crimson Stone was hidden that Blackstone did not have. This worried me. Plus, Templeton had magical abilities at his disposal. For all I knew his magic eight ball was giving him more answers than mine.

I pulled The Book from my bag and flipped through, looking for more passages about the 'pretty stone,' or even more specific, the Crimson Stone. I couldn't find anything. I felt like The Book was holding back. I stared out across the water and thought about lunch instead.

Just as my stomach started to talk back to me – I'd been fantasizing about Swiss-artichoke quiche from *The Green Bean* – I saw the ferry appear as a dot on the horizon. More activity kicked up in the terminal as people prepared to leave and workers prepared to get them on the ferry with only moderate chaos. It wasn't the biggest ferry I'd ever seen and this one only carried people. It wasn't big enough to carry cars or trucks.

It took a while for the ferry to dock and allow passengers to disembark. I kept on the lookout for Anne and Rabbit. Finally I saw them cross the gangplank and step onto the dock. Rabbit motioned toward the terminal and I watched them come through the doors.

I waited until Rabbit turned in my direction and gave a little wave. He caught the movement and taking Anne's arm, they hurried over.

"Oh Emily, I was so worried!" Anne gave me a big hug.

"I know, it was crazy and I'll fill you in on everything." I looked at Rabbit. He smiled at me, but his wary eyes kept flicking around the terminal. "Should we get a move on it?"

"Wouldn't hurt," he answered. "This way."

Anne and I followed Rabbit through a side door and we quickly moved away from the people coming and going. After putting some distance between us and the busy crowd, we stopped.

"I have so much to tell you both," I said.

"I bet, but first we have a message for you." She motioned to Rabbit and he nodded.

My heart took a little leap. "Really? From Jack?"

"He said he's been worried, and to try to keep in better touch. He got the message I sent last night. I told him you were okay after the attack on Court, and that you're going after the Crimson Stone."

"Oh boy." I imagined Jack's blood pressure was on the rise.

"I heard from Blackstone too. I sent a message about Templeton stealing the letter and told him the Fringe has the book of fairytales," Rabbit said.

"What did he say?" I hoped Blackstone didn't think I was completely incompetent for letting Templeton take the letter.

"He said to be careful, but you must find the Crimson Stone before the Fringe. He said it's definitely in Vue, and to look for a magic man."

"A magic man?" I asked.

"That's what he said. Oh, and your friend Tara sent a few messages along with Jack's." Rabbit continued. "Someone named O'Connell called her and asked if she had seen you and if you left town."

That was bad. I winced. If I survived my time in the Empire, I might not survive the legal troubles I would find myself in back home.

"There's more." Rabbit grinned. "She wants to tell you to be on the lookout for a 'gang called The Rabbits.' Her sources tell her they might have information about the missing book of fairytales."

"A gang, huh?"

He shrugged, still smiling. "We've been called worse. Your friend also said Jack is trying to keep his temper under control after the incident, but she doesn't know how long he'll last."

"Incident?" That couldn't be good.

"Yup. When they heard about the attack on the Court, Jack grabbed Blackstone and threatened to call the police unless you were brought home immediately. Tara had to intervene."

"Damn." This was bad. Jack was not one to get physical when he was angry. "What happened?"

"Blackstone told him he'd do his best." Rabbit waved a hand. "They'll work it out."

I dropped my head back and looked up to the sky. If my relationship survived this, I'd be amazed. I shook my head. "Okay, I can't worry about this now. What else?"

Anne spoke up. "Rabbit saw you in a dream on the train. Emily, you pulled him into your dream!"

I turned to Rabbit and he nodded. I pictured

the scenes from the dream. That's right, Rabbit was there. He'd opened his eyes and asked me where I was. It never occurred to me that Rabbit was pulled in like Templeton. I hadn't realized I was dreaming until after he was gone. By then, I was focused on getting Templeton.

"The good thing is it gave me a clue that you were already in Vue," he said.

"Really? How?"

Rabbit frowned. "It was strange. When I realized I was in your dream, I could see this little light flickering along the edge of it. I could hear a bell tolling the hour in the distance. I knew it was one of the towers in Vue. Then I woke up."

"But I don't understand why you were there," I started.

"Me either. This was a first for me. The minute I woke up I sent out a message to some Rabbits in the area to see if they could find you. We got lucky at about seven this morning. Someone overheard a guy talking at a breakfast counter. Apparently a 'young female Salesman' appeared in his tub the night before at the Bedrest Inn. We knew it had to be you." He laughed. I felt my face turn pink. "Anyhow, I put a Rabbit there to catch you before you left this morning. Others were on alert in the area in case she missed you."

"Incredible," I was astounded.

"Rabbits," Anne said. "You cannot beat their network. No one can match them."

"I owe you so much," I said to Rabbit. "I really mean it."

"No worries." He shrugged.

"Okay, so here's the question," Anne interrupted. "Who were you pulling into your dream?"

"Templeton."

Rabbit's black eyebrows shot up and he laughed. "I bet he loved that!"

"He was a little annoyed, for sure." I laughed too. It felt good. "I need to tell you both about it though."

"We want to hear all about it," Anne said. "But have you eaten yet?"

"A bagel this morning, but I'm still hungry," I admitted. "I'm also really low on cash. Sorry."

"Don't apologize," Anne said. "Let's go to my girlfriend's house. We can count on her to keep our secret and she loves to feed people. From there we can figure out what to do next."

❋ ❋ ❋

Anne's friend lived in an apartment not far from downtown Vue. The city itself was smaller than Matar and Anwat. It had a strong art scene. We passed many small galleries as we walked.

I told Anne and Rabbit about the statue of my father. This was the first Anne had heard about it, but Rabbit said he remembered seeing it soon after it was completed. A local artist in Vue created it in the year after the explosion.

I learned my father was a great supporter of the artist community in Vue. He supported their efforts to incorporate art in everyday life, whether it was a large mural of daisy seeds and fluff blowing from stem to sky covering the side of a building, to a series of wire statues of geese taking flight from one of the park's ponds and up into the air, or the musicians who performed there in summertime venues. He delivered a stirring speech in that very park calling on those who benefitted from the art to support those who created it.

It didn't surprise me, considering my mother's passion for painting, sculpting, and building. I told Anne and Rabbit my mother was an artist too. They just smiled and nodded.

"Lydia has inspired many people," Anne said.

"Have you seen her work?" I asked.

"You might say that." She stopped. "Here we are. This is Tuesday's building."

"Tuesday?"

"That's her name," Anne told me.

"Oh."

An old, but tidy brick building was nestled in between yet another art gallery and a spa. Downstairs hosted a bakery called *The Sweet Spot*. Just standing outside made my stomach rumble. Rabbit raised his eyebrows and glanced at my midsection. I pulled my coat around me and looked the other way.

A door leading to the upstairs met the sidewalk. We climbed the stairs to the second floor where Anne rang the bell. A moment later, a tiny but spherical woman with flour in her grey hair opened the door. She reminded me of a plump, aging hippie.

"Annie!" She clapped two pudgy hands together. "I should have guessed you were coming! All my teacups keep rattling in the cupboards when I'm not in the kitchen."

I gave Anne a funny look, but she just smiled down at her friend. "Sorry about that, Tuesday. I know we're probably imposing, but we just got to Vue and need to put up our feet while we regroup."

Tuesday leaned around Anne. "Hmm, a Rabbit and a Salesman. What are you up to Miss Annie?" Tuesday laughed and stepped back. "Come in! Come in!"

I followed Anne and Rabbit into Tuesday's huge apartment. I realized the glorious scent of fresh baked goods wasn't just coming from the bakery downstairs. Tuesday was baking up a storm in her big kitchen.

"Tuesday owns *The Sweet Spot*," Anne explained. "She experiments here in her own kitchen first."

The apartment had a partially open floor plan. From where I stood, I could see counters and plates filled with cookies and pastries. My mouth started to water.

"Are you all hungry?" Tuesday asked.

"We could eat," Anne said shrugging.

"Good! Have a seat at the table and I'll bring in a lunch puff for each of you." Tuesday waved us off to a round kitchen table stuffed into a corner and skipped off around a counter. I was surprised at how light she was on her feet. We'd barely taken off our coats and sat down when she carried over a tray with plates of food and cups for tea. The woman was surprisingly fast.

"This one is filled with a delicious veggie stuffing." She set a plate in front of Rabbit. "And for the ladies, egg and cheese filled puffs. And here's a little tea – use milk and sugar for this blend. It should go well with the pastries too. So, what do you think?" She pressed her hands together and waited, bouncing on the balls of her feet. She was a giggle in people form.

"It smells great." I dug in. It was wonderful. Tuesday could bake a delicious dish, no doubt about that. My friends agreed and Anne used the tea pot to fill our cups.

"I've been adding non-dessert pastries to the lunch menu. I'm picking up quite a crowd." Tuesday's face dimpled. "I'm always looking for people to try my new recipes."

"This is really good," Rabbit told her. "I'll tell my friends to stop here for lunch when they're in downtown Vue."

"Oh, I just love Rabbits! They are so much fun! Yes, please tell them to stop by." Tuesday gave a little hop around the table.

"Tell me," she leaned toward Anne and whispered. "What new trouble are you up to now? Rabbits and Salesmen? Unannounced visits? I smell adventure!"

"I hate to interrupt," I cut in, "but how do you know I'm a Salesman?"

"Well, aren't you?" she asked.

"Er, yes?"

"There you go." Tuesday shook her finger at me before skittering back to the kitchen. "You'll want dessert," she called over her shoulder.

Rabbit seemed unfazed and concentrated on his veggie pastry. Anne winked at me. "Tuesday is special. She's a little like your mother."

"Enough said. I won't go there then." I shook my head. Tuesday hummed as she rattled plates and checked on her ovens. I looked at Rabbit and Anne. "Can we talk here?"

"Certainly," Anne said. "Tuesday won't repeat anything."

"Well," I began, "about the dream I had last night."

"The one you pulled me into," Rabbit said.

"Yes, but remember, I wasn't trying to pull you into it. Just Templeton."

"It is strange," Anne agreed. "But go on. What happened?"

"Templeton was NOT a happy camper," I said.

"I bet," Anne replied. "Why don't you start at the beginning? How did you get off of the train in the first place?"

"Through a door."

Anne sat back in her chair. "You can door travel from a train. I don't know many Salesmen who would try it." Rabbit nodded in agreement.

"I really didn't know what else to do. I just tried to get a bead on Templeton and I think I lucked out."

"Or not," Rabbit said.

"What do you mean?" I asked.

"We think you've got a knack for door travel. Maybe you need some training, but you're already figuring out how to tap into the right energy to find the right doors." Rabbit finished his lunch puff. He looked toward the kitchen and added under his breath, "I hope she has carrot cake."

"Maybe I am getting the hang of it in some situations, but my landings are a little rough," I continued. Okay, a lot rough.

Anne chuckled. "That's right. What did the man say? A bathtub?"

"At least there wasn't any water in it. And the

man wasn't too freaked out by my arrival. I guess his nephew is a Salesman too."

"Hmm. Hopefully he won't mention you to his nephew. Word travels fast and we need to find the stone before someone finds you," Anne said.

"I know." As we finished our lunch puffs, I told Anne and Rabbit everything. I explained how I was able to pull Templeton into my dream and read the letter he stole from Blackstone. I also told them that something changed during the dream, and that Templeton seemed to take over. I told them my theory of losing focus and waking up.

"He's powerful," Rabbit said. "And he has a lot more experience than you do."

"True," I agreed.

"I don't know a lot about this kind of magic," Anne said, "but environmental stability is really important when you're doing dreamwork."

"What do you mean?"

"Well, you weren't close to your sleeping self, were you? You were on the train with us, in a way. I'm betting it created some instability in keeping control of the dream. Add to it that you started to wake up. You said Templeton knew you weren't on the train when you fell asleep?" Anne asked.

"Right. He seemed happy about it."

"I bet that's what happened then. He realized

your control was less than you thought you had. Actually – and I'm just guessing now – I bet you had about the same amount of control, but like Rabbit said, Templeton has more experience." Anne paused and turned to Rabbit. "Wouldn't it be something if she had the same abilities as our Templeton? Maybe she just needs the knowhow and some practical experience?"

"Let's not go there. I want to show you something else. I found this in my father's journal." I pulled out The Book and opened to the passage about the 'pretty stone.' "Here. I think he's referring to the Crimson Stone. Both Blackstone and my father wrote about hiding the stone in 'plain sight.' See?"

There is a Legend
about a child
who liked to play
with pretty stones.
One Stone was
Very Special.
She had to hide it,
so she put it in
Plain Sight
after breaking it into
three pieces.

Anne read the passage. "I think you're right. I wonder who the child is in your father's note. Is it you?"

"No, I don't think so. I don't remember playing with anything like that. But I do think it's a clue. He says the stone is hidden out in the open, and that it's probably in three pieces."

"But where is 'plain sight'?" Anne asked. "That could be anywhere."

"I'll send out a message to the Rabbits and see if anyone ever heard of a place called 'plain sight.' Maybe we'll get a hit." Rabbit texted with one hand.

"Maybe you can door travel to the Crimson Stone like you door traveled off of the train and to Templeton?" Anne suggested.

I shook my head, knowing it wouldn't work. I needed more than just the desire to find it – I needed to attach an emotion to it. Leaning back in my chair, I shoved my hands into my pockets. I realized I still had the business card from the antique shop. I pulled it from my pocket and twirled the card between my fingers. The shopkeeper was nice. I wondered if the hat would still be there when I went back to buy it. It really did look like it was made for me. I sighed, wishing I had the extra cash to buy it now. I loved my father and appreciated having his top hat, but I wanted one of my own. I read the card again. I hadn't noticed the shop's name before. *Common Vue.* Underneath the name a tiny tagline appeared in parentheses: *For Un-Common Treasures.* I smiled. Cute. There was so much packed into that shop – how could anyone ever find anything? Between the furniture, the piles of clothing, the jewelry poking out from everywhere...

My head snapped up. *Common Vue*. The stone was hidden in 'Plain Sight.' Common could mean 'Plain,' right? Was Vue supposed to be view? To view something is to see it, right? See, sight? Plain Sight? On the shores of Sight Sea? Could I have really figured it out? Or was I completely off of my rocker?

Rabbit grinned. "You just thought of something."

I was reluctant to share. It was such a long shot. "I don't know. It's probably nothing, but I was in this antique shop today killing time while I was waiting. The name of the shop is *Common Vue*." I showed them the card. "*Common Vue*. Common might mean plain, right? And I know it's a stretch, but Vue could be 'view' as in v-i-e-w, and when you view something, you see it. So maybe view could equal sight. *Common Vue* equals Plain Sight. What do you think?"

Rabbit didn't answer. Anne cocked her head to the side. "Well," she began, "it's a stretch, but I suppose it could be possible."

"I know." I felt like an idiot. "I'm grasping at anything at this point. It's just a coincidence and not a very good one."

"Emily, haven't you realized there is more at work here than coincidence?" Anne asked.

"I know. But this one is pushing it." I reached for the card.

"What have we here?" Tuesday exchanged lunch plates for dessert plates. She saw the card as I picked it up. "*Common Vue*! I love that old antique store. Alice owns it."

"You know the owner?" Anne asked.

"I do. Real doll of a woman. Her father was a jeweler decades ago."

I looked at Rabbit. A grin slid across his face and Anne's eyes lit up.

"A jeweler, huh?" I repeated.

"Well, officially, yes. He made the most beautiful pieces. But everyone knows he really was a magic man." Tuesday bobbed her head.

"A magic man?" I repeated. A magic man who made jewelry? This had to be a sign.

"Yes." Tuesday didn't elaborate. Instead she turned to Anne. "Shall we go to the antique store? It sounds like it could be a fun part of your adventure!"

"We certainly can, Tuesday," Anne said. "We certainly can."

"This could be it." I pulled on my coat as I stood. "Let's go!"

CHAPTER 20

Our strange little group was growing. Tuesday was a welcome distraction as we walked, pointing out pieces of artwork in the different neighborhoods. It was a pretty city. Vue was home to many of the Empire's best artists and craftsmen. Because of its location on the other side of Sight Sea, the Fringe didn't seem to have a strong presence, preferring more industrial areas closer to Matar and Anwat.

Anne chatted with her old friend as we walked. Rabbit texted, glancing up every few seconds to take in the sights and sounds. His eyes and ears missed nothing. He was always gathering information. I could have sworn I saw his nose twitching every so often.

As much as I didn't want to be distracted by thoughts of home, I let myself think about Jack. I knew he was doing his best to be supportive, but it was a lot to swallow. I understood it was hard for him to believe any of this. I was living the story, but he was only hearing it secondhand. Someday I would have to find a way to make this new world of mine more real for him. I had to do what my father had not.

Rabbit's phone vibrated with a new message and he stopped when he read the message. He looked up and our eyes met. "I think I just got some bad news."

"Now what?" I asked.

"There's been a robbery at an antique shop near Port and Main."

"Oh god. That's *Common Vue*, isn't it?"

"I think so." He went back to texting, looking for more information.

Anne took one look at our faces. "What's going on?"

"It's the antique shop. It's been robbed." I felt helpless. "Anne, this can't be a coincidence."

"I don't think so either."

Tuesday's cheery expression disappeared. Her eyes grew watery. "Oh, Alice," she whispered.

Rabbit motioned for us to continue walking. "Come on. Let's see what we can find out."

The street leading to *Common Vue* was roped off by Empire guards. We couldn't get close and the crowd of curious onlookers was growing. I could see official Empire cars parked in front of the shop, and an ambulance sat with its lights on. Guards walked in and out of the shop. From where we stood, we couldn't see Alice.

"There's no way we are getting any closer," Anne said.

I nodded and turned to Rabbit. "What do you think?"

"I'll see what I can find out," he answered. "I'll move in closer."

"Maybe the rest of us should get out of here for now." Anne was wary. "We don't want the guards to see Emily."

"Good point," he agreed. "Go back to Tuesday's. I'll meet you there as soon as I've got some answers." With that, he slipped through the mob. Effortless.

Anne, Tuesday, and I pushed back through the crowd forming behind us. I pulled my hood up as we hurried away from the chaos.

"What about Alice?" Tuesday worried. I looked to Anne for help.

"We'll wait and see what Rabbit finds out." Anne put her arm around Tuesday. "Let's go back to the apartment."

The walk was a quiet one. Anne looked anxious, Tuesday was afraid, and I was definitely a nervous wreck. It had to be the Fringe or Templeton. Someone must've figured it out like just like I had. 'Plain Sight' equaled *Common Vue*. And then they beat me back to the shop. I hoped Alice was okay, but deep down, I had a horrible feeling. I knew Rabbit wouldn't bring us good news.

So now what? I needed to know if the Crimson Stone was found. If it was, I had to find out who had it. Then I needed to figure out how to get it back. Sure. Easy.

One thing at a time. First, I needed to know if the stone was still in the antique shop. If Rabbit couldn't answer that, I'd have to go there myself. I'd have to door travel. I hoped I could land in the right place.

"As soon as Rabbit gets back," I said, "we'll figure out what our next steps are going to be. We'll come up with a new plan."

❊ ❊ ❊

It seemed as though we waited forever for Rabbit to return, but it was only a little over an hour. Tuesday sat fidgeting at the table drinking a cup of tea. I raised my eyebrows at Anne when she set the hot cup in front of Tuesday.

"This will help you relax a bit, dear." Anne put her hand on Tuesday's shoulder and I saw her lips move. I had a feeling this tea had a little something extra in it.

A knock of the door signaled Rabbit's return. He entered with a grim face.

"Alice?" I asked. He shook his head no.

"Oh!" A soft sob slid through Tuesday's lips.

"Tuesday, we're not going anywhere for now. How about you take a little rest in the other room? I know this is a terrible shock." Anne helped Tuesday to her feet. "If you nap now, you'll feel a bit better when you wake up. I'll have something to eat for all of us then, okay?"

Tuesday nodded and allowed Anne to shuffle her off to the bedroom. When Anne returned, we all sat down at the table.

I folded my arms and leaned against the table. "What happened?"

"The Empire guards are calling it a robbery-murder," he began. "The shop was open for business, so no one needed to break in. The cash register was open, and Alice was found on the floor."

"How was she," I winced. I tried again. "How was she killed?"

"It looks like she was hit over the head with something, but I couldn't find out if they had the weapon"

"Did they think anything else was stolen?"

"The shop was tossed. They think the killer was looking for something, but the guards don't know if anything was stolen. There's another employee who helped Alice at the shop. They're trying to locate her so she can go through things to see if anything besides money is missing." Rabbit shook his head. "The shop is going to be closed off for now. I'm sure the guards will keep their eyes on it."

"No strolling through the front door," Anne said.

"I guess I'll have to use a different door," I told them.

"What's the plan?" Anne asked.

"Tonight, when it's dark and people can't see in through the window, I'm going to door travel in and look around. I'll go when it's really late. If the stone is still there, I'll find it." Or at least I hoped I'd find it. "We've got to get our hands on it so innocent people like Alice aren't killed!"

Anne made a face. "I don't know, Emily. Even if you can door travel successfully into the shop, there's no guarantee the stone is still there. And if it is, you still don't know what it looks like. This is a dangerous idea." Anne turned to Rabbit. "What do you think?"

"It's definitely a dangerous idea, but it might be the only way to go about it now. We can follow on foot. Once Emily is inside, she can let us in."

I shook my head no. "I don't think that'll work. If the guards are watching the shop, you won't be able to get close."

"Maybe the back door?" Anne suggested.

"They'll probably be watching front and back," I told her.

"I still think Anne and I should follow you. At least we'll be near. If we can get closer to the shop, we will. We might catch a break."

I wasn't sure if Rabbit was right, but it couldn't hurt to have them close by.

"Okay. We'll stay here for now. I'll try to door travel tonight. I'll aim for midnight."

❋ ❋ ❋

I was ready. I felt confident. I could do this. No problem. This would be easy.

I was lying.

It was close to midnight and I'd asked for some privacy while I prepared to travel back to *Common Vue*. Tuesday gave up her bedroom and I planned to travel through her closet door right into the antique shop. I sat on the bed, my heart thumping in the quiet. I took a deep breath. Okay, I would settle myself and concentrate on my first visit to the shop. I pictured the top hat I had tried on. I would remember the friendly conversation with poor Alice. I would focus on the good vibes coming off of all the old antiques.

Right. I stood up and placed my father's top hat on my head. It slid down over my ears, but I was glad I had it. I made sure my bag was secure on my shoulder. Taking a breath, I held my hand up in front of Tuesday's closet door. Closing my eyes, I thought about the antique shop, Alice, and even her black cat Trouble. I pictured the top hat with the purple feather. I waited for the door to talk to me, to hum and vibrate and pull me through.

And waited.

Nothing.

I opened an eye. The closed door remained silent. I took another deep breath. Let's try this again. I closed my eyes and held up both hands.

I pictured the inside of *Common Vue* – the walls, the furniture, the boxes crammed full of costume jewelry.

Again nothing. This was not working.

I heard a tap on the bedroom door. Anne peeked in.

"We wondered if you had left yet," she said. "We want to make sure we leave as soon as you're gone."

"I'm working on it, but I can't get the door to hum."

"Are you focusing on your feelings about the shop?"

"I'm trying, but something isn't right." I looked at the closet door. "You know what, Anne? This isn't the right door. That's the problem. I need to find a different door."

"Do you want to try another room?"

We left Tuesday's bedroom and joined the others.

"It's not working for her," Anne told them. "It's not the right door."

"Maybe she should go find it then," Tuesday suggested.

"It's not that simple," I began.

"It probably is," Tuesday interrupted. "You're a Salesman. That's what you do." Her head bobbed up and down. She pointed a pudgy finger at me. "We all have magic inside us, Emily. You can door travel. You should just go find the right door instead of trying to turn the wrong door into the right one."

The strange little woman was probably right.

Rabbit slapped the top of the kitchen table where he sat. "Sounds like a good plan. Let's go for a walk." As we left, he looked at Anne. "Be ready to go when I get back. I'll come get you and we'll catch up with Emily at the shop."

"You make it sound so easy," I said to him as we walked out into the hall.

"I found out a long time ago that things only become complicated when people make them that way. Like Tuesday said, you're a Salesman. So, do what you do best."

We made our way out onto the sidewalk. It was bitterly cold. I carried my father's top hat in my bare hand and thought about what Rabbit had said. He meant well, but he wasn't right. Door travel was not what I did best. Loving Jack, hanging out with Tara, running my little copywriting business – that's what I did best. Door travel was a bizarre blend of making mistakes and getting lucky.

I looked down at the top hat and thought about everything Rabbit described at the scene of the train wreck. He had found the hat and kept it, but how had the hatpin found its way back to my mother's house?

"Rabbit?"

"Yeah?"

"My father's hatpin was not with the hat when you found it?"

"No."

"Oh."

"Maybe whoever delivered The Book to your mother made sure the hatpin went with it."

I thought about it. "But how did they even get the book?"

Rabbit didn't answer. He fell silent as our boots clopped against the sidewalk. Only a little ice remained after the sunny weather. I had a hard time understanding how things could change in such a short amount of time. In one week my world turned upside down. In one week I'd gone from a happy, uneventful life, to a crazy one of traveling through doors, searching for magical stones, and being chased by dangerous people who probably wanted to kill me. This was not fun.

But at the same time, I knew how important it was to keep the Fringe from getting more power. For some strange reason, I cared about the Empire already. Maybe it was in my genes. Or maybe it was because I saw how the violence in the Empire might bleed over into my world. I wanted to protect the people I loved and cared about, too.

I had to find the magical stone and make sure it stayed out of the wrong hands. I wanted to make sure people inside and outside of the Empire were safe. I didn't want the bad guys to win. I wanted to fix whatever was set in motion when I turned thirty. Templeton needed to have his wings clipped. Blackstone should never have been attacked. Elsa, Havers, and Alice shouldn't have been killed because of me. Three people dead!

And whoever killed my father needed to be brought to justice.

I had to get inside *Common Vue*.

I stopped on the sidewalk. "Do you hear that?"

Rabbit stopped and cocked his head to the side. "Hear what?"

"The hum." I looked around. "That's it." The door leading into a chocolaterie hummed faintly. It called to me as I got closer. I put my father's top hat on and reached for the knob. I could feel the energy start to crackle off of it.

"Is it the right door?" Rabbit asked.

"Yes! Go back for Anne! I'm going to the antique shop!" I grasped the knob and pushed the door forward. I felt a whooshing sound race past my ears and I stumbled, but this time I stayed on my feet. I shuffled forward and froze, holding my breath as I realized I was in a dark room. I wasn't on the street with Rabbit.

"Okay, get a grip." I shook off a shiver and waited until my eyes adjusted to the dim light. I listened, noting only a ticking clock and the normal settling sounds of an old building in winter. A couple of minutes later, I could see the outlines of stacked furniture and a door leading out to the main floor of the antique shop. I was in! I bit back my quiet celebration and tiptoed to the door, pressing my ear to it. The shop was empty.

As quietly as I could, I opened the door, wincing as it creaked. I just needed to figure out where the Crimson Stone was hidden and I could get out of there. I left the door open behind me and gently made my way through the maze of furniture. Rabbit was right. The place was tossed. Chairs were knocked to their sides and drawers had been pulled out and emptied.

I was careful not to touch anything; however, I was sure any fingerprints I left could be explained away by my earlier visit. Still, no need to add any more trouble for myself.

The counter where the robbed cash register sat was roped off with yellow Empire guard 'do not cross' tape. I stayed away. My sense was Alice had been killed there. The energy in the room now had such a desperate, painful feeling to it. For a moment I allowed myself to grieve for the friendly shopkeeper. I swallowed the lump in my throat. She'd said she knew I'd be back.

The light from the window facing the street made it a little easier to see around the room. I didn't know exactly what I was looking for, but my intuition told me that the stone would be in three pieces. If Alice's father was a jeweler and a 'magic man,' he might have known that the Crimson Stone was too powerful to leave in one piece. Would he have broken it? Was Alice the child who played with pretty stones? Did she hide it in 'plain sight'? Would I ever get an answer to any of my questions?

If I were a jeweler and wanted to break a stone into three pieces but keep it together, I would make it into a set. Maybe a necklace and a pair of earrings. I wandered, picking through a couple of jewelry boxes overflowing with costume jewelry. Of course, if the stones were set in different pieces, the potential for losing a piece of the stone increased. I thought of my own pairs of earrings that were missing mates.

No, Alice's father would've known better. It would be smarter to keep the three pieces together, like in a necklace or a bracelet. I walked toward the front of the store, stepping around a broken glass. In the window, near where the pretty top hat had once caught my eye, there were several items on display. I moved in closer to get a better look, taking care to stay out of sight in case the Empire guards were watching the antique shop.

A sign on the old rack read 'Not for Sale – For Display Only.' There were lace handkerchiefs, a couple of decorative hand mirrors, antique pens and inkwells, and several pieces of jewelry. I leaned forward, noting a necklace set at the back of the display, half-hidden by a dark-colored scarf. I carefully pushed the material to the side. Three reddish stones hung heavy in a setting of ornate silver. The necklace dangled innocently from two small hooks. I held my breath. Could it be? Could this be the Crimson Stone? The moon tossed a beam of light through the window and touched the necklace. Three crimson-colored stones glittered in the night.

"Oh, my god," I whispered. "I found it."

I was just about to reach for the necklace when I heard a noise. I stepped back from the window and dove behind a rack of vintage clothing. I waited, my heart racing. I didn't know what to do. What if it was the Fringe? What would I do? I actually hoped it was Templeton. I didn't trust him, but I didn't think he'd kill me either.

As quietly as possible, I moved around the end of the clothing rack, trying to see through the darkness. Maybe it was the building settling again. Maybe it was the wind outside. Maybe it was my imagination.

I stepped toward the counter where Alice was killed. I didn't see anyone. The door to the back room was still open. "Okay," I breathed. "It's okay, just building noises." I turned back around and ran smack into a dark figure.

"No!" I backpedaled into a display case and

lost my balance. Two strong hands grabbed me and pushed me into a table, knocking it over along with a set of dishes. I tumbled to my hands and knees with them. My bag slung forward on my shoulder, but I scrambled back to my feet. The figure moved closer and I realized he was wearing a top hat.

"Stay away from me!" I shouted. I reached behind me, struggling to find anything to protect myself and felt the chain to a floor lamp. I pulled it, causing the lamp to sway on its stand. The room filled with soft light. I hoped the Empire guards were indeed watching the building.

I looked at my attacker.

It was Tahl Petrovich.

"Looks like you have a knack for getting into trouble, Emily Swift." He took a step toward me.

"What are you doing here?" I tried to put the overturned table between us by edging around the side.

"I could ask you the same thing." He glared at me. "Of course, being a Justice in this Empire, I have far more of a right to be here than you: a lying, rogue Salesman."

"I am not a liar!" I yelled back. The bad feeling I had turned worse. "What are you doing here?"

Petrovich's gaze wandered around the shop. "I'm here to recover something for the Empire, Emily. Something very powerful. Something that cannot fall into the wrong hands." His smile was cold. "Do you know what I am looking for?"

"No." I willed my heartrate to slow down so I could catch my breath.

"See? You are a liar." Petrovich began to walk around the shop, poking through old jewelry boxes. No Empire guards came banging down the door when the light came on. Who knew what side the guards were on anyway? My only hope was that Rabbit and Anne would arrive soon.

"I don't know what you're looking for," I said.

"Then just what are you doing here?" He snorted. "Late night shopping? I know it's still here, unless you've found it?" His mean eyes narrowed. "Did you? Did you find the Crimson Stone?"

Petrovich knew. But who was he working for? The Empire? The Fringe? I had a hard time believing he was a representative of Beverly Spell. I shook my head no. "I don't have anything."

"Hmm, so you say." He continued to walk around the shop. "You couldn't find it this morning, so you came back tonight. Have you found it yet?"

"This morning?" I repeated. "What do you mean?"

"Still with the lies? Are you sure you want to keep lying to me? You will only make it worse for yourself."

I shook my head. "I was here this morning because I wanted to try on a top hat. That's why I came in here. That's the only reason why I came in here."

"Really? How interesting. And I thought the shopkeeper was lying, too." Petrovich clucked his tongue as he shook his head. "My mistake then."

"What do you mean you thought the shopkeeper was lying?" Then it hit me. "You killed Alice, didn't you?"

"Well, I only intended to question Alice. I thought she was pretending to be ignorant. Ironic that you would choose to stop at her store while you were being followed, isn't it? We probably would never have even looked here." Petrovich shrugged as if this were no big deal, just an amusing anecdote. Oh killing someone, you know. Such a lark.

Wait a minute, what did he say? "We?"

"Some associates. You've met a couple." He laughed. "But you keep giving them the slip, Emily. You know, they have little patience for chasing after you. When they catch you, it won't be pretty." Petrovich stopped walking around the room. "I want the Crimson Stone. Alice didn't have a clue. You must have it then."

"I couldn't find it in time," I told him. "I don't have it."

"How did you know it was here?"

"Templeton."

"Templeton told you?"

"Yes."

"You are not working with Templeton," Petrovich sneered.

"What do you want with the stone?" I edged away from the justice. "And I know it's not for the good of the Empire, so don't give me that crap."

"You know, you're right." Petrovich rummaged through another jewelry box. He pulled out a necklace with a lone – and presumably fake – ruby dangling from a gold chain. He squinted at it, holding it up for me to see. "This wouldn't be it, would it Emily?"

"I don't know." Maybe he would think the piece in his hand was the stone and leave. I wasn't going to hold my breath.

"No, this is cheap, costume junk. We'll just have to keep looking, won't we?" Petrovich tossed the jewelry back into the open box. "You know, Emily, you will never be a Salesman."

"Too late," I shot back. "I am one."

"You think even if the Fringe lets you live – and I doubt they will – that you have any chance of the Court approving you now? Why, you have operated in secret trying to find the Crimson Stone. You are clearly not trustworthy."

"That's not true! Beverly Spell knows the

truth!"

"Justice Spell," he said, "does not matter. When I get the Crimson Stone, she won't have any power to stop me. It's time for the Empire to go in a new direction."

"Your direction? Maybe the Fringe's direction? Let me guess, more power for them, less for everyone else?"

"You are just like your father. You believe you know what's best for everyone. You don't! Not everyone is equal, Emily. Many of us are better." Petrovich tossed out pieces of junk jewelry on the counter while he dug through a deep basket. He was ramping up. "Take the filthy Rabbits! They pay no taxes. They run wild all over the Empire. They serve no use to us. Absolutely no use! And they're extortionists! It's time they're dealt with."

"Dealt with?" I didn't like the sound of that. "What do you mean, dealt with?"

"Exterminated."

The vision that flashed through my mind terrified me.

"You really are a sick, rotten man," I spat. I made up my mind in that crystal clear moment. Even if I died in this room, Petrovich was not leaving with the Crimson Stone come hell or high water.

"She's right, Petro," said Templeton as he stepped from the shadows. "You really are."

CHAPTER 21

I jumped when Templeton appeared. Even Petrovich was startled. Templeton sighed as if he wore the weight of the world on his shoulders. "Oh come now, you're surprised to see me?"

"What are you doing here, Templeton?" Petrovich growled.

"The same thing you are hoping to do. Take the Crimson Stone." Templeton looked around. "It's quite the mess in here. What have you two been doing?"

I didn't let my eyes travel back to the necklace in the window. I was afraid I'd give it away.

Templeton strolled around the shop, picking up scarves and knickknacks. He rustled through a jewelry box. "Killing Alice White was sloppy, Petrovich. And even then you couldn't find the stone? All because you couldn't crack the code in the fairytale?"

Petrovich ignored me and followed Templeton as he wandered. "The book of fairytales is no longer of use. Tell me, Templeton. Why do you think the Crimson Stone is here?"

Templeton gave Petrovich a tired look. "One, because it is, and two, why else would you and Ms. Swift be shopping at such a late hour in a store closed off by the Empire guards? I doubt you're feeding some touristy retail addiction." He picked up a ceramic clown figurine that was more appropriate for a garage sale and viewed it with disgust.

"The Empire guards are not watching this shop. I sent them home." Petrovich's lips curled in an ugly smile.

Templeton set the tchotchke back on the counter and glided toward the front window. He hung back in the shadows as he looked at the display. I held my breath. Once again the Crimson Stone caught the moonlight as it came through the window. Templeton cut his eyes to me and smiled.

"Have you found the stone, Emily?" His voice was soft.

"No. I don't know where it is." I began to move toward the front door. I had no idea what I was going to do, but I wanted a clear escape route after I did it.

Templeton's laugh startled me. "Of course you do. You are not a convincing liar. You know exactly where it is."

Petrovich stepped in front of me, blocking my way. "You do have it!"

I shook my head no. Out of the corner of my eye I saw Templeton pluck the necklace from the display.

"Your father thought he could keep your family safe. Too bad you weren't traveling with him when he got on the train. We wouldn't have to waste time dealing with you now," Petrovich said.

"You knew about the bomb, didn't you? You set him up." How long had this man been an enemy of the Empire?

He shrugged. "He managed to get away from the Fringe during the Eve of Silence. Same with Spell. Didn't matter in the end. We knew what to do with your father."

"Except afterwards Spell got in your way, didn't she? Rallying the anti-Fringe movement?" Templeton stepped away from the window and back into the dim light of the room. "You couldn't do anything after that. The backlash against the Fringe was just too great. Spell couldn't prove anything then, but she knew about your involvement. She's kept you close all these years. Kept a watchful eye on you, Petro."

"I've had enough of this." Petrovich reached inside his coat and pulled out a gun. He chambered a round, the sound reverberating through the room. I stumbled backward as he pointed it at me. "Give me the stone, Emily."

"I don't have it."

"Now. No more games. Give me the damn stone!"

My eyes cut to the necklace in Templeton's

hand.

"Petrovich." He smirked, lifting it into the air.

Petrovich's eyes lit up. "Is... is that it?"

"Yes, Petro, this is the Crimson Stone. If you or your stupid associates would have been able to decipher the code in the legend, you would have known to look for the stone in three pieces. This necklace contains the stone." His eyes flicked toward me. "Right, Ms. Swift?"

I didn't answer. Templeton having the stone was only slightly better than Petrovich getting it. Well, maybe more than slightly, but it still wasn't a good thing. The gun pointed at my chest was a very bad thing.

"Templeton, this is your opportunity! Think of the power you'll have if you join with us. With the Crimson Stone, we could make this Empire into an unstoppable force! Everyone would have to submit to us. Let me take the stone. We'll pull together the Fringe and those who still support it. There are many! They know to trust me, and when they know you're on their side too, they'll give you whatever you want! You cannot imagine the money and power that could be yours."

Templeton looked disgusted. "Do you think I would be that stupid? I have no interest in being a part of your ridiculous cause. I have no interest in sharing power with you or anyone."

Petrovich pointed his gun at Templeton.

"That's not going to change my mind," Templeton told him.

Petrovich's eyes never left the necklace. The stones sparkled. "You will regret your decision. And I have no room for her in this Empire." Petrovich lifted his arm and pointed the gun back at me.

His hand was steady. I knew he would shoot me. He wanted to.

"I can't see how it's in your best interest to shoot her." Templeton yawned. "She's a nuisance, but her death would probably rally your opposition. Swift's daughter and all. It's not worth the bullet. Just ban her from the Empire and be done with it."

That made me take my eyes off of Petrovich's gun. I stared at Templeton. I couldn't believe what he said. He shrugged.

I finally found my voice. "You really are a jerk. You're no better than him."

"Actually, I am." With that, Templeton turned to leave the store. Petrovich pointed his gun toward Templeton's back.

"No, don't!" I took a step forward. Petrovich swung his gun back to me. I was getting dizzy.

"I think you better give me the stone, Templeton. Make no mistake. I will shoot her if you don't."

"He'll shoot me anyways." I felt as if I was going to be sick. I didn't want to be shot.

Templeton stood with one hand on the door. He lifted the necklace with his other hand and held it up to the light. After muttering a few quiet words, the stones began to shimmer.

"Do you even know how to use the Crimson Stone, Petro?" he asked. "What makes you think you can handle this kind of magic?"

"I have people who can handle it for me." Petrovich dumped the contents out of one of the wooden jewelry boxes and slid it across the top of a dresser. "Here. Put the stone into the box, Templeton. I'm not waiting any longer." The gun stayed leveled on me.

Templeton turned and took a few steps closer to Petrovich. He swung the silver necklace from side-to-side. His lip curled back. "And you really trust the people you surround yourself with? You're a fool."

"Put it into the box," Petrovich repeated.

Templeton's gaze drifted in my direction. I shook my head no. As much as I didn't want Templeton to keep the stone and leave me behind to be shot, I definitely didn't want Petrovich to have it. There were enough powerful bad guys in this world. I didn't want to be a martyr, either.

"Very well." Templeton closed the distance between the wooden box and himself. Petrovich watched him. He took his time opening it and adjusted the soft cloth inside.

"No more stalling," Petrovich ordered.

Templeton raised an eyebrow. "As you wish."

I watched as Templeton lowered the necklace into the box. He carefully turned the three stones so that the pieces fit together as they nestled into the satin. I heard a gentle click.

Templeton had reunited the three gem pieces into one 'pretty stone.'

I saw Petrovich frown. I realized he didn't understand that three gems in the necklace could be brought together as one stone. We all watched as it turned a vivid crimson and the light inside the stone started to move like tongues of fire.

"What are you doing?" Petrovich cried. He turned the gun toward Templeton and this time he pulled the trigger. Templeton was fast and dove behind the overturned table. I made my own escape behind an antique desk, hunkering down and sitting with my back against it.

I heard another shot and the sound of furniture being slammed. I poked my head around the desk's corner just in time to see Templeton take a hit to the chin. He swung back and Petrovich's gun was knocked loose and skidded into a corner. The Crimson Stone burned bright in Templeton's grasp.

"Give it to me!" Petrovich yelled, reaching for Templeton's hand as the two fell to the floor. Templeton was a lot stronger than Petrovich, but Petrovich was on top, giving him some leverage. He slammed Templeton's wrist against the floor, making him grunt in pain. Templeton's fingers relaxed just enough and the stone skittered across the floor.

Without thinking, I scrambled out from behind the desk on my hands and knees, grabbing the necklace and pulling it toward me. As my fingers wrapped around the Crimson Stone, it vibrated in my hand. I held on for dear life as I knelt, watching the two men struggle.

The door to the antique store smashed open and Rabbit barreled in shoulder first, stopping short when he saw Templeton and Petrovich fighting on the floor. Anne was right behind him. Before he could react, Anne grabbed his arm and cried out, "Rabbit, she's holding the stone! Emily, put it down! Put it down!"

Flames filled the stone and I could feel the energy throbbing in my hand. Heat pounded through my wrist and up my arm to my shoulder. I knew I shouldn't be able to hold onto it. The stone was made from magic. I sucked in a breath as the energy filled my chest. Sparks flew from the stone as I held it tightly.

Petrovich and Templeton were back on their feet and Anne's cries caught their attention. Whipping around, Petrovich let go of Templeton and glared at me. "Give it to me, you little witch!"

I wrapped both hands around the stone, feeling the energy circle through my body and down my left arm. I was afraid of Petrovich, but I was more afraid of what he would do with this kind of magic. I could feel it. I understood it. It was a force forged from all elements at work in this world, but it burned the brightest with fire. In my hands I held absolute power.

Petrovich had to be stopped. I could use the Crimson Stone to bring about a cleansing fire. The energy was wild, but already I could feel how to harness it. I could be an instrument of its power, a conduit. I held it up toward Petrovich as I kneeled. The stone began to hum. I thought about The Book and my father's words. I remembered the story of the girl who broke the pretty stone into three pieces.

Templeton climbed to his feet. His right arm was bleeding, and he held it with his left hand. Blood seeped through his fingers. His icy-blue eyes glittered like diamonds in the snow.

Use it, Emily, he said inside my head. You can stop him.

I can stop him, I repeated silently.

I didn't know any magical words or spells, but Petrovich was an enemy of the Empire. He had my father's blood on his hands. He was a killer. I stared at him, forcing away my hatred and instead focusing on the justice he deserved.

"Tahl Petrovich, never again will you have

the power to harm anyone in the Empire. You will no longer sit on the Salesman Court. You will never be able to deceive the people who truly do serve the Empire. You will be brought to justice. You will pay for your crimes!" The stone's hum swelled, filling the room with its song.

I felt the fire erupt through me and surround me. My hair lifted and crackled with static electricity. I held onto the energy as long as I could before releasing it toward Petrovich. The whole room flashed in a burst of crimson flame and Petrovich was blasted backward against a wall. He screamed in pain as he fell. But he quickly staggered back to his feet, lifting his hand. He had recovered the gun.

"No! I won't let you have it!" On his face I could see patches of pink where the fire had swept against him. The smell of burnt hair hit my nostrils. Petrovich pointed the gun at me and pulled the trigger. In an instant I was on the floor and Templeton was on top of me, his body covering mine. At the same time Rabbit dove at Petrovich, slamming him across a table. The gun went flying again. Anne ran after it and picked it up. She pointed it at Petrovich's head with shaking hands.

"Emily! Emily!" she called frantically.

I lay on my back staring into the strange depths of Templeton's almost translucent blue eyes. His breath was hot and labored on my face and his body was heavy on mine. The stone was still held tightly in my hand. My body hurt from being slammed into the floor, but I felt no other pain. I wasn't shot.

"Templeton! Are you shot?" The words tumbled out of my mouth in one breath.

"Just once." He rolled off of me and moved into a kneeling position, before rising from the floor and dragging me to my feet with his good arm. "He missed this time." Templeton looked at Rabbit and gave him a curt nod. Rabbit's glittering eyes registered the moment. His swiftness saved Templeton.

Rabbit held Petrovich to the table, bending his arm behind his back. I was surprised by the lean man's strength. Containing Petrovich looked almost effortless. Anne had calmed down, but her hands still shook as she held the gun on Petrovich. Templeton took it from her. "I should shoot you now and spare you the Fringe's retaliation," he said to the fallen justice. "You're useless without the stone and you know too much. The Empire won't protect you from them."

"Don't underestimate my power," Petrovich spat.

"Don't underestimate hers," Templeton shot back.

Hers?

Templeton looked at Rabbit. "Let him go. The

Empire will deal with him. Spell will see to it."

He reluctantly let Petrovich up. I remembered what Rabbit had told me about the scene of the train explosion. Now we knew Petrovich played a role in causing the carnage.

Petrovich stood, and although he struggled to keep his balance, he moved to the door to make his escape. I could see that the fire touched his hands and neck as well as his face. The burn marks were turning a vivid red against his skin. He gave Templeton a vicious look. "This is not over," he said.

"Wait, you're letting him go?" My mouth popped open. I held the Crimson Stone to my chest. It still vibrated, but the energy was controlled.

"Trust me, he's not going far." Templeton smirked. Two Empire guards appeared at the door. The first one grabbed Petrovich's arm and pushed him against the wall.

"What do you think you're doing?" Petrovich yelled as he tried to wrestle free. "Get your hands off of me!"

"Tahl Petrovich, by order of the Salesman Court and at the request of Justice Beverly Spell, you are hereby under arrest and charged with treason against the Empire. You will submit to this order immediately," the arresting guard said. The second guard pulled Petrovich's hands behind his back and put a pair of handcuffs on his wrists.

"I will not allow it! Do you know who I am? I will see both of you dead! Take these off of me! You will pay for this!" Petrovich nearly foamed at the mouth in his rage. Spit flew from his lips. I realized the fire had also burned hair off the side of his head. I looked away.

The first guard nodded to the second and they dragged him out through the smashed door. Rabbit pulled a chair from their path.

"We'll make sure he's returned to the Court immediately," the first guard said to me as he looked over his shoulder. Petrovich continued to fight on the sidewalk, attempting to kick the men. The second guard jabbed him in the stomach with his club. "We've dealt with worse."

I nodded and we watched them disappear into the night. I leaned against the desk; my heart had finally stopped racing. But I was still in shock. I looked at Templeton. "How did the guards know where to find him?"

"I told Spell you were in Vue. I'm sure she's had you closely followed just like Petrovich had you followed." He was holding his arm again. His shirtsleeve was soaked in blood.

"You need to get to a hospital," I told him.

Templeton scowled. "I have someone who can take care of this scrape."

Rabbit shook his head, grinning. He put his hands into his pockets. Clearly he knew

Templeton in ways I did not. "Emily," he began, "what about the stone?"

I looked at the magical stone in my hand. I'd finally found it. I could still feel its potential even though the flame inside had now shrunk to a mere sparkle. But a power pulsed just below the surface. Holding the Crimson Stone was frightening and exhilarating at the same time. A part of me wanted to see what else I could do with it. That's why it was so dangerous for one person to have all of the pieces. It was a temptation better avoided.

"That's right," Templeton said. "I'd better take it now so you don't hurt yourself. Why don't you set it in the box and I'll be on my way. Places to go. Bleeding, you know."

"No." I raised my eyes to his.

"No? Emily, in spite of what just happened, we both know you can't handle that kind of magic. You will be under constant threat from enemies who want it. You'll be reckless if you try to protect yourself and your family. You won't be able to keep it safe. And we both know that I can. Give it to me and I'll take good care of it. Come now." He motioned toward the box.

I shook my head. Templeton was partially right. The fact was, no one could handle this stone and not be affected by such awesome power. And, although I hated to admit it, Templeton laid out a possibility that could come true: I might behave recklessly if I tried to protect the people I loved when under attack.

I thought about my father's words, what he had written in The Book. I said to Templeton.

"There is a Legend
about a child
who liked to play
with pretty stones.
One Stone was
Very Special.
She had to hide it,
so she put it in
Plain Sight
after breaking it into
three pieces."

With that, I released the clasp so that the stone opened into what appeared to be a necklace with three different gems. I removed them from the chain. The flame was gone and I examined how each piece sat in the silver. The pieces would remain in their individual settings, but I could separate them from one another by releasing tiny little hooks. And that's what I did. Templeton watched as I walked over to the jewelry box. I placed one piece inside and closed the lid, securing the latch so it would not open.

"This time, we're not going to put anything in plain sight," I told Templeton. Turning to Rabbit I asked, "Can you take this piece and hide it where no one will ever find it? Take it far away from here. Don't tell anyone, not even me, where you put it."

Rabbit's nose twitched as he took the box. I looked into his kind, shining eyes. I was so grateful to him – for everything he had done. I was truly in his debt.

"Thank you, for everything." I placed my hand on his arm and squeezed. Rabbit nodded. Without a word, he shoved the box inside his jacket and made his way to the front door. A moment later he was gone. I knew he would do exactly what I asked. My father trusted Rabbit. So did I.

Did I trust Templeton? Not so much.

"You are making a mistake, Emily," Templeton warned.

"I'm not." My eyes flicked to him before I turned to Anne. "Can you take a piece to Beverly Spell? She'll make sure it's kept safe. I don't think anyone will follow you, but I'm not so sure about me. I think when the word gets out about Petrovich's arrest, the Fringe will ramp up the search for the stone. I'll need to go one way and you'll have to go another."

A box of old silk scarves sat on one of the shop's antique tables. I picked a small black scarf from the pile and wrapped it around the stone piece. I tied the ends and held out the scarf to Anne.

"Are you sure?" Anne asked, sliding a vintage shoulder bag from a beat-up hall tree. She held it open and I dropped the scarf inside.

"I'm totally sure. Anne, I don't know what I would have done without you." I hugged her. "Please be careful."

"Oh, don't worry about me." Anne gave me a sly look. She was resourceful. "Where are you going now?"

"Eventually? Home. Where I belong." I could feel Templeton's eyes on me.

"Then I'll meet you there." She grinned. "I seem to remember my kitchen going up in smoke a day or two ago. Maybe Kincaid needs a new café – one with a daily brew." Anne winked and wrapped her coat tightly around her, pulling her new vintage bag over her shoulder. "I'll call you from the train station in Kincaid."

I nodded, smiling back. "I'll come get you."

Anne looked at Templeton, a white eyebrow raised. "She used that stone quite nicely, didn't she? I guess there are two Salesmen who can handle magical items now."

Templeton didn't acknowledge Anne's words. Instead he gestured to the last piece of the stone, still in my hand. "And your brilliant plans for this one?"

I wrapped the third piece in another silk scarf and pushed it deep into my pants pocket. I ignored his question. "Shouldn't you get some medical attention before you bleed to death?"

Templeton snorted and turned away. Stepping through the mess, he found his top hat among the overturned furniture and dusted it off. He grimaced as fresh blood seeped out onto his sleeve.

"You have a lot to learn, Emily." He bowed to Anne and before I could respond, Templeton walked to the back of the store and put his hand on a closet door. He paused with his back to us, but instead of turning around, he simply stepped through the door and was gone.

"Good riddance," I said.

Anne gave me a funny look as she moved to the front of the shop. "He saved you, Emily."

"Rabbit saved me. If Rabbit hadn't tackled Petrovich, the gun wouldn't have been knocked out of his hand. Petrovich would have shot me." I began to pack up my bag. "Let's get going."

Anne frowned. "Emily, Templeton stepped between you and Petrovich. He is the one who would have been shot, not you." She shook her head. "Emily, don't you realize? Templeton jumped in to protect you."

I finished pushing the last few items I needed into my bag. My father's top hat was pretty squashed, but useable. I glanced up at Anne. "I'm sure he had a motive for that."

Anne sighed. "After the guards left, Templeton had Petrovich's gun. He could have stopped you from breaking the stone and giving pieces of it to Rabbit and me."

This was true. Still, I had to assume that Templeton only did what served him. He admitted that he only worked for himself. Then again, I thought about what he said about Beverly Spell having me followed in Vue. He was the one who told her I was here. And he knew that Spell was on to Petrovich. At some point I would have to learn more about his relationship with the justice.

"I'm not going to try and figure it out now," I said to Anne. "Come on. I don't want the Fringe to show up."

"You're right." She nodded. "Will you be okay traveling by yourself?"

"I'll be fine. I'm going back to Tuesday's apartment to see if I can spend the rest of the night, though." I pulled my bag over my shoulder. "I want to say good-bye to someone tomorrow morning before I leave for Kincaid."

Anne gave me another curious look but didn't ask me what I meant. Instead, she left the same way as Rabbit and I followed a few seconds later. The air outside was cold and dark. The sky was still black with pinpricks of stars. The streetlights were out, and I hurried away from *Common Vue*. I would go straight home in the morning, but first I wanted to say goodbye to my father.

CHAPTER 22

It was early in the morning, but the sun was shining as brightly as it did the day before. It was glorious. I stopped at a corner coffee vendor and picked up bitter coffee flavored with Styrofoam. It didn't matter; I knew I was going home. I would not need to wait for the Winter Solstice and the North Door to be opened. I would curl up in Jack's arms and let him hold me tight all night long. I would snuggle with the Furious Furballs in the morning and stay in bed until noon. Tara and I would park our butts at *The Green Bean* for a week and drown ourselves in latte bliss.

I would decide on what to tell my mother about this adventure.

From the park bench, I gazed up at the statue of my father. The look in his eye was far away. I guess my father had always been far away. My mother and I weren't included in the Empire. I could only guess the reasons why he chose to do that. He probably hoped to protect us. Even Petrovich hinted as much.

I pulled my father's journal from my bag. The Book had literally opened doors to a new world. I wondered if my father knew it was going to happen this way. Why else would he have left all of those messages?

Turning through the pages, I ran my fingertips over the first map I'd found. I traced my father's drawing with my finger. He served this world. It meant something to him. I never knew my father's parents. Which one was the Salesman? I had so many questions for Blackstone when I returned home. I hoped he had the answers.

I continued to page through The Book. So many things made sense now. Anne Lace was my new friend; Rabbit was someone I could count on for help. I turned another page.

Templeton.
Not in Matar during EoS?
Friend?

I blew out a breath. Templeton. I pulled a pencil from my bag and wrote under my father's note:

We still don't know.

I wasn't alone in the park. I could hear the sound of someone walking along the sidewalk. They were heading my way. I pushed The Book back into the bag and pulled up the hood on my jacket. I was prepared to run if I needed to. Templeton appeared from around the base of the statue. He paused when he saw me. A moment later he sat down.

I stared at my father's statue. I hadn't expected Templeton to show up and I didn't know what to make of it. He wore his long dress coat and carried his top hat in his left hand. I wondered if his arm had been properly cared for. I assumed he went for help when he left *Common Vue*. Templeton was not a fool.

"He really was a great man." I nodded toward my father.

"He was better than most of them."

I turned and studied Templeton's profile as he sat looking up at the statue. I could see no affection or sadness in his face. I wondered if he ever felt anything for anybody.

"Do you know who killed my father, Templeton? Was it Petrovich? Is he the one who actually put the bomb on the train?" I was tired, but I was going to keep asking until I got an answer.

Templeton sighed. Leaning back against the park bench, he faced me. He didn't speak right away. He choose his words carefully.

"Your father was targeted by the Fringe because he had such a strong influence here in the Empire. The truth is, Emily, the actual person who put the bomb on the train was most likely a nobody – someone who was merely a foot soldier in the Fringe's cause. He – or she – might have been among the casualties in the explosion all those years ago or died later during the backlash that followed. I doubt even the most powerful members of the Fringe know who actually planted the bomb. Petrovich probably doesn't know either."

I nodded and looked at my father's statue. I believed Templeton, but I had a hard time accepting justice would never be served. And, although Templeton didn't say it, we both knew the person who did it still might be alive, carrying the dirty truth with them.

"Did he know about the Crimson Stone?"

"Your father kept a lot of secrets."

"That's helpful." I rolled my eyes. "I'd just assumed my father knew where the stone was hidden. It was in The Bo– I mean, there was a reference in his travel journal about the stone."

Templeton lifted a shoulder. "Powerful men don't share their secrets."

"What are you doing here now?" I asked.

"I wanted to let you know that the piece has been delivered to Beverly Spell. Anne can be quite resourceful when she needs to be. She made it to Court in record time. She's boarding the train out of the Empire as we speak."

I didn't bother to ask how he knew these details. "I see. Good. And your arm?"

"Attended to."

"Good." I knew I should thank Templeton for jumping between Petrovich's gun and me, but I just couldn't. I didn't want to be in his debt. I supposed I was no matter what. Still, I didn't need to admit that to him.

"Something else?"

"I've been wondering about last night. In the

shop." I figured if anyone knew how I could hold the Crimson Stone, Templeton would be the person to ask.

"Yes?"

"Why could I hold the Crimson Stone? According to Blackstone, Salesmen are not able to handle magical items."

"I can," he said.

"Yeah, I know. So?" I waited.

He avoided looking me in the eye. Instead, he tilted his head back and stared into the clear morning sky. "It appears you have certain abilities."

"Abilities?"

"I won't guess to what extent, but you obviously have some magical inclinations. Perhaps it's in your bloodline. From your mother's side, I would guess. Anyhow, although you are quite sloppy, you do seem to have a natural affinity for door travel. Not like me, of course. But there's something there." He scowled.

"Trust me, Templeton, I'm nothing like you."

"And now you are returning to Kincaid?" He ignored my comment.

"I am."

"And just how do you plan to do that?"

I pulled my father's top hat from the bag at my feet. I smiled. "Oh, I'll think of a way."

Of course, Templeton didn't return the smile, but I caught a flash of amusement run across his face. "Why, Emily, you're not approved by the Court for travel."

I shrugged. "I wouldn't have had any issue if you hadn't pulled the Birthmother stunt. Why did you do that?"

"You were becoming quite the little pain. It was necessary to delay you. Well, at least try to delay you. Besides, it's my understanding the repeal is imminent. The Court is moving fast. You should have your Salesman approval in, oh, say a week or two." Templeton stifled a yawn.

I sat forward at this news. "Really? How will I know? Will I be called back to Court? Will Blackstone find out first? Does he give me my own top hat? Can I choose it instead? There was one with a purple feather in the antique shop. I don't know if it can be used as an official Salesman hat, but I really liked it. I'd use my father's, but it's just a bit too big. And I think I should have my own anyway." In my excitement I rambled on. Ugh. I hated that Templeton had better knowledge of my Salesman status than I did. Especially after everything that happened in Vue.

Disgusted with my outburst, Templeton rolled his eyes and stood to leave. "I'm sure the Court will find an appropriate way to notify you." He picked at yet another imaginary piece of lint on his sleeve, suppressing a wince. His arm probably hurt. "Well, Emily Swift, this is goodbye. This past week has been tolerable. I'm sure you'll do something moderately interesting in the future and our paths will cross again. In the meantime, try not to make any more trouble for yourself – especially if you are still holding onto a certain piece of stone." His eyes cut to me.

"Yes, it's been a pleasure for me as well." I said, looking for my own piece of imaginary lint. Templeton sighed as if pained. He tipped his hat to me and walked out of the park. Hopefully, out of my life.

I stood after Templeton disappeared from view and walked to the base of my father's statue. Placing my hand on the cold stone, I looked up into his unseeing eyes. "Bye Dad. I'll keep your hat and my piece of the pretty stone safe. Maybe I can help keep the Empire safe, too."

The statue had nothing to say in return, so I took my leave. I walked out of the park and began to stroll along the busy sidewalk. I was looking for the right door.

I thought about home. I pictured my wonderful Jack, the Furious Furballs, my weird mother, and my best friend. I felt their love for me, their willingness to help and support me even though they were scared and didn't want me to go. I reached out with my thoughts and my hopes and my dreams for all of us. I let the energy stretch out of my body, seeking and looking. Feeling my way home.

And I heard a hum.

A door leading into an apartment building began to buzz as I walked by. I smiled as I turned the doorknob and stepped through.

❋ ❋ ❋

Two weeks passed since I stepped out of the pantry and into the kitchen. I found Jack standing at the counter in a pair of boxers and a white undershirt. He held a spoonful of vanilla ice cream halfway to his mouth. I told him we had to stop meeting like this.

I would have scolded him for eating ice cream for breakfast, but he was too busy kissing me. I was home! Yay! And I was home in one piece! Double yay!

Blackstone was eager to see me, of course, but I told him he'd have to wait. He understood but encouraged me to keep in touch. I promised him no more door travel until I heard from the Court. At least I would do my best. Blackstone reminded me to keep my emotions in check and I shouldn't have too much of a problem. His sources in the Empire reported that after Petrovich was arrested, he was immediately taken before the Salesman Court and held without bail. He was being investigated for his role in the slaying of Elsa Haus and Alfred Havers. He would go on trial for the murder of Alice White and for treason against the Empire after the New Year. If found guilty of either, the punishment would be death.

The Fringe had retreated. For now. I hoped that with the Crimson Stone broken into three pieces and hidden separately that the book of fairytales would have no more value to them. It had yet to be recovered.

I was a real-life Dorothy back from Oz to Jack, my Mom, and Tara. The day I returned from the Empire, my mother drove into town and Tara closed the bookstore so she could come straight over. Everyone listened to my story in half-disbelief and half-fascination. I'll admit to scaling down on some of the drama for Jack's sake. I think he was on to me, but decided to be okay with not knowing every dangerous detail. Tara was eager to visit the Empire, Jack said 'not on your life,' and my mother demurred. She said it would probably be better if she stayed home for now.

As for telling my mother about the Empire's version of Daniel Swift, I tried. The words just did not come out as planned and finally I said: 'He was a great man who did many great things.' Mom simply replied, 'of course he was, darling.' Then she hugged me, rocking us both gently in her embrace.

My legal worries were resolved quickly. Detective O'Connell paid me one last visit to report that a suspect in the Elsa Haus murder and Rene Blackstone attack had been taken into custody. When I pressed him for more information, he told me that another authority had taken over the case and he was no longer privy to details. He also suggested that I work on keeping a low profile moving forward.

I admit I was a little surprised at O'Connell's news and it made me wonder: how far did the Empire's reach extend?

Anne Lace arrived in Kincaid and I picked her up from the train station as planned. She stayed with Jack and me for several days before securing a loft apartment downtown. Tara was helping her look for a storefront to open a new café: *The Daily Brew Too*. They were hoping something would open up near *Pages & Pens*. I was so glad my new friend would be close. Because of my experience with the Crimson Stone, Anne put out some feelers for a teacher who could assist me in understanding some of the abilities I seemed to have. In the short term, she provided me with some gentle sleeping tea to help keep my nights free of dreams.

I was also very popular with three felines – well, at least for a couple days. William, Mystery, and even little Mischief followed me from room to room. I guess they missed me too.

My father's traveling journal, The Book – capital T, capital B – sits in my office in an engraved wooden box on a shelf. It bears the name Swift with a little top hat sitting at an angle on the 'S." The box was a gift from Tara to help preserve this priceless piece of my father's legacy. I take it out every couple of days and look through the pages. It's my connection to my father, but also the Empire. There are many mysteries yet to be revealed and sometimes, I find new passages that I swear I have not read before.

I take my responsibility for my piece of the Crimson Stone very seriously. I'll be honest, I'm not sure what I should do: keep it so I know where it is at all times, or do something radical, like toss it in one of the Finger Lakes here in New York? Or maybe I should bury it somewhere in the Adirondacks and hope it stays hidden forever. I know I was one of the heroes in this story, but I admit it: I'm a hero without a clue as to what to do next.

For the time being I'm keeping it. But I'm not telling anyone where it is.

And Templeton? He had been M-I-A since that morning in the park. That is, until another thud woke me from a sound sleep a week before Christmas.

"Oh, no. Not again." I looked over at Jack, blissfully unaware. He snored softly with both arms flung above his head. How anyone could sleep so soundly, I'll never understand.

I glanced at the clock. Imagine that, six in the morning. I slid out of bed and grabbed my robe. William appeared from the hallway and stretched.

"Did you make that noise?" I scratched his chin. He closed his eyes. "Probably not. Well, let's go see what's up now."

I shuffled down the stairs. Nothing seemed out of place as I walked through the living room and into the kitchen. Maybe it was just my imagination, or maybe I was dreaming again, regardless of Anne's soothing tea. I hadn't had any memorable ones since I returned from the Empire, though. No scary doors, no dark places, no whispers.

I contemplated whether or not to go back to bed. I decided to make some coffee when I noticed the pantry door was slightly ajar. I walked over and pushed it open. Everything looked okay. Hmm. I decided to check the dining room.

Flicking on the light switch I received quite the pleasant surprise. There, sitting in the middle of my dining room table was the pretty top hat I tried on during my happier visit to *Common Vue*. I touched the curved brim. The pink bow and the purple feather were just as perfect as I remembered.

An official envelope from the Salesman Court sat by the hat. I slipped my finger along the crease and opened it. The letter inside stated

I'd been approved for door travel and would be assigned a Senior Salesman for my initial training. I was to report to one Mr. Rene Blackstone, Record Keeper and Warden of the North Door, after the New Year for advising and to set up my training schedule. At the bottom of the page Justice Beverly Spell added a note: The Empire thanks you for your recent service.

Recent service, indeed. But I got the hat! The Hat! Capital T, capital H.

I couldn't help it; I was excited. How in the world the Court knew that I wanted this one didn't matter. I supposed they had their ways.

I scooped it off of the table. Just as I was about to place it on my head, a folded piece of white paper tumbled out of the hat and landed on the floor at my feet. I picked it up. What in the world?

I unfolded the paper. Familiar, slanted handwriting appeared in black. I felt the corners of my mouth turn up.

The note simply said:

You've been approved by the Salesman Court, Emily.
Enjoy your hat.
T.

The end.
(For now...)

ACKNOWLEDGEMENTS

I am incredibly fortunate to have a loving husband who encouraged me throughout the creation of *Door to Door*. Thank you, Gordon, for everything, and in particular: that car ride from Long Island to Rochester when Emily's story started to take shape. I am grateful for you every day.

A big thank you goes to Jill Arent of Jill-Elizabeth.com for cheering me on and saying *"yes!"* without hesitation when I returned as the prodigal writing-buddy, asking if she would read my manuscript. Her feedback was exactly what I needed to complete this book. You are truly valued and a dear friend, Jill.

Finally, many thanks to EBookLaunch.com for designing the book cover for *Door to Door*. You captured my vision perfectly.

BOOKS IN THIS SERIES

Door to Door Paranormal Mystery Series

Door To Door

First in series!

Seventeen years after Emily Swift's father died, a door is opened to a new world, an Empire led by peculiar men and women called Salesmen – transporters of magical items. These Salesmen have the unique ability to travel from place-to-place, and even world-to-world, simply by stepping through the "right" door. Now that Emily is thirty, it turns out that she can "door travel" too, stumbling unplanned into kitchens, bathrooms, and alleyways as her connection to the Salesman Empire is revealed.

Fueled by the cryptic notes and sketches in her father's journal, Emily discovers the real reason behind his death: he was targeted and assassinated by the Fringe, a terrorist group of rogue

Salesmen.

Through The Door

Coming in 2021.

Emily Swift is back - and so is Templeton! When Lydia goes missing, it's a race between Emily and the Fringe to catch up to Emily's wandering mother. Add the dead body of a hated art critic into the mix and things go from bad to worse.

Will Templeton join Emily in rescuing Lydia? What will it cost her? Is the price too high?

Doors Wide Open

Also coming in 2021!

Emily Swift faces her biggest challenges yet in this fast-paced installment from T. L. Brown.

ABOUT THE AUTHOR

T. L. Brown

T. L. Brown is the pseudonym for the author who writes the cozy paranormal mystery series called Door to Door. She was born in snowy Western New York where she developed a love of reading and writing. She holds a Bachelor of Arts from the University of Pittsburgh in History - Political Science.

After college, she moved to Rochester, New York and began to write a story about an average thirty-year-old woman who found herself caught between two worlds: the known one and a new, often dangerous place known as the Empire. That character became Emily Swift.

Ms. Brown now lives with her husband in the beautiful Finger Lakes of New York State dreaming up new stories and quirky characters that make life all the more interesting. She believes that magic still exists, you just need to look in the right places.

FIND T.L. BROWN ONLINE

Visit WriterTracyBrown.com to learn more about the Door to Door Paranormal Mystery series and to connect with the author in her social media channels.

Made in the USA
Middletown, DE
14 April 2021